PRAISE FOR

ᴛʜₑ STORM KEEPE

D0485359

"Doyle's writing glows, with the pitch-perfect barbs the young people sling at each other, the atmospheric weather events, her masterfully delineated characters—including the island itself—and a page-turning plot. Heart-wrenching and heart-stopping, this is one gorgeous novel" —*New York Times Book Review*

★ "Doyle's prose explodes with lyrical language as she deftly explores themes of loss, guilt, and how memory weighs on one's soul. . . . Doyle proves with this exquisite debut that she is a middle-grade fiction author to watch." —*Booklist*, starred review

★ "Doyle infuses every aspect of the novel with the richness of Irish folklore and culture: readers will be captivated. . . . [A] modern yet timeless fantasy." —*School Library Journal*, starred review

★ "Fans of Harry Potter or Percy Jackson can add Fionn Boyle as a generous and brave hero from the Emerald Isle." —*School Library Connection*, starred review

"Imaginative and exhilarating." —Rebecca Stead, Newbery Award–winning author of *When You Reach Me*

"Magical in every way." —Eoin Colfer, bestselling author of *Artemis Fowl*

"Catherine Doyle is one to watch." —Lauren Wolk, Newbery Honor–winning author of *Wolf Hollow* and *Beyond the Bright Sea*

"The engaging construction of magical time travel and Doyle's beautifully descriptive prose will enchant those looking for an atmospheric magical adventure." **DISCARD**

"Irish legends collide with modern times in a fast-paced, magical tale about the ordinary becoming extraordinary. . . . A distinctive fantasy with depth, humor, and heart." —*Kirkus Reviews*

"Doyle's vivid imagery and colorful language engages the senses as she weaves together an atmospheric setting. . . . A beautiful blend of Irish legend and self-discovery." —Shelf Awareness

Books by Catherine Doyle

The Storm Keeper's Island
The Lost Tide Warriors

The STORM KEEPER'S ISLAND

Catherine Doyle

Errol Hassell Library
~~18200 SW Barn Road~~
~~Aloha, OR 97007~~

BLOOMSBURY
CHILDREN'S BOOKS
NEW YORK   LONDON   OXFORD   NEW DELHI   SYDNEY

BLOOMSBURY CHILDREN'S BOOKS
Bloomsbury Publishing Inc., part of Bloomsbury Publishing Plc
1385 Broadway, New York, NY 10018

BLOOMSBURY, BLOOMSBURY CHILDREN'S BOOKS, and the Diana logo
are trademarks of Bloomsbury Publishing Plc

First published in Great Britain in July 2018 by Bloomsbury Publishing Plc
Published in the United States of America in January 2019
by Bloomsbury Children's Books
Paperback edition published in January 2020

Text copyright © 2018 by Catherine Doyle
Illustrations copyright © 2018 by Bill Bragg
Lettering by Patrick Knowles

All rights reserved. No part of this publication may be reproduced or transmitted in any form
or by any means, electronic or mechanical, including photocopying, recording, or any
information storage or retrieval system, without prior permission in writing from the publisher.

Bloomsbury books may be purchased for business or promotional use. For information on bulk
purchases please contact Macmillan Corporate and Premium Sales Department at
specialmarkets@macmillan.com

ISBN 978-1-5476-0253-7 (paperback)

The Library of Congress has catologed the hardcover edition as follows:
Names: Doyle, Catherine.
Title: The Storm Keeper's Island / by Catherine Doyle.
Description: New York : Bloomsbury, 2019.
Summary: Fionn Boyle, terrified of the sea, must spend the summer with
his older sister, Tara, and their grandfather on Arranmore, an island that has
been known to make people disappear, and seems to be restless again.
Identifiers: LCCN 2018024284 (print) • LCCN 2018030597 (e-book)
ISBN 978-1-68119-959-7 (hardcover) • ISBN 978-1-5476-0011-3 (e-book)
Subjects: | CYAC: Brothers and sisters—Fiction. | Grandfathers—Fiction. | Islands—Fiction. |
Supernatural—Fiction. | Ireland—Fiction.
Classification: LCC PZ7.1.D69 Sto 2019 (print) | LCC PZ7.1.D69 (e-book) |
DDC [Fic]—dc23
LC record available at https://lccn.loc.gov/2018024284

Typeset by RefineCatch Limited, Bungay, Suffolk
Printed and bound in the U.S.A. by Sheridan, Chelsea, Michigan
2 4 6 8 10 9 7 5 3

To find out more about our authors and books visit www.bloomsbury.com
and sign up for our newsletters.

For my grandparents,
Captain Charles P. Boyle and Mary McCauley Boyle
of Arranmore Island

PR⊕LOGUE

In a field full of wildflowers, a boy and a girl stood side by side beneath an ancient oak tree. The sky was angry, the thunder growling like a beast.

"Are you ready?" asked the boy nervously.

The girl raised her chin, her wheat-blonde hair sweeping down her back in a curtain. "I've *always* been ready."

They pressed their palms against the gnarled trunk. The tree began to quiver, its branches stretching as it shook itself awake. There was a brief silence and then a crack exploded above them. A whip of lightning leaped from the clouds and split the center of the tree in two. Flames erupted along the bark, climbing across the branches and devouring the leaves until everything was a bright, brilliant gold.

"Betty?" said the boy uncertainly. "Should we—"

"*Sssh!*" hissed the girl. "It's about to say something."

The tree began to whisper. It was much louder than

the boy expected—the crackle and hiss of surrounding flame slowly turning into words. "Sssspeak or be sssspoken to."

The girl asked her question. As the tree considered it, she grew restless, tapping her fingers against the charred bark. The air grew heavier, a veil of mist curling the strands around her face.

The tree did not speak to the girl again.

Instead, it turned its attention to the boy and climbed inside his head. He fell to the ground, twisting and writhing, as a vision unfurled in the blackness of his mind.

He was standing on the edge of a headland with the clouds gathering in his outstretched hands and the wind wreathing his body. He felt the sea rushing through his veins, leaving salt crystals in the lining of his heart.

He knew that he was changed forever.

Betty had been wrong.

The island had chosen him.

He tried to blink himself awake but the tree tightened its grip on his mind. Another vision pushed its way through. Something they had not asked to see.

"Watch," hissed the tree. "Pay attention."

A boy appeared before him. He was a little younger, but he was wearing the same nose and the same eyes. In one hand, he held an emerald as green as the island grass. In the other, a crooked staff that pointed out to sea. They stood apart from each other, looking but not really seeing as ravens filled the sky in plumes of feathers. The earth cracked beneath their feet and a shadow crept across the island and buried them in darkness.

The boy woke up. Back in the field of wildflowers, it was pouring with rain.

"Betty," he said, a droplet landing squarely in his mouth. "You won't believe what I've just seen."

The girl was standing over him, her narrowed eyes like burning coals. She kicked him in the ribs. "Don't you mean what you just *stole*!"

"Stop!" He twisted away from her as she kicked him again. "I need to tell you something. Can you stop, please? *Ow!* Listen to me. I saw ravens, Betty. I think . . ."

The girl wasn't listening. She was stalking away from him, through wildflowers and sodden grass, her chin tipped to the weeping sky.

The boy wanted to call her back, to tell her this was much bigger than her—that it was bigger than both of them—but she had disappeared into thin air, leaving only the faintest ripple behind.

The boy tried to swallow his fear. Somewhere deep inside the earth, the darkness was rising again, a darkness more terrible than anything the world had ever seen.

It was too late to stop it now.

Chapter One

THE SLEEPING ISLAND

Fionn Boyle sat hunched on a plastic chair with his arms tucked into his sides and his chin tucked into his chest, and tried not to be sick all over his shoes.

The ferry groaned. Fionn couldn't help noticing the rust around its edges, the flaking blue paint, how the horn sounded like a dying cow. He tried not to imagine how much seawater he would have to swallow to drown from the inside out. Tara wasn't watching him just then but Fionn knew sisters could smell fear. If he hurled his lunch up, he'd never hear the end of it.

To make matters even more grim, Fionn was wedged between two nattering old ladies, and his phone was useless in his pocket. No coverage. Not even one bar. Sometimes the old ladies would stop and chew on a secret like it was too big to swallow. Sometimes Fionn could feel their gazes prickling on the side of his face, like they were waiting for him to join in. Mostly the waves roared and drowned out all of it.

That was the worst of all: the ocean right underneath him. In his most gruesome nightmares, it would suck him up and gulp him down and he would wake suddenly, dripping in sweat.

The sea air burned in his lungs and stung his cheeks as he watched the mainland fade away, first to a green smudge on a gray horizon, and then to nothing at all.

Already, Fionn missed the Dublin smog, the clang of roadwork, and the half-finished tram tracks cutting up the city and flinging tourists from footpaths. He never thought about whether he liked it or not—the noisiness of a city constantly in motion—only that it was familiar, and to Fionn familiarity meant home.

This was anything but familiar.

Tara stood at the bow of the ship, her feet planted on the railings like she was about to launch herself into the ocean. Her dark hair whipped through the air, loose and tangled, like ropes. She turned, searching the cluster of passengers for him. "Come here, Fionny! Look at these waves! They're *huge!*"

Fionn shook his head. The ferry bobbed and his stomach went with it—up and down—until the contents of his lunch started to climb up his throat.

"Don't be such a baby!" Tara taunted.

Fionn and his sister were close in age. Fionn could even remember a time when they felt almost like *friends*. He supposed they'd had something in common until the day she turned thirteen and he stayed eleven, and suddenly she was much too wise and too clever to hang around and play video games with him anymore.

I'm mature now, Fionny. My interests have changed.

Fionn didn't know how Tara measured maturity but he was the one cooking dinner for the three of them most evenings, while Tara pawed Nutella out of the jar like Winnie-the-Pooh and shrieked the walls down any time she saw a spider.

Tara smirked over her shoulder and then stepped higher on the boat railings, peering over the waves, until it looked like she was going to dive in, just to show him she could. Fionn thought it might be nice if she tipped over, and drowned a little. Not enough to die, just enough so that a fish could come along and eat the part of her brain that caused her personality to be so terrible.

He went back to staring at the blurry horizon—a fixed point to help with the sickness. His mother said it would help with the motion of the boat. That was the last thing she told him before their goodbye back in Dublin, when her eyes were clear and her smile was sad. Then all of a sudden they were in their neighbor's car, Fionn's nose pressed up against the window, as they trundled across the country and left her behind.

Fionn waited for the island to appear. The one she used to tell them about when he was younger, her eyes glassy with some faraway look. Sometimes the island was a beautiful place. Sometimes it was a sad, unforgiving place that held nothing beyond the memory of his father, long ago lost to the sea. All Fionn ever knew for sure was that Arranmore haunted her, and he could never figure out whether that was mostly a good thing or mostly a bad thing. Only that places can be just as important as people. That they can have the same power over you if you let them.

Tara left her perch at the front of the ferry, skipped across the deck, and bent down until they were almost nose-to-nose. "Do you have to look so depressed about all this?"

Fionn didn't like the way his sister threw the word around like that. *Depressed.* Like it was a color he was wearing. Like it was something you could be, and then not be, by choice. Besides, it was easy for her to be excited about this. She had visited the island last summer and had *somehow* managed to make friends.

"I don't want to go," he grumbled. "I'm not going to pretend I do."

"You never want to go anywhere," Tara pointed out. "All you do is sit inside and play video games that you're *bad* at anyway. You're so boring."

Fionn wanted to say he wished he could stay behind with their mother, that he could sit beside her even when it felt like she couldn't see him. He wanted to say he wasn't *bad* at video games; that he was, in fact, excellent.

Instead, he said, "Shut up."

Tara slid a Mars bar from her pocket—the result of a gas-station shopping spree on the way to the ferry, old Mrs. Waters snapping open her floral purse full of coins, smiling at them with her toothy grin. *Get whatever you want, my loves.*

She took a bite, her words soupy from half-chewed caramel. "It's an adventure, Fionny." She glanced from side to side, then dropped her voice. "This place is magical. Just wait and see."

"You only think it's magical because you met a *boy* last year," said Fionn with deep, abiding disgust.

Tara shook her head. "No, *actually*, I think it's magical because there are *secrets* on the island."

Fionn tried to waft the smell of chocolate away from his nose. "What kind of secrets?"

"Can't tell you!" she said, eyes gleaming with triumph.

Fionn sighed. "I can't believe I'm going to be stuck with you all summer."

"Well, I wouldn't worry because I obviously won't be spending any time with you." She wrinkled her nose, her freckles hunching together. "You can hang out with Grandad."

"I already like him better than you," said Fionn quickly.

"You don't even know him yet."

Fionn opened his fist to reveal his crumpled-up ferry ticket. "I like this piece of paper better than you."

Tara brandished her Mars bar at his nose. "You're so immature."

"I am not." Fionn waited for her to look the other way and then threw the piece of paper at her. He watched it tangle in the ends of her hair and felt a little better then. Across the bay, a seagull dipped and swirled, its wing skimming the waves. It released a savage cry, and as if called to attention, the island rose to meet them.

Pockets of dark green grass bubbled up out of the sea, climbing into hills that rolled over each other. Gravel roads weaved themselves between old buildings that hunched side by side along the pier, where the sand was dull and brassy. The place looked oddly deserted; it was as if the entire island was fast asleep.

Arranmore.

It was exactly how Fionn imagined it: a forgotten smudge on the edge of the world. The perfect place for his soul to come to die.

Tara flounced back to her perch and Fionn felt himself deflate, like a giant balloon. He watched the faraway blurs on the island turn into people, shops, houses and cars, and too many fishing boats to count. He tried to picture his mother here, in this strange place, wandering along the pier, ducking into the corner shop for bread or milk. Or even standing on the shore, looking out at the ocean, with her arms pulled around her. He couldn't imagine it, no matter how hard he tried.

When the ferry had finally groaned its way into port, Tara bounded on to the island without so much as a backward glance. Fionn hovered on the edge of the pier, his spine stiff as a rod. Something was wrong. The ground was vibrating underneath him, the slightest tremor rattling against his soles as though his footsteps were far heavier than they really were. The breeze rolled backward and twisted around him, pushing his hair into his eyes and his breath back into his lungs, until he had the most absurd sensation that the island was opening its arms and enveloping him.

Fionn searched the jagged lines of the headland. In the distance, at the edge of the bay, where briars and ferns tussled on a low, sloping cliff, a cottage poked out of the wilderness. The smoke from its chimney curled into the evening air like a finger.

The wind pushed him across the pier. The smoke kept rising and twisting, gray against the sun-blush sky.

It was beckoning him.

Fionn could almost hear the whispering in his ears: a voice he had never heard before, a voice thrumming deep in his blood and in his bones. A voice he was trying very hard to ignore.

"Come here," it was saying. "Come home."

Chapter Two

THE CANDLEMAKER'S COTTAGE

Malachy Boyle's house was breathing; Fionn was almost sure of it. It was rising and falling behind the tangled briars, peeking out at them every so often. The smoke was still curling into the sky, but there was no sign of Fionn's grandfather.

"Hurry up," Tara grunted. Her suitcase was spitting rocks at Fionn as she hauled it up the narrow road. "I want to get there sometime this century!"

"Does he not know we're coming?" Fionn was half watching the road and half watching the house up ahead. "Shouldn't he have met us down at the pier?"

"He's old," said Tara.

"Can he not walk?"

"Do you want him to carry you, like a baby?" The determined *thu-thunk* of her suitcase punctuated her words. "Or can you not climb a hill by yourself?"

"I'm not by myself, am I?" Fionn snapped. "I'm with Lucifer herself."

"Shut up," Tara hissed.

"I just think it's rude," Fionn mumbled. "We're supposed to be his guests. And we don't even know where to go."

"I know where to go. I've been here before, only last time I didn't have *you* slowing me down."

Fionn rolled his eyes. They had been delayed by almost five minutes when a bee landed on Tara's shoulder. It chased her around the headland, and she went shrieking and hopping, like it was some great big grizzly bear.

"Lead on then, Columbus," he said, stomping up after her.

Fionn didn't think his expectations could possibly get any lower. And yet.

The cottage was small and squat, wedged deep into the earth, and swamped in a mess of trees and thorns. The edges of stonework peeked out in parts, where the white paint was peeling. The roof was made of slates, but around the edges, some had chipped and fallen into cracked gutters. The windows were cloudy with dirt and the sills were stuffed with headless flowers, their stems bending over into the garden like they were searching for their lost petals.

It was an explosion of chaos and color, and Fionn hated every inch of it. He wanted to be back in Dublin with his mother, in their cramped apartment, listening to their upstairs neighbors pretend they weren't harboring a secret pit bull terrier and deciding what takeout to order.

They passed an old letter box, inscribed with faded Irish: *Tír na nÓg.*

The Land of Youth.

Ironic, thought Fionn. And then he made a mental note to double-check what the word "ironic" actually meant before he said it out loud in front of Tara.

The gate let out a low whine as he closed it behind them.

"It's grim, isn't it?" Tara didn't bother to whisper despite the fact they were now standing in what some people might call a "garden," but which seemed to Fionn more like a salad. "And inside is just as depressing."

Depressing. That word again.

Fionn did a slow-motion turn. "Why would anyone choose to live here?"

"Well, I suppose this is the only place that would have me."

Fionn stopped turning. The blood vessels in his cheeks burst open.

His grandfather was standing at the entrance to his cottage. He was a giant of a thing—tall and narrow with a shiny bald head, a large face and a nose to fit it. It was the same nose Fionn had been cursing in reflections for as long as he could remember. An oversized pair of round, horn-rimmed glasses sat along the tip, making his eyes seem bigger and wider than they really were. His arms and his legs were impossibly long, but still somehow dwarfed in an oversized tweed suit. He looked like he was all dressed up to go somewhere, only he'd been all dressed up for fifty years and now the suit was falling apart on him.

His grandfather threw his head back, opened his mouth until Fionn could see all his teeth—the graying and the white—and laughed. And laughed and laughed and laughed, until Fionn imagined his laughter was sweeping around him in a tornado, the winds of it playing his heart like a fiddle.

And then Fionn was laughing too. It was awkward and forced, but if he laughed then he wouldn't have time to think about how this didn't feel so much like an adventure but a prison, or how his mother had been left behind inside a faceless building in Dublin surrounded by professional-type people wearing expensive sweaters and fancy spectacles. He laughed to keep these thoughts from turning into something sad and ugly that looked and sounded very much like crying.

Fionn would not cry in front of Tara.

This was not going to be a crying sort of vacation. Even if it wasn't really a vacation at all.

When the laughter sputtered out, his grandfather took one long, lingering look at him. "Well then," he said, dipping his chin. "At last we meet."

He stooped underneath the low doorframe and beckoned them inside, his finger crooked like the plume of smoke that had led them up the cliffside.

Tara charged up the path, tossing an insult over her shoulder. "Congrats, Fionny. You've finally found someone as weird as you."

"Watch out for that bee!" The weight on Fionn's heart shifted as Tara yelped and danced her way into the cottage.

Fionn shut the door and nearly toppled into a coatrack, where hats and umbrellas hung like props, all covered in a thick layer of dust.

"Oh," he said, staring wide-eyed at the shelves that

stretched floor-to-ceiling around the small living room, continuing into the kitchen, which was visible through a wooden archway.

Every inch of space in the already cramped cottage belonged to a shelf, and all the shelves were filled with candles.

Each one was labeled in swirling calligraphy. *Autumn Showers* and *Summer Rain* huddled between *Foggy Easter* and *White Christmas*, while others like *Unexpected Tornado at Josie's 12th Birthday Party* or *Sean McCauley's Runaway Kite* were oddly specific. There were labels whittled right down to the briefest window of time, like *Flaming Sunrise, February 1997* or *Tangerine Twilight, August 2009*, and some were vague Irish words like *Suaimhneas*, which meant "Peace," or *Saoirse*, which meant "Freedom."

One candle simply read *Fadó Fadó*—"Long, long ago." That could be anything. It could mean the Ice Age, or the Bronze Age, or that time in Ireland when all the monks were doodling manuscripts and hiding in big round towers for some reason Fionn couldn't remember.

Fionn's attention was drawn to *Angry Skies Over Aphort Beach*, a candle that looked as if it had been carved from a raging storm. It was dark gray around the base, the clouds gathering in climbing swirls, until the wax bubbled around the edges, fading into a deep violet. A streak of silver lightning zigzagged through the middle, and the longer Fionn stared at it, the more it seemed like it might leap off the shelf and crackle in the air around him.

"You'll be having tea then," said his grandfather. It wasn't a question but it brought relief to Fionn. Some things were the same everywhere in Ireland.

Tara retreated to a corner of the living room, searching for a phone charger in her bag, the way a dying man would scour the desert for water.

Fionn ducked under a beam and wandered into the hallway, where the house tapered off into three more rooms and the walls seemed to bend inward, as though they wanted to tell him a secret. There were candles here too. Some were tiny—the size of his baby finger. Some were rainbow-colored, and others had grass growing out of them. There were oddly shaped ones too—like raindrops and umbrellas and little moons pocked with craters. There were clouds so round and fluffy Fionn had to poke them to make sure they were made of wax and not vapor.

Back in the living room, a single candle was blazing above the mantelpiece. It was the largest in the cottage—a big waxen slab sitting snugly in a thick glass trough, as deep as Fionn's misery. It was pale gray, but in the center, around the wick, the wax was marbled with streaks of blue—turquoise and sapphire and aquamarine. There were lines of sky blue that bled into sea blue and even, Fionn couldn't help but notice, shades of the color of his school uniform—puke navy.

It was the only source of light now that the sun was dipping somewhere behind the tangle of trees outside. Fionn couldn't place the scent of it, but it tickled something in him.

It reminded him of sea air, but it didn't sting his nostrils in the same way. There were other things too. Water? No. Not *just* water. Fionn clenched his eyes shut. He felt as though the answer was buried somewhere in his bones, and if he closed his eyes and concentrated hard enough he might be able to drag it up from the depths of him and wrestle it from the tip of his tongue.

Rainwater. Yes. But from a storm—something that whirls and rages and slams itself into windowpanes. There was the sea again—right in the heart of it, but it was choppy this time, like froth on a restless wave or—

"Earth to Fionn!" Tara clapped her hands in front of Fionn's face and he startled, jumping backward and knocking a candle from its perch by the head of the armchair. The aroma evaporated at once and Fionn found himself wondering if he had hallucinated it.

Through the archway, his grandfather was filling mugs with tea. "Didn't your sister tell you I was a candlemaker?"

Fionn glared accusingly at Tara.

"I thought I wasn't supposed to talk about that stuff outside of Arranmore," she said dismissively. "And honestly, I don't think he'll care that much about the candles. No offense."

Fionn's grandfather reacted like Tara had just thrown a dart at him, his left eye twitching as he watched her flounce off down the hallway in search of a working socket.

"She doesn't mean to be so terrible," said Fionn. "Mom says she'll grow out of it. But it might take a while. She's only just grown into it."

His grandfather clapped him on the shoulder. "Don't you worry, Fionn. I am well used to the frigid wind of teenage apathy."

"Don't take it too personally. She's just never cared much about candles." Fionn didn't finish his thought, which was that he didn't care about them either, because like goldfish, and math and his sister, candles didn't do anything of note. And also, he wasn't over a hundred years old, or searching for a last-minute Christmas gift for someone he had completely forgotten about.

"And anyway, I thought you worked on the lifeboats,"

Fionn said, remembering. This was one of the few things he knew about his grandfather—that like all Boyle men (except for one), Malachy Boyle loved the sea and the sea loved him, that he grew up around the lifeboats and then went to work on them when he turned eighteen. "Like Dad did when . . ."

When he was alive, he wanted to say, but the words stuck in his throat. There was something about being in the place where his dad died that made the sadness of it seem fresher to Fionn.

"I used to but I prefer to stay indoors now. I am not as young as I once was." His grandfather had returned to the mugs, dipping and discarding the tea bags in the sink, before adding a splash of milk to each and handing one to Fionn. "You look a wee bit green, lad. Or are you just very patriotic?"

Fionn followed him into the living room. "The boat ride here was really choppy. Lots of people were feeling sick."

His grandfather gave him a knowing look as they sank into opposite chairs.

"Okay ... maybe I'm a little ... scared of the sea," Fionn conceded. He took a too-hot sip and nearly spat it back out. "I don't like the waves. Any of it, really."

His grandfather continued to watch him, his head

cocked to one side. The light from the candle flickered along his skin, casting shadows that crawled across the side of his face.

"Does that make me a bad Boyle?"

His grandfather *hmm*'d under his breath, his gaze passing over Fionn and settling on the wall behind him, where a photograph of Fionn's grandmother smiled down at them. "In my experience, there is no fear—however small—to be ashamed of. Your grandmother suffered very acutely from anatidaephobia, did you know that?"

The moment Fionn heard the word, it flittered away from him like a butterfly. "What's . . . that?"

His grandfather steepled his hands in front of his lips. "She was afraid of being watched by a duck."

Fionn stared at his grandfather. "What?"

"Anatidaephobia," his grandfather repeated. "The fear that, somewhere in the world, a duck is watching you."

". . . What?" Fionn said again.

"Crippling, *crippling* thing." His grandfather took a noisy sip of tea that seemed to go on and on. "It did her in in the end."

"Mom says she died of a broken heart."

His grandfather stroked his chin thoughtfully. "No. It was the duck, Fionn. I'm almost sure of it."

"You're joking?"

His grandfather's composure flickered, his lips giving way to a grin. He chuckled, and Fionn found himself joining in, relief making the laughter spring out of him a little too loudly.

His grandfather tapped the side of his mug. "Now *that* and *only* that is an absurd fear."

Fionn sank into his chair, privately relieved that he wasn't afraid of ducks.

"You'd best get used to the sea though, lad. It's every-where up here."

Fionn's smile was faint. "I guess that's the thing about islands, isn't it?"

"That, and they're often packed with extraordinarily handsome old men."

The silence settled around them, and for a while there was nothing but the dull roar of the ocean and the furious tap-tapping of Tara's phone as she desperately tried to fashion a social life out of a half-dead island. Fionn's grandfather watched him in the waning light. He was drumming his fingers along the buttons of his shirt, tapping his own silent rhythm.

"So," he said after a while. "How are things back in Dublin, Fionn?"

"Not very good. But I suppose you probably know that since Mom's sent us here . . ." Fionn's gaze was resting on the hearth of the fireplace. Something was beginning to rumble in the back of his mind. "She was too tired . . ." He trailed off, unwilling to say the rest. *She was too tired to be our mom.*

It didn't seem fair to say it, even if it was the truth and they both knew it. Their mother was just taking a vacation. It was a strange sort of thing, Fionn thought, to take a vacation not from a place, but from people. But it was going to make her better. She was not the shadow behind her eyes.

His grandfather was still drumming his fingers. "I'm sorry, lad. I know you don't have a choice about being here. You don't have a choice about any of it . . ."

Fionn couldn't tear his gaze away from the fireplace. There was a thought percolating somewhere in the back of his mind, and it was an important one, drip-dripping out.

The armchair creaked as his grandfather leaned forward, his elbows resting on top of his knees. "But the island is a place like no other, Fionn. You'll come to see how special it is . . ."

Fionn was staring so hard, he was forgetting to blink.

The fireplace was empty.

There was no soot, no metal grate, or even a fireguard. The cottage was cool, not bathed in the warm afterglow of a fire.

Fionn looked up at his grandfather. "Grandad, if there's no fire in the grate, where was the smoke coming from before?"

His grandfather smiled. It was an odd kind of smile that lifted the hairs on the back of Fionn's neck. The candle flickered in the sides of his vision, the flame seeming to grow taller and narrower in response to his answer.

"Where did the smoke come from?" he said again.

His grandfather laughed, but this time it was a dry, dusty sound. Like it came from somewhere else, not deep in his belly, like before. He rose from his chair, unfolding his long limbs, and wandered back to the kitchen, where half-peeled carrots suddenly demanded his attention.

Fionn glanced again at the empty grate, uncertainty swimming inside him like a fish.

Chapter Three

THE BEASLEY BOY

"Bartley Beasley just stepped off the ferry," Tara announced the following morning, when Fionn was shoveling porridge into his mouth. His hair was stuck to his forehead and his eyes were still full of sleep. He had tossed and turned all night, haunted by the faraway sounds of waves crashing against the cliffs. In his dreams, he imagined watery fingers creeping up over the headland and dragging him down into a bottomless ocean.

"Ah, *Bartley Beasley* ...," said their grandfather, who was chopping a week-old banana into his porridge. "How could I forget such unnecessary alliteration?"

Tara stopped texting long enough to glare at him.

He chuckled as he ate a banana slice off the end of his

knife. "Are there any more boisterous Beasleys coming to the island this summer?"

"I heard they're very bewitching," said Fionn.

His grandfather smirked. "How *beguiling*."

"If you *must* know, Bartley has a younger sister," said Tara very seriously. "It's her first time visiting Arranmore, so I said I'd help show her around."

"Will she be barefoot?" asked Fionn.

His grandfather sipped his tea, peering at Tara over the rim of his mug. "Or perhaps . . . barnacled?"

Fionn snorted.

"*Oh,*" said Tara, her eyes narrowing in delayed understanding. "You're *so* funny. Ha ha *ha*. Well, I hate to disappoint you but her name is Shelby, so you two can stop acting like *boneheads*." She rolled her eyes and got up from the table, whipping her plait over her shoulder and stomping back to their bedroom, muttering things about prejudice and immaturity.

Fionn's grandfather had the good sense to look sorry. At least until Tara disappeared, and then he turned to Fionn, and said, "Was that very belligerent of us?"

"We're blameless," said Fionn, shaking his head.

Usually, Fionn knew better than to insult the great Bartley Beasley, the boy Tara was not-so-secretly in love with. The boy who came to Arranmore last summer and gave her a blue-thread bracelet that she never took off. Even to shower. Which was obviously *gross*. Bartley lived in a big glass mansion in Bray, wore boat shoes instead of sneakers, and at fourteen, was already training for the Irish Olympic Swim Team. He had overly gelled hair that swooped upward in a perfect swirl, so people could be reminded of his richness at all times.

Bartley Beasley was also the first boy Tara had ever kissed. Fionn wished he could un-know this information, but he had happened upon it accidentally, when he was eavesdropping on one of her phone calls six months ago.

For these reasons, Fionn considered Bartley to be the worst person of all time. This did not, however, mean he wasn't insulted when Tara decided to join Bartley and his sister an hour later, without inviting him to come along.

"We have plans, Fionny. We're going on a secret adventure."

"I like adventures!" Fionn tried not to sound desperate.

Tara merely looked at him, her freshly glossed lips sliding into a frown, her too-yellow sweater making her look like a lemon.

"This is different. And I don't have time to explain everything right now."

Fionn couldn't bring himself to beg. He couldn't

stand the thought of Tara knowing how badly he wanted it.

"Go and hang out with Grandad." She gestured toward the back garden where their grandfather was bent over his workbench, melting wax chippings for new candles. "Since you find him so funny."

And then she left him alone, surrounded by candles that grouped together in silent judgment, as if to say, *See? Even we have friends.* Fionn considered this strange, new loneliness and wondered whether it was worse than being back in the apartment in Dublin, watching his mother watch television, without really watching it at all.

He decided that it was.

So he ran outside, his socks sinking into the overgrown grass, and watched his sister wind her way down the headland, toward adventure. He thought about calling out to her, or putting his shoes on and running after her, but in the end, he just stood there, listening to the seagulls.

He ignored the rumbling inside him, the feeling that his bones were stretching through his skin, trying to get to the sea.

At eleven thirty, his grandfather pottered in from his workstation to find Fionn flipping through an old encyclopedia (letters Q to Z), trying to pretend he cared about volcanoes. He shoved a five-euro note into Fionn's hand, his fingers mottled in gray wax, and dispatched him to the shop for emergency tea bags (*Twinings, not Lipton, or I'll send you packing*).

"Can I go later?" Fionn asked. "Or maybe tomorrow?"

"Mount Vesuvius will still be here when you get back." His grandfather gestured to the window, where a slash of sunlight was peeking through the dirty panes. "I don't want you to miss any of it."

"Any of what? The deceptively cold sun?"

His grandfather yanked the front door open and that strange island wind whistled through the archway, wrapping itself around Fionn.

"You can take that sarcasm with you too. Bury it under a rock before you get back here with my tea bags."

Fionn laid the encyclopedia down slowly. "I really want to know what happened in Pompeii though," he said wistfully.

His grandfather opened his arms and made an explosion noise. "Big eruption. Everyone died. Tragic stuff."

"Spoiler alert," grumbled Fionn. "Do you want to come with me?"

His grandfather was already retreating to his workbench, his answer thrown carelessly over his shoulder. "Nope."

Fionn glared at the five-euro note, trying to figure out just how necessary this errand was. He once read that humans could survive up to ten days without food and water. Tea, he wasn't so sure about.

When he shut the front door behind him, the wind pushed him out of the garden, past briars and brambles that scraped him goodbye. He fixed his gaze on the horizon beyond the headland and nearly swore when the cliff edge started to roll toward him. He blinked and found it back to normal again, the ocean far below him minding its own business.

It's a short walk, he told himself, as the sea roared, droplets hitchhiking on the wind until he tasted the spray on his tongue.

When he looked down at the ocean, it was still as a lake—flat and shiny in the morning sunlight.

It's just an island.

It *was* just an island. Even if sometimes there were birds squawking in the sky but when Fionn looked up, they had disappeared entirely, replaced by a cloud or—

A seagull dipped over Fionn's head, startling him into the kind of jump that only happens in silent movies. It definitely hadn't been there a moment ago, but when he tried to find it overhead it was gone, leaving nothing but the echo of its cry on the wind.

Was *this* the secret Tara was referring to? The island shifting and stretching and blinking as if it was *alive*?

Or was it withdrawal from *Minecraft*?

Fionn was paying close attention to how the grass grew tall and then short in the same moment, how sometimes the patches by the road were lush and green, and then dried up and brown at second glance, like a drought had sucked them dry. Sometimes there were flowers lining his way, like purple-tipped soldiers, but when he blinked for too long, the air shimmered and they disappeared.

What on earth was going on?

The next time he saw a flower, he yanked it out of the grass so fast he fell backward, sliding down the hill and scuffing his gym pants with clouds of dirt. He glanced around. *No witnesses. Phew.* He leaped to his feet and clamped the limp flower in his fist. *Ha!* His miniature green hostage. Proof that he wasn't losing his mind.

By the time he reached the pier, where shops and houses crowded together like little old ladies looking over the port, Fionn had a fistful of purple flowers in his hand. He was so busy Sherlocking the island, that he didn't notice the girl springing directly into his path, until he was almost nose-to-nose with her.

"Oh!" said Fionn, skidding to a stop. "Sorry. I didn't see you."

The girl was just as tall as Fionn and looked around the same age too. She had sandy hair that fell straight past her shoulders, a wide, curved mouth and big bright eyes that were studying him very closely. She pointed her half-eaten ice cream at his nose. "My impressive powers of deduction tell me that you are Tara Boyle's little brother."

"Only by blood," Fionn lamented. "I'm Fionn."

"Shelby," said the girl, around a mouthful of Creamsicle. She inclined her head in the direction of the shop, where Bartley and Tara were peering over a case of ice creams. "They've been in there for *ages*. And there's only about six options."

Fionn could tell from Shelby's elaborate eye-roll that they both suffered from the same affliction—sibling-related-annoyance. He decided that he liked her.

"Where are you guys going?" he asked casually, trying to keep the gnawing curiosity from flashing in his eyes.

"To find the Sea Cave." Shelby's braces winked at him in the sunlight. Her eyebrows were perfectly arched so that in her excitement she looked like a cartoon character. "Bartley couldn't find it last year but that's only because he didn't have *me*. I have an amazing sense of adventure, which my teacher likes to refer to as 'a proclivity for time-wasting,'" she said, while making finger quotes in the air. "But that's only because she doesn't understand me on a deep, human level. And also because she's extremely boring."

Fionn stared at Shelby Beasley for longer than was socially appropriate.

She stared right back, her eyes glowing even brighter. "It should be quite simple, really. It's not like the island is that big. But don't say that to Bartley because it makes him feel very incompetent about the whole thing. I don't suppose you have any clues as to where it might be, do you?" she added hopefully.

Fionn shook his head. "You could always look at a local map?"

"You must be joking! We'd *never* find it on a map!" Shelby waved her ice cream around at the preposterousness of such a suggestion. "It's hidden for a *reason*."

"Oh. And why is that?"

"Because it's magical," said Shelby, like it was the most obvious thing in the world.

Fionn waited for her to smirk but she pressed her mouth into a hard line and watched him with the same intensity. "Why are you making that face at me?" she asked.

Fionn tried to smooth his features but his eyebrows kept hunching together. "Did you just say the Sea Cave is *magical*? Did I hear that correctly?"

"Clear as a bell," said Shelby, unfazed. "I had elocution

lessons as a child. It was either that or fencing and since I'm not a sixteenth-century monarch, I chose the speech stuff."

"What's so magical about it?" said Fionn, focusing on the important part.

"Well, I'm sure an avid geologist would tell you all caves are magical in their own way. But *this* cave grants wishes."

"That sounds ... far-fetched," said Fionn, with much suspicion.

Shelby frowned. "You don't believe me?"

"Nope. But I do think you were right about the fencing lessons."

She gestured at the crushed flowers in his fist. "Can I see those?"

Fionn handed them over.

Shelby rotated the wilting bouquet, grimacing at it from every angle. "My mother would lose sleep over these," she muttered. "My father bought her pink roses instead of red roses one year for Valentine's Day, and she didn't speak to him for a week. *These* would haunt her. Now, florally, I don't like to discriminate, but I will say I prefer flowers that aren't so ... how do I put this delicately? Miserably and irreparably squished."

"They're not intended for human appreciation."

"Good. So you won't mind parting with them then."

Before Fionn could answer, Shelby chucked the flowers into the air. They fell like confetti, fanning out around them in an array of wilted stems and crumpled petals.

"What was the point of—" Surprise batted the end of Fionn's sentence away.

He gaped at the flowers as they disappeared into the earth, stalk by stalk by stalk, the petals following in silent succession, like they were waiting their turn.

He smudged his feet along the gravelly dirt, just to be sure they weren't still there, hiding somehow. Then he scrunched his nose up toward his forehead. "Where did they go?"

"Look." Shelby skipped to the edge of the road, and Fionn swiveled like a robot, his gaze unblinking as it followed her.

The flowers were resprouting along the grassy edges, popping up one by one.

Shelby whipped them out of the grass and shoved the new bouquet in Fionn's face. "Explain that," she said triumphantly.

Fionn took the flowers from her and rotated them. He was silent for ten very long seconds. So, he hadn't been imagining it all up on the headland. The strangeness wasn't in his mind but in the earth around him. He shook his head in dawning belief. "I . . . I'm not sure I can explain it."

He thought, perhaps, that was the point of magic.

Magic.

Goodness.

Shelby took a self-satisfied bite of her Creamsicle.

Fionn squinted at the new flowers in his fist. The closest he had ever come to magic back in Dublin was finding money at a bus stop. And even then, his mother had made him split it with Tara, who completely wasted her share on yogurt-covered raisins. "Where does it come from?"

Shelby yanked the end of her ice cream from her mouth. "Wait. Do you mean you haven't even heard of *Dagda*?"

"I only just got here yesterday," said Fionn defensively. *And I think my head is about to explode.*

What *else* had he missed out on?

"Well, shouldn't someone have at least mentioned him before now? You're a *Boyle*. This is where you come from."

Fionn glanced inside the shop, where Tara was *finally* paying for her ice cream. Bartley Beasley was swaying behind her, like a big, clingy palm tree. His sister had had plenty of time to tell him about Dagda, whoever Dagda was, and she hadn't bothered. It had just been *Bartley Bartley Bartley* all year round.

At Fionn's look of dismay, Shelby waved her hand around, the last dregs of her Creamsicle blurring to streaks of orange and white. "Never mind. You're here now and we've come this far. I'll just tell you." She rolled her shoulders back and beamed so wide the sun sparkling along her braces momentarily blinded him. "A long time ago—like way before roads and Snapchat and computers and even houses and stuff, two ancient sorcerers fought each other right here, on the shores of Arranmore. Their names were Dagda. *Woooooo!*" Shelby made an exaggerated thumbs-up, before flipping the gesture upside down. "And Morrigan. *Booooo!*"

"You really are a fantastic storyteller," said Fionn.

Shelby snorted, then inclined her head in the direction of the pier. "After Dagda defeated Morrigan, he left his magic behind. It's gathered in different places across the island. The Sea Cave is one of his gifts." She took the final bite of her ice cream, licking the ring of orange from around her mouth. "Our granny says if you can find your way in, the cave will grant you a wish. But it's really difficult to find, not to mention *extremely* treacherous. Which makes it the perfect summer adventure!"

"A magical wish," said Fionn quietly. A kernel of

wonder had ignited inside him, and it was warm and golden as the summer sun. "So...you can wish for *anything*?"

Shelby's eyes were glowing again, both of them dwelling in the dazzling light of absolute possibility. "Of course," she said a little breathlessly. "It's *magic*, isn't it?"

Fionn's heart was thumping so loudly he wondered if she could hear it. He was afraid to believe it ... afraid to *hope*, and yet ... he kept glancing at the flowers in his fist. Remembering the empty fire grate ... "So, how are you going—?"

"Boyle!" Fionn was interrupted by the unceremonious arrival of Bartley Beasley, who stalked out of the shop with all the confidence of a male runway model. He elbowed Shelby out of the way, and looked down on Fionn through the column of a long, slim nose.

He gestured to the flowers in his fist. "Trying to woo my little sister, are you?"

Fionn dropped them like they were on fire. "What! No."

Bartley's laugh came out in exaggerated syllables: *haw haw haw*. He had already opened his snow cone, and had a faint ring of red around his mouth. "Relax, Boyle. Don't have a heart attack."

Now that he was face-to-face with his sister's crush,

Fionn *really* couldn't understand what all the fuss was about. He was every bit as annoying as his profile photo had suggested. Okay, Bartley was tall (his hair adding at least three inches) and was wearing a nice (if a bit posh) sweater, but he still looked like a bird. He had a pointed chin, small, beady eyes, and a pinched mouth that didn't seem used to smiling; it wasn't broad and bow-shaped like Shelby's, who looked as though she lived on the edge of a joke.

Bartley tapped the side of his nose. "I see you've inherited Malachy's honker."

Fionn glared at the perfectly coiffed hair on Bartley Beasley's head and wished a plague of head lice upon him. As if in answer, the wind whipped up, pushing Bartley's hair from its overly gelled swirl, until it looked like he had fallen into a clothes dryer face first.

"Fionn!" Tara charged out of the shop with her Häagen-Dazs ice-cream bar pointed at him like a sword. "What are you doing here? You better not be embarrassing me!"

Fionn wanted to say, *Your sweater is doing that all by itself,* but instead he said, "Shelby was just telling me about *Dagda.*" He narrowed his eyes, his lips twisting with fresh hurt when he added, "Thanks for filling me in."

Tara glared at Shelby. "I was going to do that."

Shelby stared at her Converse, her bright hair falling around her face like a curtain. "Oops."

"*When?*" demanded Fionn. "You've had plenty of time to fill me in."

"Don't be so dramatic. I was getting around to it."

"Did you tell him where we're going, Shel?" said Bartley accusingly.

"Of course I did."

"Blabbermouth," he said viciously. "Why don't you learn how to actually keep a secret for once in your life or will I get Gran to send you home so you can't ruin all our plans?"

Tara jabbed her finger at Fionn's forehead. "Do *not* tell Grandad where we're going or I'll cut up all your T-shirts. He'll kill me if he finds out."

"Why don't I just come with you?" Fionn suggested, his heartbeat galloping at the thought of that wish ... of the impossible things he wanted.

"No," said Bartley flatly.

The word landed square in Fionn's chest.

"No," echoed Tara, twisting the knife. "It's the *Sea* Cave and you're terrified of the ocean. You cried when you heard we had to come out here on the ferry."

Fionn inhaled sharply. His eyes were prickling. His eyes should *not* have been prickling. Even if Bartley Beasley had just slammed the friendship-door in his face, even if his sister had just blown his deepest secret up like a balloon and floated it between them to impress him, even if Shelby was suddenly looking at him like he was a wounded animal. Fionn took a deep breath and freed his fingers from the fists at his side. Then he said, "Tara still plays with her dolls when she thinks no one's home."

Tara nearly choked on her ice cream.

"And they're always stealing each other's boyfriends and slapping each other!"

Bartley stared at Tara with unconcealed horror.

"Sounds scandalous," said Shelby.

"Fionn!" Tara gasped, her cheeks rapidly turning pink.

"You started it!" said Fionn.

"I did not, you absolute *gremlin*." Tara turned from him, tugging Bartley by the sleeve. "Come on. Let's just go."

Fionn didn't say anything else. He just stood there and watched them walk away from him.

Shelby twirled her ice-cream stick in mournful farewell to Fionn. Bartley whispered something (probably unhilarious) to Tara that made her laugh like a hyena and Tara ignored Fionn entirely.

Fionn stared after them, the flowers crushed at his feet, and hated how badly he wanted to go with them.

Instead, he went into the little shop across from the pier and picked out a box of Twinings tea bags and a milk chocolate ice-cream bar.

The shopkeeper smiled at him as he slid the items across the counter. He had creased, papery skin and gray hair that stuck out in every direction, as if he had been electrocuted. "Well, if you're not Malachy's grandson, I'll eat my hat."

"You're not wearing a hat," said Fionn, failing to return the full wattage of his smile. "But you're right about my grandad, so I suppose it doesn't matter. I'm Fionn."

The shopkeeper's laugh sounded like a wind chime. It went on and on and on. "How is Malachy doing? I haven't seen him down here in a while. Usually Rose from over the hill does the shopping for him."

"He's great, thanks," said Fionn automatically. He had been trained to give this answer whenever people asked after his mother, so it had tumbled out unbidden. He didn't really know if it was true or not.

"Any word on the coming storm?" asked Donal.

Fionn shook his head. "Um, I don't think so."

A man wandered out from one of the aisles and set up camp at the magazines by the door, momentarily distracting them from their conversation. He had the reddest hair Fionn had ever seen. It was redder than a cherry. Redder than a fire engine. And as if that wasn't enough color for one person, he had a matching beard-ful of it too.

The shopkeeper eyed him warily, his lips folding into a frown. "Peculiar-looking fella, isn't he?" he said, dropping his voice.

Fionn glanced over his shoulder to get a better look. The man's crimson hair was braided into a series of intricate knots and his beard reached all the way down to his collarbone, ending in two miniature plaits. The cheek that Fionn could see was bright red, probably owing to the thick black turtleneck he was wearing on such a warm day.

"Beard as big as Dagda's, I'd say," muttered the shopkeeper, as he swept the tea bags and the ice cream into a paper bag.

Dagda again! Did everyone know except him?

Fionn handed over the money. "Thanks."

The shopkeeper shook his head as he slid the bag toward him. "On the house, lad."

Fionn glanced at the crumpled fiver still in his fist. "Are you sure?"

"For the Storm Keeper." The shopkeeper winked. "Tell him Donal sends his best."

"I will," said Fionn, tucking the strange nickname in the back of his mind and the paper bag under his arm. When he turned around, the red-haired man was staring at him, a magazine dangling limply in his hands. Fionn kept his gaze on his feet, hoping he hadn't heard what Donal had said about him. He felt guilty enough by association.

"You're just like him, you know," Donal called after him. "It's uncanny. I had to do a double take when you first came in."

Fionn paused in the doorway.

"Your dad, I mean," said Donal, his voice a little thicker than before. "He went to school with my son. That's a long time ago now. Feels much shorter somehow." He shook his head, like the melancholy was a hat he could remove. "It must be wonderful for Malachy to see him again in you . . ."

Fionn didn't wait to hear the rest. He waved a hasty goodbye, ignoring the crushed flowers on the way out, and not noticing when they resprouted along the headland on his way home. He didn't want to think about his father—how they had the same eyes and the same face and the same nose.

How they had never got to meet.

Fionn had seen the photographs, had marveled at their sameness as he grew. But he didn't want to be a stand-in for his father. He just wanted to be *Fionn*. More than that, he wanted his father to be unchained from the lifeboat at the bottom of the sea and stand in for himself. He wanted it so badly it rocked him to sleep most nights and woke him up most mornings. All his life, it had dwelled in the sliver between his soul and his heart— where desire dissolved into impossibility.

When he got back to the cottage, Fionn stowed the tea bags beside the kettle, where another full box leered back at him. In the living room, he sank into his grandfather's chair and reopened the encyclopedia. The words swam off the page as his eyes glazed over, thoughts of the wish he'd make crawling out of his head and sitting on his chest.

Chapter Four

THE WOMAN WHO FOUGHT
THE SEA

Just after midnight, Fionn sat bolt upright in bed with a scream trapped in his throat. He wiped his brow, his gaze traveling the length of the shoebox he and Tara were sharing. Moonlight seeped in through a crack in the curtains, casting strange shadows across the walls.

Tara sighed and turned over in her bed. Fionn knew she hadn't found the enchanted Sea Cave earlier, but whatever she did get up to had kept her away for most of the day.

We're going to try again tomorrow. That's the thing about adventures, Fionny. They take a bit of time.

This time, Fionn hadn't asked if he could go with her.

He knew she would say no. She was still stewing about the doll thing. Plus, the fact remained: he was afraid of the sea. And now everyone knew it.

It needled him that Tara was right. He was not brave. He didn't know how to be brave. Whenever he watched *The Lord of the Rings*, he imagined himself as a lone rider galloping away from a battle while all the other characters were marching into it. When everyone else was in Helm's Deep, he'd be back in the Shire, making a sandwich.

Even so, he couldn't stop thinking of the Sea Cave. If there really was a wish hidden somewhere on the island, would he have enough courage to go and get it? What if he met the same fate as his father? He had fallen asleep imagining himself crawling inside it, through seaweed and seafoam, shouting his wish at the top of his lungs. It was only when the dream turned to visions of a cave swallowing him up like a mouth, that he lurched wide-eyed from his sleep.

He slipped out of bed and into the hallway, trailing his fingers along the shelves of candles as his grandfather's snores echoed through the little cottage.

In the living room, Fionn was surprised to find the giant candle still blazing on the mantelpiece. It was a fire hazard, surely, and yet, considering the way the wind was squeezing itself through the cracks in the walls and howling down the chimney like a banshee, the candle was probably the least of this place's problems. He watched the flame for longer than he intended to. The sea settled in the air around him, and Fionn opened his mouth and tasted a storm on his tongue.

His gaze was drawn to a shelf tucked away in the corner of the room, where a small, dark-blue candle was peeking out from behind a lopsided wax snowflake. It was round and squat, like a piece of fruit, with a silver thread zigzagging through the center.

The label glinted at him in the dimness.

Evelyn, it said.

Fionn climbed on to his grandfather's chair and plucked the candle from the shelf. Why would he name a candle after his mother? And why was it hidden away in the farthest corner of the cottage?

He traced the silver streak with the pad of his thumb as he lifted the wick to his nose. There was no smell. He hopped off the chair and found a box of matches at the end of the mantelpiece. He lit the wick and the flame sparked with a faint *whoosh*. The scent enveloped him: hurried strides across damp earth, grass collecting between toes, the bite of an unforgiving wind. And there beneath the rest of it, two different kinds of salt: warm teardrops in a freezing ocean.

What on earth . . . ?

Fionn held the burning candle in his hand until his curiosity yawned and stretched itself into action. A rogue breeze had slipped underneath the front door and was curling around him.

It pressed itself against his back.

Walk, something inside him said.

He waded out into the night.

This way.

The air shimmered as he pushed through it, the wind shoving harder until he was running so fast his feet were barely touching the ground. The flowers shrank into the earth around him and the grass grew until it brushed his ankles. He didn't notice his bare feet scraping on the rough earth, or the cold seeping through his pajama bottoms. He followed the moon with the flame in his hand and the wind at his back as the island swept by him.

He stumbled past sleepy houses and little cars, the secondary school and the corner shop and the pub. The island was beautiful dappled in moonlight. It looked like a black-and-white painting, punctured with amber flecks, where stragglers were still awake, reading or watching television. They winked in and out as Arranmore rose and disappeared above him, and a new one crept up from the ground.

When the wind finally settled, Fionn hovered on the edge of the beach and watched the sea get angry. The waves swelled, spraying the pier with foam as thunder rumbled through storm clouds so dark they ate the stars.

There was a girl standing in the middle of the sea. The fractured moonlight danced on the crown of her head, and dark hair tumbled down her back, tangling and swaying like ropes.

Fionn hopped over the wall and ran on to the beach, panic guttering in his throat.

"Tara!"

The wind took the name from him and gobbled it up.

"Tara!" She was so far in, he didn't know if she could wade back out again. Not with the waves tugging at her elbows. She started flailing her arms, like she was trying to beat up the sea with her fists. The clouds swirled lower, static crackling along their underbellies as the thunder growled like an angry bear.

Fionn raced to the edge of the beach, where it curved into the sea in a peninsula. The candle was still clamped in his fist, the flame fighting the wind the way his sister was fighting the sea. The wax was melting over his knuckles but he didn't feel it.

When he reached the end of the peninsula, the waves dipped and Fionn saw a bump protruding from the girl's stomach.

He looked at her face. More closely, this time.

"Mom?" This time, the storm didn't steal the name. It spluttered out all on its own.

Fionn's mother was screaming at the sea. The sky was roaring back.

"Mom!" Fionn waved the candle in the air, like a flare. "Mom! Come back!"

A wave crashed against her and she fell backward, a hand cupping her swollen belly. She scrambled to get back up but another one washed over her head, burying her from view.

Fionn launched himself into the water. The waves spat in his eyes and tangled salt in his hair, pushing him back to shore. The harder he tried to get to his mother, the harder the ocean fought back.

And then from the darkness came a flash of pale skin and long limbs. Fionn's grandfather appeared as if from nowhere, hurtling across the strand like an Olympic athlete and flinging himself into the sea headfirst.

He resurfaced ten strides later, his bald head shiny with droplets. He seemed so much younger now, so agile and fearless. The wind didn't steal his warnings the way they had taken Fionn's—they tornadoed around and around, as loud and stubborn as a ship's horn.

"Evelyn!" He yelled, his arm looping around her as he tugged her backward. "Come out of there before you drown, Evie!"

Fionn tried to wade toward them but the sea danced around him in a prison of salt and brine until he lost his balance. He dropped the candle and the flame went out.

The island inhaled.

Fionn's grandfather disappeared and took his mother with him. The tide sank and the clouds evaporated into a star-laden night. Without the clash and clamor of a troubled sky, Fionn could hear his heartbeat in his ears. He remembered to be afraid, and once he did, the fear climbed down his throat and stole his breath.

He was in the sea! And the sea was going to drown him! He stumbled backward and tripped on a rock, his body twisting as he fell. He landed face-first in the ocean and inhaled a lungful of seawater. A wave rolled over him. And then another.

Come out of there before you drown, Fionn!

It wasn't his grandfather's voice now; it was his own.

Fionn dragged himself from the water, spluttering

and vomiting onto the sand. He crouched there, shaking and panting, until the stars in his vision winked out. Then he rolled onto his back and stared out at the empty sea. It was calmer than he had ever seen it, the sky above a star-speckled obsidian.

He got to his feet. He had only been underneath the water for a few seconds, but the sea had made the most of it. He was sopping wet from head to toe. Crystals of salt were stuck to his eyelashes and streaks of seaweed had woven themselves into his hair.

He trudged home, wincing from the pain in his feet.

Slowly, slowly, the world reset itself.

He did his best not to think about the island as it watched him go by. What it had taken from his family all those years ago. Why his mother had waded into the sea and screamed at it like that.

Where was she now? Was she there, or here?

Where was his grandfather? Swimming underneath the tide like a fish or at home in bed where Fionn had left him?

Where am I?

In the cottage, Fionn peeled off his wet pajamas and changed into new ones. He dried his hair with a tea towel in the little hallway outside his grandfather's bedroom, listening to the steady rise and fall of his snores. How could he have been in two places at once? Fionn couldn't wrap his tired brain around it.

In the kitchen, he made himself a cup of tea, then took it through to the living room where he watched the candle on the mantelpiece with a new sliver of mistrust. Why was it lit? And what was it doing to him? He peered around the dusky room, half expecting a ghost to unfold from the patchwork chair. It was stupid to leave a candle burning at night. Hadn't anyone ever told his grandfather that?

This thing could kill us all.

Fionn set his mug down.

Then he stood in front of the fireplace and blew the candle out.

It exhaled like a sleeping giant and pushed a breeze through the cottage that rattled the windowpanes. Fionn felt it on his ankles as he sank into his grandfather's chair.

There. That's better.

Exhaustion swept over him as the tea settled into his bones. Sleep dragged him to a dark place, where he forgot his name and the island along with it, until—

"HELP ME!"

Fionn jerked awake to the sound of his grandfather

shouting the walls down, his fingers scrabbling to light the candle on the mantelpiece. Spittle was gathering at the sides of his mouth and his breath was stuttering out of him in labored gasps.

"WHAT HAVE YOU DONE!" he shouted, his fingers slipping and sliding as another match snapped in half.

Fionn sprang to his feet and grabbed the matches from his grandfather's shaking hands. He lit the candle on the first strike. The flame hissed as it climbed toward the ceiling, raging and thrashing as if it was angry with him for blowing it out. The darkness broke apart and flecks of dust floated around Fionn's surprised face.

He shuffled backward. He was afraid of his grandfather, wild-eyed and unkempt in his mismatched pajamas. He was so much frailer than the man Fionn had seen in the ocean, dipping and diving like a fish. He towered over him now, the light bleeding back into his eyes as he took Fionn by the shoulders and pulled him close.

"I will tell you this once and once only, lad. As long as you live here in this house, as long as you live on this island, as long as you draw breath and pump blood around your body, you are never, *ever*, to touch that candle again." He brought his nose right up to Fionn's, two sides of the same coin staring into the same deep blue eyes. "Do you understand?"

Fionn could feel his pulse in the tips of his ears. "I understand."

His grandfather turned and stalked out of the room like a storm cloud, his footsteps thundering back to his bedroom where he slammed the door behind him. Fionn froze in the middle of the living room, surrounded by hundreds of candles that peered over him judgmentally.

His sister stood across from him in her Hogwarts pajamas, her arms folded across her chest. "I told you never to touch that candle, Fionny."

Fionn wanted to launch himself across the room and shake her and shake her and shake her until all of her meanness fell out.

He swallowed the quiver in his throat. "No, you didn't."

"Oh," she said, shrugging her way back into the darkness. "Well, I meant to."

"You didn't tell me anything!" Fionn called after her, but she was already gone.

In the seething silence, Fionn's mind started to whirr. The truth was unavoidable now—he had seen it. He had *lived* it. Arranmore was full of secrets.

The island was full of impossibility.

Be brave.

The island had magic.

This is your adventure.

And he was going to find a way to use it.

Chapter Five

THE SHRIEKING SKY

The following afternoon, Fionn woke to find his sister had left without him again. After a lonely breakfast of marmalade-smothered toast and milky tea, he found his grandfather stirring a pot of melted wax in the back garden. It was little more than a patch of land wedged between an old wooden shed, a couple of rusty bicycles and some hundred-or-so overgrown plants, but there was something oddly cozy about it.

The sun peered over his grandfather, sprinkling its rays along the mottled workbench and glinting off the back of his bald head.

"Welcome back to the land of the living," he said,

without looking up from the wax. "For a while there, I thought you were nocturnal."

Fionn watched him work, lulled by the steady movement of his arm as he stirred. Around and around the stick went, back and forth.

"I haven't slept that long in ages."

"That'll happen here," said his grandfather, his eyes narrowed in concentration. "Sometimes."

Fionn cleared his throat. "I'm sorry about last night. For blowing out the candle above the fireplace. I didn't realize it was so important . . ."

This was not so much an apology, but a question.

"I know."

His grandfather's response was not so much an answer but a door closing on the topic.

"Do we have any bandages? My feet are killing me."

His grandfather kept stirring, the wax turning milky and smooth as the last chippings melted away. "I'll have a look once I've finished this."

Fionn stalled, his hands dug into the pockets of his jeans. He was waiting for his grandfather to look up at him. When he didn't, Fionn said, "Don't you want to know what happened to my feet?"

His grandfather reduced the flame on the burner but

didn't shift his gaze from the wax. Like he was afraid something might happen if he did.

"I expect you cut them when you went out last night."

Fionn pressed his lips together. He was searching for something beyond the quiet hiss of flame, the distant trilling of a bluebird—the perfect *ordinariness* of this moment. He could sense the whisper of magic writhing underneath it but he couldn't figure out where it was coming from or what it would turn this candle into once it was sitting on one of his grandfather's shelves.

"Aren't you wondering where I went?"

"Do you want to tell me where you went?" his grandfather said, gently shaking the pot, the wax lapping lazily against the sides.

"I want you to ask." What Fionn really meant was, I *want you to care.*

His grandfather removed his horn-rimmed glasses and slid them onto his head. He looked at Fionn.

"I know where you went."

Fionn swallowed. "Oh."

"I know *when* you went, I should say." He drummed his fingers along the workbench, a frown tugging at his mouth. "And I'm sorry, Fionn. I didn't think you'd burn that candle. I expected you might try one. But not that one. I don't even know where you found it," he said, still tapping. "I knew you wouldn't ask first though. That I was sure of."

Fionn knew he should have said sorry then, for taking something without asking, for burning it up and dropping it in the sea, but this moment was so much bigger than that, so instead he said, "I saw you last night down by the beach. But you were here. You were asleep. And I saw my mom in the sea. But she's back in Dublin in that place."

His grandfather's eyes were glinting. Fionn understood that spark, the reflection of the sun in his irises. It was wonder. "But she wasn't always there, Fionn. And I was not always here."

Fionn glanced again at the wax. It was sitting innocently between them, gathered up in a neat little puddle. There was a dull throbbing in the base of his skull, the two sides of his mind jostling for what to believe.

"Where did I go when I burned that candle?"

"You followed the storm." His grandfather said it very casually, as though he was describing a piece of carrot cake he had eaten after lunch. Then he stood abruptly, forgetting about the pot on the workbench as he strode past Fionn and beckoned him inside the cottage. "The island is made up of many layers, Fionn. All of the moments that have gone before us. Last night, by burning that candle, you chose a different layer to visit and in the process, you lost this one." His grandfather stopped in the middle of the living room and swiveled around to face him, a look of triumph on his face. "It is as straightforward as that."

"That is the most complicated thing I've ever heard," said Fionn, but in the corner of his mind—in the space that was becoming more and more open to such impossibilities—Fionn could believe it. The grandfather he had seen last night was not the grandfather standing in front of him now. His mother had not been his mother—but the woman she was right before he was born, just after his father drowned.

"Let me put it very plainly, Fionn. As long as it happened before on Arranmore Island, it can happen again. I just have to catch the weather before it fades away." His grandfather snapped his hand open and shut, like he was trying to catch a fruit fly. "The people are not the focus of the candles, but sometimes I end up catching them too. You see, when you record the weather, you record the world."

Understanding dawned on Fionn, slow and lazy as the rising sun. "Storm Keeper," he remembered. "That's what the shopkeeper called you."

His grandfather grinned. "The storms are my favorite."

Fionn scanned the shelves, a thousand different moments gathered before him, smells and storms and people bundled into wax, all lined up like history books in a dusty old library. And all he could think to say was, "Why do you record any of it?"

His grandfather chewed on the corner of his mouth and Fionn thought he could sense a secret, trying to get out. But in the end, all he did was shrug again. "Well, why *not*?"

Fionn looked at the candle blazing on the mantelpiece and licked the sea from his lips. "It's a weird kind of magic." He didn't want to say *pointless*, but the more he thought about the Sea Cave, and how *helpful* it would be, the more he wished he was outside hunting for it, instead of wondering at the usefulness of candles that showed things that had already happened. *Painful* things.

Thoughts of the Sea Cave brought ugly reminders of Tara's secrecy. It was still festering inside him, like an open wound. He shouldn't have to swallow all this in one big bite—magical caves and weather from long ago—if this was his history then he should have grown up with it . . . had a chance to get *used* to it.

"Why did no one bother to tell me any of this stuff?" he demanded. "Why have I never known about Arranmore?"

"Because it's a secret," said his grandfather, as though this was the most obvious thing in the world.

Fionn glared at him. "Well, why isn't it still a secret?"

"Because you're here now," said his grandfather cheerfully. "I thought it might be better if you discovered the candles first, like your sister did. It helps dispel any suspicion that I might be lying when I inform you that you are standing on a hotbed of ancient magic that contains possibilities beyond your wildest dreams and so must be kept fiercely secret from all those who dwell outside Arranmore." At Fionn's look of alarm, he threw his head back and laughed. His cheeks were still twitching when he said, "And now that we are both official islanders, you may set aside your seething indignation and ask me anything you want."

Fionn took a deep, purposeful breath. "I want to know *exactly* who Dagda is. Tell me everything. And start from the beginning."

His grandfather arched an eyebrow. "The *very* beginning?"

"I want to know *everything*," said Fionn firmly.

What he really meant was, I *want to know more than Tara.*

His grandfather trailed his finger along the rows of candles behind the armchair, stopping at a mottled cylinder that was dark and murky around the bottom and green along the top, where the wax puckered in on itself. It looked more like a clump of grassy dirt than a candle and was certainly the least impressive one in the entire cottage. Even the streak of silver zigzagging across the middle was lopsided. *Fadó Fadó*, the label said. "Long, long ago." He plucked the candle off the shelf. "Perhaps it's better if I just show you."

Fionn eyed the candle with unconcealed suspicion. Such a messy, murky *blob* couldn't possibly be the holder of the island's story.

His grandfather stalked past him, swung open the front door and stepped out into the garden. When Fionn didn't follow him, he turned around, his brows drawing together. It suddenly felt as though there was a barrier between them, a gossamer-thin veil hanging from the doorframe of the cottage. The fire of Fionn's resentment was melting away, and in its absence there were other things tugging at him—uncertainty and hesitation. "What do I have to do?"

"You just have to walk, lad." His grandfather held out his hand. "Will you do that, Fionn? Will you walk with me?"

There was more in that question than those five words. There was hope and caution and excitement . . . and something else. Something cloudy and gray that felt a little like sadness. In the end, the decision wasn't difficult.

Fionn was standing alone in the dusty little cottage and he decided that he would much rather be with his grandfather, wherever he was going. "Yeah," he said. "I'll walk with you."

Fionn stepped over the threshold and took his grandfather's hand. "Hold on tight, lad."

Together, they lit the candle.

This time when the flame fizzed to life and the wind whirled around them, Fionn was expecting it.

"Where exactly are we going?" he asked as the cottage gate creaked open for them.

His grandfather waved the candle above them like a flag. "Back to the very beginning, Fionn. The first storm."

The wind whooshed them onward.

The road disappeared under their feet and rolling meadows of emerald-green grass rose in its place. When Fionn looked back, the cottage had dissolved into a field of wildflowers.

"Once you light a candle, the wind takes you back to the time it contains. You simply have to go with it." His grandfather relaxed against the wind, like he was reclining his seat on an aeroplane. "Once you arrive you must take care not to let the flame die or you'll find yourself back in the present. And don't let go of me either, or you'll be dumped out on your behind!"

Fionn was too out of breath to respond. Even though the wind was doing most of the legwork for him, he was struggling to lean into it the way his grandfather was. He wondered how long they would be herded like this, and more importantly, if there was a bench where they were going.

As they made their way down the headland, the last of the houses disappeared, and big, sprawling oak trees sprouted in their place. The grass grew well past Fionn's ankles and then his knees, while the sky turned to a dappled, milky white. It wasn't long before civilization was pulled out of the island like threads in a tapestry.

Arranmore became a wild, rugged thing.

When the wind lulled, they slowed to a walk.

Fionn had lost all sense of the familiar, and the silence was making him jittery. He glanced at his grandfather, at the crisp edge of his shirt collar, the little woollen balls along his sweater, the gloopy candle in his hand. "Not really your best work, is it?"

His grandfather harrumphed. "I am *certainly* not old enough to have made this candle, Fionn. *Fadó Fadó* is the oldest one we have."

"Is that why it's so ugly looking?"

"Every time we burn it, it remakes itself," said his grandfather. "Over the years, it's lost its shape."

Fionn poked the clump of wax. "Why does it do that?"

"Because Dagda created it." Fionn wasn't sure whether his grandfather meant the storm they were chasing or the candle itself. Perhaps they were the same thing. "It's the very root of our history, Fionn. I think he intended for us never to forget it, no matter how time marches onward."

By the way his grandfather was now strolling through the long grass, his hand swinging Fionn's back and forth, Fionn could tell he had been here before. He wasn't jumping out of his skin every time an oak tree sprouted up beside them and he was completely unconcerned by the disappearance of every single house and shop and road and *person* who brought their Arranmore—the *right* Arranmore—to life.

If this was the very root of their history, then their history was a feral island full of trees and plants and little else.

Fionn's attention was drawn to the forest, where swaying branches shook their leaves, as if saying hello. "Have many people burned this candle then?"

He was trying to imagine his father in this place, studying the same ancient trees, or his mother, who had held on so tightly to the secret of Arranmore she must have squeezed it out of her memory before she came to

Dublin. That, or she had kept it from Fionn all his life, and the idea of her doing such a thing lit a furnace so hot and uncomfortable in the pit of his stomach that he didn't dare dwell on it.

"You'd be surprised how few people care about the past, Fionn."

"I bet I wouldn't." Last year, Fionn had dodged history projects about the First World War and the Renaissance by faking the measles twice. He picked up a stick and flung it over his shoulder, where it landed in the bough of a tree and sent birds squawking from their nests.

His grandfather glared at him. "Don't mess with this layer or the island will kick us out."

Fionn abandoned the perfectly sized rock he was trying to pluck from the grass. "Fine."

They came to a halt at a bend on the headland, where the island dipped toward a beach that stretched on and on, the sand unblemished and golden along the frothy shore.

Across the deserted cove, Fionn could make out a stone fort, and hundreds of thatched dwellings and animals—horses and cows and sheep—wandering around it all. Smoke rose above the camp into the sky, painting it with thick gray clouds that swelled and swirled and clung to each other—the early makings of a storm.

The past had settled around them, and there was life here, between the trees and the fields. Ancient life.

"Oh," said Fionn quietly. "We're not alone."

His grandfather glanced sidelong at him. "We most certainly are not."

Then the sky started shrieking.

Chapter Six

THE LAST SORCERER

The throaty *kraa*-ing of ten thousand ravens flooded the air like a terrifying aria. Fionn's fingers itched for the rock he had left behind, anything that might keep a bird or ten from pecking his eyes out. "I suppose you should explain this."

His grandfather squeezed his hand, while the flame in his other one twisted and thrashed. "A very long time ago, the world found itself under threat from a very powerful sorceress called Morrigan. One of a rare and precious few, Morrigan was born with ancient magic in her veins, a gift that was intended to help protect our world. But as she got older, something happened that caused it to go wrong. Her magic twisted, until it became dark and dreadful and all-consuming. She began to draw her power from the souls of others, wearing them around her like a cape so that she could control them."

Fionn's mouth had gone curiously dry. "What did she want?"

"Morrigan believed her magic gave her the right to rule over ordinary people. To take their souls at will, and leash their bodies to hers, like guard dogs." His grandfather sucked a breath through his teeth. "Power is an ugly thing, Fionn. It's intoxicating and addictive and if you're not wary of its lure then it can lead you down a very dangerous path. As Morrigan grew, so did her twisted magic. She didn't just want to be feared. She wanted to be *worshipped*, like a god. To the exclusion of all others.

"She came for the other magic-born first, swift as a knife and stealthy as night. Those who sensed her coming couldn't hide from her; those who saw her couldn't run fast enough. Parents and children were slaughtered in their beds. Brothers and sisters were burned side by side. Thousands died in the first wave of her terror. More were stripped of their humanity and remade as Soulstalkers. They became cold-blooded and cruel beings, bound to her for all of eternity, chasing souls she would never release . . ."

"I don't remember this from my history book," muttered Fionn, his eyes still glued to the sky. "Why did we spend so much class time studying stones with weird swirls on them?"

"Because it is very hard to believe in magic until it grips you by the shoulders and shakes you awake, Fionn."

Fionn's spine was as stiff as a rod. If he was asleep before, he was wide awake now. "What happened?"

"After months of slaughter, Morrigan brought her reign of terror to Ireland, in pursuit of the final sorcerer. She turned the country upside down, uprooted forests and fields and boulders and hills while her ravens scoured the skies, but as hard as she searched, she could not find the last surviving magic-born."

"Dagda," guessed Fionn a little breathlessly.

His grandfather nodded. "Dagda was a benevolent sorcerer. He drew his power from the elements and bent nature to his will. While Morrigan was out terrorizing the land, Dagda was moving inside storms and traveling through rivers, amassing a secret force. Powerful as he was, he was not strong enough to face Morrigan's growing army alone. So, he found five clans to fight one final battle with him. A war to end all wars."

The warmth left Fionn's cheeks in little prickles. "Just . . . *five*?"

His grandfather's answering smile was entirely serene, as though to him this number was perfectly reasonable and not drastically optimistic. "Dagda chose the bravest clans he could find. There were the Boyles, the Beasleys, the Cannons, the Pattons, and the McCauleys. He brought them here, to a wild and forgotten island to draw Morrigan away from everyone on the mainland." He rolled back on his heels, his gaze traveling upward. "On the day she arrived, her ravens turned the sky black."

Just as he said it, the ravens' shadow crawled over them like a veil, and the island fell into darkness. On the horizon, hundreds of boats rose up out of the water like a tsunami, their black sails spilled out like a slick of oil.

The wind blew a shiver down Fionn's spine. He glanced across the beach, where hefty dark clouds were still puffing into the sky like smoke from a steam train. "They'd better get their act together," he said nervously.

His grandfather pointed the candle toward the middle of the fleet, where the ravens were gathering. They dipped and swirled in a tornado of black feathers until from within, a figure emerged as though it had formed from the birds themselves. She stood on the bow of the foremost warrior boat, her long black hair bleeding into strange shadows that billowed from her like a cape.

"Morrigan." The word tasted acrid in Fionn's mouth.

"Darkness incarnate," his grandfather whispered. He squeezed Fionn's hand. Fionn squeezed back.

The candle was over half-melted now, streaks of emerald-green wax dribbling over his grandfather's fingers, but the flame was still flickering vigorously.

Fionn decided it was a good time to ask a question. "Can you die in a memory, Grandad?"

"They're not able to see us, if that's what you're asking." Before Fionn's shoulders could untense, he added, "But you can die in any layer of Arranmore. They're all as real as each other."

Fionn grimaced. "Fantastic."

Across the cove, a battle cry rang out.

The clouds arced over them, bruised around the edges, where shades of indigo and violet bled into gray and black. Fionn could feel the static building in the air, the answering hum of activity thrumming in the earth around him.

The ancient clans had emerged from the settlement and were gathering along the shore. There were thousands of them—many more than Fionn was expecting, but still not enough to match Morrigan's fleet. Over half of them were brandishing torches. "Everywhere Morrigan went, the darkness came with her," said his grandfather in a low voice. "Their fire helps protect them from her hungry shadows."

Fionn glanced at the flame in his grandfather's fist and willed it to climb higher.

Their attentions were seized by a sudden, powerful gust. As if from nowhere, a man as tall as Fionn's grandfather appeared at the helm of the islanders below. He had thick white hair that rippled past his shoulders and a beard that looked like a runaway cloud. He was striding so fast it seemed as if the wind was carrying him.

The storm clouds moved with him.

"Dagda," whispered Fionn, the name wreathing his bones in warmth. He remembered to breathe again.

"Dagda," said his grandfather with quiet reverence. "Giver of gifts."

Dagda stopped at the water's edge and raised his wooden staff. An almighty roar ripped through the sky, the clouds opening like the maw of a snarling lion.

Fionn could feel the power vibrating through the soles of his feet.

Dagda stepped into the ocean, his white hair tinged green from the glowing emerald set into his staff. His clans fanned out on either side like the wings of a great eagle, their torches and spears raised to the sky. As if tugged by an invisible string, the sea retreated to make way for them. Waves rolled backward in great arches, crashing against Morrigan's fleet and upending three of the boats along the frontline. Soulstalkers spilled into the ocean, like toy soldiers.

Morrigan howled. The fleet quickened their advance, the hulls cutting through the water like butter, while iron spears soared through the storm.

Dagda swept his staff above him and the wind took the spears and flung them back out to sea. The islanders marched on, pushing the shoreline out.

The war-boats made it to the shallows.

"They're really going to fight all those Soulstalkers," said Fionn breathlessly. "They don't even look *human* anymore."

Dagda's cry rang out again and a gust carried it into the sky, where the clouds were beginning to spark with electricity. The clans charged on Morrigan's warriors, their answering cries echoing in every chamber of Fionn's heart, until a small, unused part of him felt like racing down to the beach to join the battle. "Let's get closer!"

His grandfather's grip was tight as a handcuff. "We can't."

"Why not?"

As if in answer, the clumpy candle's flame sputtered, once, twice, and then went out.

The island inhaled.

The wind splintered the storm and the islanders dissolved into another layer, taking their battle cries with them. Fionn gaped at the shimmering sand, the sudden, jarring emptiness before him.

"Why did it go out?" He pointed accusingly at the candle. "There's still wax left! Did you blow it out?"

His grandfather released his hand and touched the lighter to the candle. "Watch."

Fionn twined his fingers in the bottom of his grandfather's sweater just in case the flame lit up again and he was left behind. No matter how his grandfather held the lighter to the wick, it wouldn't work. The wax remained untouched, a ring of green hovering above the darkness underneath. "The candle never burns past this point," said his grandfather. "The memory stutters and the flame fails. Then it starts to remake itself again."

Disappointment bubbled up inside Fionn. It was like watching a film and missing the best part. His feet were itching to carry him down to the cove. "Why does it fail?"

"Nobody knows. Who can say what it's keeping from us?" mused his grandfather. "Perhaps the flame is too weak to protect us from Morrigan's darkness, even in memory."

They turned from the beach, Fionn kicking stones into thin air as they trudged home. "I feel cheated."

"Well, we do know what happened. We have the stories." His grandfather nudged him in the ribs. "Dagda and Morrigan fought on the shores and in the sea surrounding Arranmore. Neither one was strong enough to kill the other, but somehow Dagda found a way to best her in battle. How he did it remains a mystery to this day. By all accounts, he was on the brink of defeat, and then the tide turned suddenly. He buried her deep beneath the earth, but he went down with her, spreading out every last drop of his magic against hers, like a shield, so that she could not rise again. In her defeat, the remaining Soulstalkers fled back to the mainland. Their souls stopped stirring underneath the earth. Over time, they forgot their leader and her resting place along with it."

"Wait." Fionn stopped abruptly. "They *both* had to die?"

His grandfather kept walking, his strides long and leisurely as the island peeled over them, the wind guiding them back home at a much more leisurely pace. "They are not dead, Fionn. Only buried."

"But if they're not dead, does that mean Morrigan could *come back*?" said Fionn, jogging to keep up.

His grandfather's jaw tightened. He glanced sidelong at him, a shadow flitting behind his eyes, gone as quickly as it came. "That's why I'm here, Fionn. And you. And Tara and Bartley and Shelby and all the islanders. If that darkness should return, it will be up to us to defeat it."

The wind whirled busily around them as the island reset itself, but Fionn was barely paying attention to the landscape now. He was halfway to a heart attack. "It sounds to me like we're sitting on top of an evil volcano that could blow at any moment!"

"Well, you don't have to be quite so Pompeii about it."

"But I sprained my wrist from playing too much *Mario Kart* last year! And you lose your glasses every other hour! And what would *Tara* do? Nag Morrigan to death?"

His grandfather clapped him on the shoulder, as though he was trying to press a morsel of strength into him. "Morrigan can't rise on her own, and the island is designed to help us if anyone ever tries to help her."

"The *island*! What can the island do?"

"There's magic here," he said, his brow quirked. "Or haven't you noticed?"

"Like *candles*?" said Fionn in an unusually high-pitched voice. He was suddenly keenly aware of the ancient power-crazy sorceress buried somewhere below his feet. His palms were sweating; he wiped them on the sides of his jeans. "What can *they* do to protect anything?"

Houses rose up from the ground like plants. Roads swallowed grassy fields as the pier and its boats re-formed, the land stretching and groaning as layers of time peeled over it. His grandfather wasn't looking where he was going, but the island seemed to be doing that for him. Instead, he was watching Fionn, with a peculiar expression on his face.

"Dagda drew his power from the elements, Fionn.

Nothing on Arranmore is inconsequential. No blade of grass, no drop of rain, no wisp of cloud. There is magic in *everything*." He pressed his lips together, like there was a secret underneath his tongue, swelling and swelling, until he chewed it up, and then simply said, "There is magic in memory."

Fionn opened his mouth to protest but his grandfather spoke over him. "Watch your feet." He linked his arm. "Don't look at the island while it's changing. It's terribly rude. Now where was I? You can find Dagda's magic all over the island. Gifts, we call them, though in truth they belong to the island, not to us."

"Like the Sea Cave, you mean?"

His grandfather glared at him over the bridge of his spectacles. "Aye. But as I have *told* your sister a thousand times, you are not allowed to go anywhere *near* the Sea Cave. It's much too temperamental. And besides that, the deeper into the island you go, the nearer you are to Morrigan, and that is never a good thing."

The cottage appeared up ahead. The island was growing steadier but Fionn's heart was thumping wildly.

"So, Dagda left an evil sorceress *somewhere* underneath the ground and gave us a moody, dangerous cave to defeat her?"

"Don't be trivial, Fionn," his grandfather said. "This is *serious*."

"I know it's serious!" said Fionn desperately. "That's my whole point!"

His grandfather smiled, the darkness in his warning dissolving between his teeth. "Well, he left a flying horse too, if that makes you feel better."

"Are you *joking*?"

They stopped just outside the garden. The briars had re-emerged in their tangled, messy glory and the seagulls were freewheeling through the sky above them.

Fionn's grandfather leaned against the gate, wobbling uncertainly as though the grass had suddenly been pulled out from underneath his feet. "Oh dear."

Fionn hovered next to him, anxiety buzzing inside him like a hive of bees. "Grandad?"

"Sorry, lad," he huffed. "I find I'm suddenly not feeling myself."

Fionn threaded his arm through his. "Can I do something?"

His grandfather looked at him. Then he looked at his hand, frowning at the dried rivers of green wax striping his fingers, the candle stub still in his palm. He held it out to Fionn. "What is this? Is it yours?"

Fionn stared at the melted candle. "I—no. I think it belongs to Dagda . . ."

His grandfather blinked at him.

Fionn took the candle and shoved it in his back pocket. "Let's go inside."

In the living room, his grandfather wandered over to the fireplace and perched on the arm of his chair, his breathing trundling noisily through his nose. "What were we talking about again? It's on the tip of my tongue."

"Magic," said Fionn quietly.

"Magic," his grandfather muttered.

Fionn pressed his back against the front door. He was only just noticing how musty it was inside the cottage. The air was stale and there was dust spiraling in the thin slants of sunlight that had managed to slip inside. It was still unnaturally dark, the flame on the mantelpiece casting strange shadows along the wall. They were a thousand miles away from where they had just been. A thousand layers too, and Fionn was surprised to find himself yearning for that oak-lined walk, the easy flow of conversation that had come with it.

"I think I need to close my eyes for a bit."

"Sure," said Fionn quickly. If he had learned anything from his mother, it was not to make a person feel bad for feeling bad. It only made the whole thing worse. "I'm pretty tired too, actually. I mean, we did just take a thousand-year round trip. That's like flying to California five times in a row. You're probably jet-lagged," he suggested. "Or time-lagged."

"Time-lagged," his grandfather repeated, the edge of his mouth twitching. "I like that." He took himself away to bed, pottering down the narrow hallway and shutting the bedroom door behind him.

Fionn watched him go.

Then he started in the corner of the living room and inched along the shelves, trying to read every single candle label. As long as it happened before on Arranmore Island, it can happen again. Above the armchair, the portrait of his grandmother smiled down at him. There was a candle nestled on the lip underneath. It was small and round—a pebble the color of midnight—with a rainbow arcing across the middle.

Winnie's Moonbow, the label said.

Winnie Boyle had visited Fionn twice in Dublin when he was just a baby. Fionn couldn't remember his grandmother but his mother said she smelled like roses and smiled like sunshine, spoke like a poet and laughed like a pirate. Fionn stared at the little wax pebble for a long time. In a cottage full of sunsets and blizzards and everything in between, he had already found his mother and his grandmother. Who else had the candles caught over the years?

They stood in silent reverie, the labels winking back at him as he trailed his fingers over them and yet, no matter how hard Fionn searched, he couldn't find the one he was looking for.

The one that bore his father's name.

Chapter Seven

THE HUNGRY SHADOW

Fionn sat cross-legged on the sand and watched the Arranmore ferry glide out to sea. The sound of bagpipes wafted from the pub up on the road, where islanders were singing and laughing, and down by the water's edge, two little boys with pasty legs and yellow sun hats were giggling uncontrollably as they fired clumps of sand at each other. The sun was sitting in the sky like a plump orange, its edges feathered by cloud as fine as cotton candy. It was turning the back of Fionn's neck a rosy pink, but he didn't notice.

He was thinking about the Sea Cave.

He had been thinking about it for the last two days, wondering just how much trouble he would be in if he went behind his grandfather's back to find it, and more importantly, whether he should risk disturbing an ancient sorceress. He had come to the decision that it was worth searching for. For one thing, he had heard that the Beasleys' grandmother was perfectly fine with her grand-children adventuring to the Sea Cave, and for another, Fionn's grandfather seemed prone to being overly cautious. Already he was reaming off lists of things Fionn shouldn't do while out and about, checking on him several times during the night, and frowning at him over dinner as though he was expecting him to suddenly flip a table or throw his dinner plate across the room.

So, Fionn had reached the following conclusion: some things, and impossible things most especially, were worth the risk of punishment.

He had come down to the beach after breakfast, drawn to the spot where the ancient Battle of Arranmore had taken place, in the hope that the cave might be hidden in the rock face nearby. But the tide had rolled out and taken his hope with it. Now he was staring so hard at the waves, his eyeballs were beginning to vibrate.

The little boys went tumbling past him, the leader brandishing a miniature green shovel while the other squealed helplessly in pursuit. A harried-looking woman with a face full of freckles jogged after them, her arms laden with towels and buckets and shoes. When she passed Fionn, she smiled distractedly before stopping to do a double take over her shoulder. "Hang on. Are you—?"

"I'm Fionn," he said, before old ghosts could rise up between them.

The woman brushed the hair from her eyes with the heel of a jelly sandal. "You look ... Well, I thought for a second—"

"I'm Malachy's grandson," he said quickly.

"Oh. *Fionn.* Of course, that's right. You're Evie's boy."

"Yeah," said Fionn, puffing his chest up.

"I'm Alva Cannon." She tried to rearrange a towel-stuffed bucket to shake his hand but thought better of it at the last second, hitching it up her arm and smiling apologetically. "Evie was a few years ahead of me in school. She used to tutor me in French on the weekends. I was useless at it," she added sheepishly. "How's she doing? I haven't seen her since ... well ..." She trailed off.

"She's great, thanks," said Fionn automatically. "So you grew up here too?"

Alva nodded proudly. "Been here all my life. I teach English and history up at the school."

"Have you heard of the Sea Cave by any chance?"

"Dagda's cave?" said Alva, her attention flitting back to

her boys, who were digging themselves into a giant hole. "Find me an islander who hasn't."

"Do you know where it is?" said Fionn eagerly.

She leveled him with a dark look. "That place is hidden for a reason, Fionn. Your mom wouldn't want you to go looking for it." At his look of disappointment, she added, "Did you say you were staying with Malachy?"

"Yeah. I'm here for the summer."

"Just the summer?" She drew her brows together. "I assumed you—" She was interrupted by a high-pitched squeal. One of her little boys had just taken a plastic shovel to the face. "Ronan! Put that shovel down this *instant!* Sorry, Fionn," she called over her shoulder as she scurried toward the commotion. "Send my regards to the Storm Keeper! You can tell him he was right about the terrible twos!"

"I will," said Fionn, but Alva Cannon was already out of earshot, corralling her boys off the beach in a flurry of flailing arms and wriggling legs.

Fionn tried not to dwell on his frustration. If it was that easy to find the Sea Cave, Tara would have got to it already. He had time still. Nothing but time.

So what if there was an evil undead sorceress simmering somewhere underneath the ground? If no one else cared about her then why should he? She hadn't set foot on this beach in hundreds of years. Maybe even *thousands*. They couldn't even get to her with the candle.

I *wonder why?*

He pulled the remains of Fadó Fadó from his back pocket and rolled it along his fingers.

Why make something that can't be used?

He blinked in surprise—twisted the candle this way and that, just to be sure. There was at least an inch of fresh green wax bubbling along the top. The candle was remaking itself.

Fionn jolted as an idea jumped out of his head. If he burned those remade minutes down here on the beach, he would see so much more than he had seen when they were stuck up on the headland peering over the past. He would get to walk beside Dagda. He could answer his rallying cry and stand shoulder to shoulder with his ancestors.

There would be boats racing toward them. Ravens shrieking overhead ... and there would be her. Fionn shuddered at the memory of Morrigan, the shadows that moved with her across the sea.

It's just a memory.

She would still be at sea when the candle ran out again.

So, be brave.

He could do this. He *had* to.

Tara would squirm with envy when she found out.

Fionn's heart was thumping wildly. The wind had picked up, and a faint breeze was curling around his ears as if to say, Go on. Try it.

The beach was deserted now. It was just Fionn and the storm in his palm.

He rolled onto his feet and touched the lighter to the wick.

The candle fizzed into life.

The island inhaled.

The wind slammed into him like a sledgehammer and Fionn went face-first into the sand. He lay in a semi-conscious heap, the flame flickering vigorously as a thousand islands whipped over him, one after another after another. When he roused himself, his mouth was full of beach and the beach was full of war.

The battle cries had returned, but they were closer now—so close that Fionn could smell the tang of dried leather mixed with fresh blood. The sea had rolled back on itself and taken the empty warrior boats with it. Soulstalkers and clansmen were fighting in the shallows, where spears slashed at swords and heads rolled into the sea.

The sky was a deep, bruised purple. Dagda's storm

clouds pressed down on Fionn as he staggered to his feet, their underbellies crackling with whips of electricity.

The wind was prodding him, sharp and pointed like a finger. *Walk*, said a voice inside him. *They're here somewhere.*

Thunder growled through the sinking sky.

They're waiting for you.

Fionn didn't venture too close to the Soulstalkers, though he could see them well enough in his periphery: flashes of wild hair, and empty eyes that seemed to look through the world instead of at it. A wrongness squirmed inside Fionn. He was in the midst of something that should not exist—shells without souls, humans devoid of humanity.

The Soulstalkers wielded swords glistening with blood. Arms and legs were visible beneath swathes of leather and sheepskin fastened like battle armor. Some were taller than others, some quicker on their feet, but they moved with unnatural fluidity, and each one had been branded with twisting black swirls that crawled along their shoulders and up their necks. Where Fionn could see flashes of bare chests, there was an imprint of a raven tattooed in black.

The islanders were smaller and thinner, with wafer-thin skin stretched over sharp bones. They seemed so *breakable* in comparison, but somehow they were holding the line. Fionn watched one hurtle into the waves with nothing but a stone-tipped spear. She landed on the back of a Soulstalker and swung from his neck, dragging him backward into the ocean. She moved around him in a circle, her spear twisting, like she was stirring the sea. The ocean was twisting too. She raised her weapon as if to strike, and the water leaped into the air, pouring itself down the Soulstalker's throat and into his body until his limbs splayed out like a starfish, and his face turned blue. He sank into the sea, like a boulder.

It was over in less than twenty seconds.

The islander bared her teeth to the sky as a cloud rushed down to meet her, wreathing her body in wisps of purple and gray before seeping into her skin.

Fionn closed his jaw. She was *human*. Like *him*. And she had drowned a Soulstalker twice her size without even touching him! A realization struck him as a spear went flying past his nose, weaving unnaturally before impaling itself in the heart of a Soulstalker one hundred paces away. He hadn't seen *any* of this up on the headland with his grandfather. The candle had burned past all the new wax, and it was burning still—the flame burrowing its way into the darkness underneath.

This definitely wasn't supposed to happen.

The battle had moved on and somehow Fionn had moved with it.

The wind was growing impatient. It dragged him along the strand, away from the frenzied clash of sword on stone. Up ahead, the ravens had formed a shrieking black circle. Fionn held the candle out like a lantern, as a gust jerked him through the middle like a puppet, through beaks and feathers and beady eyes, until he found himself standing in a cove with two ancient sorcerers.

The rest of the battle faded to white noise as Fionn's breath bulleted out of him.

They can't see me. They can't see me.

Morrigan hovered across from him, wearing a cape sewn from his worst nightmares. In the shifting darkness, Fionn could make out the imprint of contorted faces stitched together like patchwork, each one stretched into a gaping, screaming mouth.

Even invisible, Fionn could not hide from the sheer terror of Morrigan. The souls engulfed her skeletal body, pulling the warmth from the air and turning it into something cold and dreadful. Her hair was slick and black and endless, her skin so pale, the light shot through it and glistened along her glacial bones.

Fionn thought he might throw up. He tried not to imagine his own face bursting from his body to join the others.

Be brave.

He shuffled forward on shaking legs.

She can't see me. She can't see me.

Morrigan's bloodless lips were moving around muttered incantations, her obsidian eyes trained on the figure kneeling before her.

Dagda, Fionn realized.

His head was bent to the earth, his white hair obscuring the side of his face, so Fionn couldn't tell whether he was conscious or not. Only that he looked more human than he could have ever imagined. Weak, *breakable.* His staff lay forgotten beside him, the emerald stone half covered in sand.

The darkness speared Fionn's heart as he inched toward it. Step by step, sweat turning to ice on his brow, shadows kissing his fingertips. The fear was almost paralyzing, but now that he had made it here, *somehow,* he had to know. He had to see how it had ended.

Morrigan was unspooling Dagda's soul, her incantations turning guttural with need. Strands of light had burst from the sorcerer's chest and were floating through the air in gleaming, gossamer threads. As they moved toward her, they turned oily and black, seeping through her teeth as she gulped them down.

This was not how the story was supposed to go.

The shadows around Morrigan were growing while Dagda's light was dying.

Something was very, very wrong.

The wind slammed its fist into Fionn's back. *Do something!*

"Hey!" Fionn brandished the dying flame in his fist. "Get up! She's going to kill you! Get up and fight!"

Dagda slumped forward, his body shuddering as the last thread of light left him.

No no no no no!

"Get up!"

He couldn't hear Fionn. Of course he couldn't. But what else was he supposed to do?

Do something!

Fionn slammed his fist into Dagda's back. "Do something!" he roared.

Fionn's fingertips jolted. A spike of warmth surged up his arm and exploded inside his chest.

The island hiccuped.

Morrigan turned her endless gaze on him.

The world shrank to two obsidian pinpoints.

Fionn fell to his knees, a scream guttering in his throat as an icy fist closed around his heart.

Dagda staggered to his feet.

Morrigan blinked between them, the shadows around her faltering for a precious, fleeting second.

Dagda pointed his staff at her and a bolt of searing bright light speared her chest.

The candle in Fionn's fist went out. Morrigan's howls chased him through the layers, as the world tilted and then went black.

Chapter Eight

THE STRANGE TOURIST

It was almost an hour before Shelby Beasley found Fionn huddled in a ball at the end of the beach.

She tapped him on the shoulder. "Are you doing your best impression of a sea turtle or do you have an awful stomachache? I can't tell. Groan once for turtle, twice for food poisoning."

Fionn raised his head.

The dying sun haloed her face, the edges of her mouth creased in an exaggerated frown. She glanced behind her. "Do you want me to get your sister? Bartley's walking her home. I said I'd give them a minute to say goodbye."

Somewhere in the very back of Fionn's mind, a little

voice said, *Gross.* He got to his feet, his knees still knocking together.

"I'm fine. I just ... I must have fallen asleep." He turned his face to the ocean, his breath tripping as he watched the waves lapping against the shore. The beach was deserted. The battle was long over.

They had survived.

He had survived.

Mercifully, Shelby was not at all like her older brother. She waved his strangeness away, her braces glinting at him when she said, "I suppose there's nothing wrong with a bit of fresh air. I love the way it smells like seaweed here. You don't really get that back home, do you?"

Up above, the gulls were making their little pterodactyl noises. "I suppose not," said Fionn distractedly. He could still feel the imprint of Morrigan's gaze inside him.

She had *seen* him.

One minute he was invisible, the next he was trapped beneath her stare.

He had felt it in his bone marrow. He couldn't shake the sensation off, no matter how many years stood between them now.

She felt unbearably *close.*

To him. To all of them.

"Shelby," he said urgently. "Can you tell me what else Dagda left behind to protect Arranmore?"

Shelby blinked in surprise. "Not one for small talk, are you?"

"The gifts," pressed Fionn. "I need to know about the gifts."

"Okay . . . ," she said slowly. "Well, there's the Sea Cave, for that which is out of reach. But you already know about that thanks to yours truly."

Fionn nodded fervently. "Keep going . . ."

"Um. There's the Whispering Tree, for that which is yet to come."

"What does that mean?"

"It shows you the future. Kind of. I'm not exactly sure how it works, but my gran says you can ask it any question and it will tell you the answer. She visited it *ages* ago and she's still angry at it. How you can be mad at a tree, I have no idea," mused Shelby. "But I did see her threaten a sheep once, so I suppose I shouldn't be too surprised."

Fionn blew out a breath. "Okay. Good. What else?"

"The Merrows, for invaders that may come." Shelby sounded more sure of herself now. Her eyes were twinkling with that same impossible wonder. "And before you ask, merrows are *not* mermaids. My gran is very precise about the whole thing. Apparently, they're more like monsters than humans. They don't have many dealings with us." Shelby grimaced. "Which is probably a good thing. I've only just got over my fear of dolphins and their creepy smiles. And anyway, we don't have any business with an army of sea barbarians, do we?"

An *army of sea barbarians*. Fionn's shoulders relaxed.

"Then there's Aonbharr, the flying horse, for danger that cannot be outrun." Shelby beamed so wide it looked like the sun was shining out from behind her face. "If I had my way, we'd be looking for *him*, but Bartley's still stewing over the pony that bucked him off during his eighth birthday party. My mom says he has pony-related post-traumatic stress disorder but I don't think that's a real thing. It probably doesn't really matter either way, because he's *obsessed* with that stupid cave." She took an exaggerated breath before adding, "I'm assuming you already know about the Storm Keeper?"

"Yeah, yeah. The weather stuff," said Fionn dismissively.

Shelby looked at him strangely. "Then that's all of them, as far as I know."

Fionn was starting to feel better. There really were things in place to stop Morrigan. *Useful* things.

And Bartley Beasley was afraid of ponies. H*a!*

"Thanks, Shelby."

Shelby shrugged. "Glad I can be of some use today."

"No Sea Cave yet?" Fionn fished.

She shook her head mournfully. "I wish Bartley would let me take over for a bit. He's terrified that if he's not leading the way, one of us will steal the dumb wish."

Fionn tensed. A new breed of anxiety was suddenly spider-walking up his spine. "There's only one wish?"

"Well, one per generation. That's why Bartley's so picky about who he takes with him. I'm family and Tara . . . Well, she's loyal to him because of their . . . romance." She wrinkled her nose. "But he sees you as a threat. It's my gran's fault putting the old family rivalry in his head. Don't take this the wrong way, but she's been poisoning him against you for as long as I can remember. Well, both of us actually, but I like to think for myself." She smiled apologetically. "If I had my way, we would all go."

"Don't you want the wish though?" said Fionn, trying not to appear too offended by all that unearned Beasley hostility. "If there's only one, how come Bartley gets it?"

"I want the *horse*," said Shelby with renewed excitement. "I love my gran but whoever gets that wish will end up having to answer to her. She's the reason Bartley's so obsessed in the first place. And I'm no one's puppet."

"But why would—"

"Hey! Shelby!" As if summoned by the mention of his

name, Bartley Beasley appeared on the headland with his chin in the air and his hands on his hips. He marched toward them. "Uncle Douglas has the barbecue on! We have to go!"

"Speak of the devil," said Shelby.

"Literally," said Fionn.

"What are you doing over there with that weirdo, Shel?" yelled Bartley. "Stop annoying my sister, Boyle!"

"I'd better go before he gets even more cranky," she said, backing away from him. "See you around, Fionn!"

* * *

When Fionn made it back to the cottage, there was a raven sitting on the chimney and a man loitering in the front garden. Fionn recognized him immediately by his flaming crimson hair. It was scraped into a ponytail today but his beard was as full and vibrant as it had been in Donal's shop, and he was still wearing the weird sweater despite the warm day. He was inspecting the briars, twirling the thorns between his fingers, like a poet scouring for inspiration.

"Can I help you?" said Fionn, slowing to a stop.

The raven *kraa*-ed as it flew away.

Fionn tried not to jump out of his skin.

It's just a bird. I'm not afraid of birds.

The man regarded him with an easy smile—a full set

of bright white teeth made all the whiter against the shock of red. He released the thorns and dug his hands in his pockets. "I'm looking for the Storm Keeper."

Fionn tensed. Perhaps it was the unexpected raven or the memory of Morrigan's gaze branded in his mind, but he was suddenly on high alert.

"Alas, your sister says he's not here," the man went on. He was slimmer than Fionn remembered, his shoulders bony and his chin sharp, his body carved with angles instead of curves. "Or was she lying to me?"

"Sorry, who are you?"

The man's chuckle was a musical arpeggio. "Forgive me, Fionn. I often forget to introduce myself. I'm Ivan. I arrived a couple of days ago from Dublin." He dipped his chin, his hands still dug into the pockets of his jeans. "I am just *fascinated* by the history of this island."

Fionn didn't know which made him more uncomfortable—the familiarity with which he was speaking to him or the fact that he hadn't blinked since they began their conversation. "What brings you here?"

"Curiosity," said Ivan, stepping into his path. Fionn tried to place his accent but he couldn't. It was easy and fluid, a singsong cadence that made it seem as though he might burst into song at any moment. He didn't sound like he was from Dublin. "If I'd have known where all the good

Irish weather had been hiding ... I would have come a lot sooner."

"Don't get used to it. The weather here is just as unpredictable."

A glint sparked in Ivan's eyes. "Is that right?"

Fionn got the feeling he had just made a misstep. Uneasiness was grumbling in his stomach, the events of earlier creeping over him again. He needed to be inside in the comforting dimness, away from human interaction. "I'd better go."

Ivan didn't move out of his way. "Do you happen to know when your grandfather will be back? Your sister didn't seem to have a clue."

"No idea."

His beard twitched. "I was under the impression he never left the house. Isn't that why Rose from over the hill does his shopping for him?" he said, plucking the detail from Fionn's previous conversation with Donal and holding it over him now like an interrogation lamp. "At least, that's what I *heard* ..."

There was a long, lingering silence.

Fionn glared at Ivan. "What exactly did you want to talk to my grandfather about?"

Ivan smiled, the word coming through his teeth. "*Caves.*"

Fionn's chest tightened. Ivan's smile was suddenly too loud, his beard vibrating from the effort of it, and there were beads of sweat dripping down the sides of his face.

"Well, I'll let him know you came by," said Fionn, arcing purposefully around Ivan and striding into the cottage. "Have a nice day."

Chapter Nine

THE RESTLESS ISLAND

Fionn's grandfather had squeezed himself into the gap between the windows in the living room, his shoulders hunched together so he looked as narrow as a green bean. "*Pssst,*" he hissed. "Stay low."

Fionn shut the front door behind him. "He's leaving."

His grandfather pressed his face against the windowpane, like the worst spy of all time. "*Finally.*"

"What a weirdo," said Tara from inside the kitchen. She was reclining across two chairs, scrolling through her phone. "It's like he's trying to kidnap you or something."

"He's probably just an aggressive breed of tourist." He unstubbed his nose from the pane. "*Where* is he off to with a beard that big? Is he trying to outdo Dagda himself?"

"And that *turtleneck*," added Tara with equal disgust. "It offends me."

Fionn hovered between them with his fists bunched by his sides. "I need to tell you both something."

"What do you want? A musical introduction?" said Tara.

Fionn cleared his throat, his heartbeat suddenly galloping faster than a racehorse. "I came face-to-face with Morrigan today. I burned the rest of Fadó Fadó."

His grandfather, who was loping away from the window like an exaggerated cartoon, paused mid-tiptoe.

"You are such a liar," said Tara through the archway. "You can't burn the end of Fadó Fadó."

Fionn set his jaw. "I'm *not* lying."

His grandfather spun around, his attention honed on Fionn like a laser point. "Explain . . ."

The memory was still looming over Fionn like a shadow. There was an aching fullness in his chest and he couldn't tell if it was a pool of unshed tears or the scream Morrigan had trapped in his throat.

"I saw Morrigan," he said stiffly. "I went back to the battle and watched the clans fight the Soulstalkers. I saw one of them control the sea without even touching it. They were using magic."

"The candle burned," said his grandfather quietly. "After all these years."

Fionn swallowed the lump swelling in his throat. "All the way to the end."

His grandfather blinked once, slow and heavy.

In the kitchen, Tara's chair scraped across the tiles.

"Then I found them," Fionn went on quickly. "Morrigan *saw* me. She looked right at me and I *felt* it." He clutched his heart, as if he had been punched. "Then Dagda hit her with something and the candle died and I think I must have passed out but when I woke up I was still on the beach and the rest of the wax had melted all over my hand. The candle's gone, Grandad. I'm sorry."

He raised his hand as Tara marched through the archway.

She grabbed it and turned it over, tracing the rivers of inky black wax with her finger. "This could be anything."

"Why would I lie? I'm not *you*." He turned to his grandfather. "You believe me, don't you?"

His grandfather lowered himself onto the side of the armrest, his knees creaking in the silence. He didn't speak for a long time. He stared instead at a spot on the floor, his eyes glazing as though he was traveling somewhere else inside his head. Fionn counted his own heartbeats—ten, thirty, fifty, until—"Yes, Fionn. I believe you."

"*What?*" said Tara, aghast.

"I touched Dagda," said Fionn, spurred on by his

grandfather's unexpected support. "He was on his knees and then I don't know what came over me but I sort of thumped him in the back and my fingers jolted and that's when Morrigan looked at me! She got distracted and then Dagda leaped to his feet . . ." He trailed off.

His grandfather was staring at him as though he had just confessed to murder.

Fionn slammed his teeth into his bottom lip. "But she's gone, isn't she?" he said shakily.

"There's no need to be afraid," said his grandfather, quickly stretching his lips into a smile. "No need at all, in fact. I'm right here with you. You're home now, lad."

"I'm sorry, but *why* are you even humoring this?" Tara interrupted. "You've said it yourself, Grandad. We can't be seen in other layers. We're like the wind!" She turned on Fionn. "You did not go and play with Morrigan and Dagda earlier. You threw that candle in the sea and then made up a stupid story about it because you felt left out."

"And what did you do?" Fionn fumed. "Run around the cliffs all day so you can scoop out that wish and hand it to your idiot *boyfriend* on a silver platter? If you *cared* about your family you wouldn't give it away so easily!"

Tara's lips twisted. "You have no *idea* what I care about."

"*That's enough!*" said their grandfather sternly. "If I

wanted to experience death by pointless bickering, Winnie and I would have had a second child."

Tara scowled at him. "That candle doesn't burn for anyone! Why would it burn for *him*?"

"Because I'm better than you," said Fionn.

"You *wish*."

"Dagda, give me *strength*." Their grandfather rolled his head from side to side like he was trying to knock all the stress out of his brain. "I want you both to listen to me *very carefully*. And this time, when I say *listen*, I *mean* it, Tara." Tara looked at her shoes. Fionn smirked at her forehead. "There are forces at work here that I don't fully understand yet. The island is restless. There are reports of other layers peeking through, things appearing and then disappearing. The tides are keeping their own rhythm. The weather is as unpredictable as ever, the birds even more so. I've seen more ravens this week then I have in years . . ."

Fionn's cheeks began to prickle.

"It definitely wasn't like this last summer," mumbled Tara.

"It's never this bad. Even before a storm." He tipped his head back to the ceiling, his eyes shut tight as if he was sleeping.

"I think that's why that Ivan guy's come," said Fionn.

"I hope he's just a tourist chasing rumors, but it is

important to be wary of everyone. Morrigan took a great many souls to her grave. She has her followers, even now." He snapped his eyes open. "I want you both to be very careful. Don't burn any candles unless you're with me, and don't speak to anyone you don't know. Keep your heads down." He leveled Fionn with a dark look. "*Especially* you, Fionn. Can you both do that for me?" he said wearily. "*Please?*"

"We will," they chorused.

"And for the last time, stay away from that *blasted* Sea Cave."

"We will," they lied.

That night, the island sang Fionn a lullaby. A woman called out to him through the layers, pulling him through time and over sea. He tumbled from dream to dream, the melody bringing him to the edge of a jagged cliff, where he was serenaded from the cavern beneath his feet. Fionn followed the woman's song until he stood beneath a great, black hole, the yawning entrance as sharp as fangs.

A shadow leaped inside, and Fionn stumbled after it, sure it was his father.

Chapter Ten

THE SUSPICIOUS WISH

The following days brought dull weather and fruitless searching. Now that Fionn knew there was only one wish simmering inside that cave, time was of the utmost importance. He bought a local map of Arranmore from Donal and set about marking the cliffs that might harbor a cave entrance. Rather inconveniently, they covered most of the coast.

Even when he managed to overcome the hour-long walk and the pesky wind that came with it, Fionn's investigations were still beholden to the tides, which seemed to rise higher every day, as though they were trying to swallow the island. Tara spent most of her time with the Beasleys, tracking the rock face just as unsuccessfully, until the evening she returned with a smirk so wide it pinched her cheeks. "I told you I'd find it before you," she said to him when they were lying in bed that night.

"Has he taken it?" he asked in alarm. Was it all over already?

"We haven't found a way down to it yet but we will when the tide goes out."

There's only one wish! Fionn wanted to scream. *And you're letting him steal it from us!*

He curled his fingers in his blanket and swallowed the desperation bubbling inside him. He would not yell. He would not beg. He scrunched his eyes shut and held on to his carefully curated silent treatment, eventually falling asleep to the sound of her texting furiously.

The next morning, he woke to the sound of church bells ringing.

Dong dong dong.

They breezed up the headland and swept under the doorway, echoing off the walls of the little cottage and vibrating underneath the floorboards. Fionn could feel them on the soles of his feet when he rolled out of bed. Though it felt like an age since he had left Dublin, it was only his second Sunday on the island. His second Sunday away from his mother.

Sometimes, back home, when she was feeling up to it,

she would take the three of them to the Temple Bar Food Market, and they would spend the morning wandering the stalls, sampling the crêpes, and ranking them out of ten. It was here, one drizzly Sunday, that Fionn discovered bacon jam for the first time and Tara found chicken eggs that were dyed bright blue. Once, their mom bought a giant bag of toffee marshmallows and they took turns seeing how many they could stuff in their mouth at the same time. Fionn had emerged victorious with eleven, but his mother (trailing with seven) swore she would have won if it had been green olives, which were her favorite food. Tara had demanded a rematch and Fionn had helpfully suggested that she should try and keep her nine marshmallows in her mouth for as long as possible so they could all have some peace and quiet.

Dong dong dong.

He dressed in gym pants and his favorite gray hoodie. He wore his best sneakers too—the ones his mother got him from the Nike outlet shop for his eleventh birthday. They were black with lime-green ticks running up the side. *Adventuring shoes,* she told him when he unwrapped the box, eyes gleaming with happiness.

If only she knew where he was planning to take them.

Bartley and Shelby came by just before midday,

arriving in the midst of an argument about how Bartley had been using Shelby's hair conditioner without her permission. Fionn was hovering in the garden, pretending to inspect the headless flowers.

"Boyle!" said Bartley, while Shelby waved at him. "I didn't know you had a green thumb. Is this what you do when we go exploring? Gardening like an eighty-year-old woman?"

The wind whipped into a sudden flurry and the rosebush bent over Fionn, its petals brushing the edge of his earlobe as though to whisper, *Do you want me to fight this Beasley kid?*

"That's sexist," said Shelby. "He could be acting like an eighty-year-old *man*."

"Shut up," said Bartley, banging on the front door.

"Knock louder," said Fionn. "So everyone on the mainland can hear you too."

Bartley cut his eyes at Fionn, his lips curling into a sneer. "Don't worry, Boyle. We'll tell you *all* about the cave after we get in."

"*If* you get in," said Fionn.

Bartley smirked at him. "You sound jealous, Boyle."

"I'm not jealous," Fionn said quickly.

"What would you wish for anyway? A friend? I doubt there's a cave magical enough to pull that one off. You could try wishing for a backbone though. Or maybe shoes less embarrassing than last year's cast-offs."

"Bartley, you wear boat shoes," said Shelby.

Fionn smiled blandly. "I assume you'll be wishing for a personality, Bartley. Though your face could probably do with some divine intervention too."

Shelby trapped her laugh on the back of her hand. It hiccuped in her shoulders and turned her face red.

Bartley glared at her as Tara flung the door open. They tumbled into each other in a mismatch of hoodies and flailing limbs. Bartley frantically checked his hair was still in its little swirl, before extending a hand to help her to her feet.

"And they say chivalry is dead," said Shelby.

"Ready?" Bartley said, when they had righted themselves again.

Tara tightened her ponytail. "Ready."

"To the lighthouse!" said Shelby, glancing at Fionn.

"Shut up!" said Bartley viciously.

Fionn rolled his eyes.

"See ya later!" said Shelby.

"Good luck with the encyclopedias, Fionny," said Tara. "Don't eat them if you get hungry!"

They took off down the headland.

Fionn counted to a hundred in his head. Then he followed them.

He was almost at the church when he lost sight of his sister and instead found himself standing face-to-chest with the tallest man he had ever seen. He was broad too, with beefy arms and wide shoulders that took up twice the width of an average person and he had an oversized mustache that looked not unlike the sweeping end of a kitchen broom.

"Fionn Boyle," he boomed, his familiar beady eyes flashing with triumph. "At last we meet!"

"Um. Hello," said Fionn awkwardly. The man looked enough like Bartley for Fionn to make the family connection but his accent was island-born, which meant he was perhaps not Bartley's father, but his uncle, Douglas.

Before he could ask, a tall, sinewy woman with long silver hair elbowed the man out of the way.

"It has been a long time since I saw you, Fionn Boyle," she said, studying him with small, coal-like eyes. "A very long time indeed."

Fionn scrunched up his nose. "I think you've got me confused with someone else."

"My name is Elizabeth Beasley," she said, extending a dainty hand. Fionn was surprised by how strong her grip was, how vigorously she shook it. "I'm an old friend of Malachy's."

The mustachioed man snorted, and Fionn was

reminded of his presence on the periphery of their conversation. Demoted, but still very much there.

"How's your summer going?" asked Elizabeth sweetly.
"Is the island being kind to you?"

"I, eh, yeah. It's—"

"Douglas and I would *love* you to meet someone," she
interrupted.

Douglas beckoned at someone over Fionn's shoulder.
"C'mere," he grunted. "Come and meet the Storm Keeper's
grandson."

To Fionn's surprise, Ivan slipped in front of him, as
though he had materialized from thin air. He had combed
his beard into submission, and his red hair had been braided
away from his face. He had paired his usual black sweater
with a smart blazer and jeans, but he still looked a hundred
degrees too hot for the weather. "We've met," he said cheerily.

"Ivan is a distant cousin of ours," said Elizabeth.

"*Really?*"

"I think he knows more about this place than I do,"
she added, laughing. "He's very invested in the family's
future. Or perhaps I should say the *island*'s future."

Fionn stared at Ivan with renewed suspicion. "I
thought you were interested in the history of Arranmore."

Ivan grinned at Fionn. "Haven't you heard, Fionn?
History always repeats itself."

"Except in the case of Boyle Storm Keepers," said Douglas, his oversized mustache twitching doubly fast now. "And before you get any wild ideas, boy, that gift is going to pass to my nephew. I don't care if everyone thinks you're the one. Things are going to change around here very soon..."

Fionn blanched. *What?*

Douglas winked at Ivan, a sharp laugh cutting out of him. "He just needs a little extra help, that's all."

Elizabeth's smile disappeared in the lines around her mouth. "How's your grandfather, Fionn? We haven't seen him down here in a long while..."

Ivan held his static smile, his eyes misted over as though he was looking through Fionn—to the future, or the past. Or perhaps both. "I'm sure the next Keeper will be less... elusive."

"Of course he will," said Douglas knowingly.

The next Keeper...

Fionn's heart was hammering in his chest. What had he missed? And why were the Beasleys so smug about it? He had to find out where Bartley Beasley was and just what exactly he was going to wish for.

"Excuse me," he said, turning from the three of them. "I have somewhere to be."

"Not the cave, I hope," Douglas called after him. "A

scrawny little kid like you wouldn't last two minutes down there. There's a *storm* coming, you know."

Storm. He said it with such gravitas that Fionn stopped in his tracks. He glanced at the sky. "I don't see any clouds."

Elizabeth's laugh was a sharp titter, the mating call of an evil bird. "This is a different kind of storm, Fionn."

"Island-brewed," said Ivan breathlessly.

Douglas smirked. "The first in nearly twelve years."

Fionn turned on the heel of his shoe. "What?"

"Oh, I'm sure Fionn doesn't want to talk about that," said Elizabeth, her smile indulgent. "Especially after what happened to poor Cormac."

Fionn's heartbeat stuttered. It had been a long time since he had heard his father's name out loud. It hovered in the air between them, like a wisp of cloud. Fionn wished he could hook it in his finger and take it away from these horrible people.

"We thought the magic was going to pass to him all those years ago," Elizabeth went on. "The island was wide awake. The storm was brewing. And then ... well ..." She dropped her voice, the ends of her bright hair floating around her face like snakes. "I suppose he shouldn't have gone out in that lifeboat. He was looking for trouble."

Fionn desperately wanted to say something brave and

defiant but his bottom lip was trembling and he couldn't help thinking of his father being pulled into the eye of that storm. How terrified he must have felt, how desperately *alone* he was in those final moments.

"I believed it was Cormac I saw at first all that time ago, you know ..." The veneer of politeness was gone. She was smiling openly, enjoying the grief on Fionn's face. "But he never remembered it. And now I see you're *just* like him. There really is no diluting those ... *strong* Boyle features. Except ...," she went on, her dark eyes narrowing.

Fionn stood frozen, pinned to her viperous smile. "Except what?"

Elizabeth Beasley peeled her lips back. "Except Cormac wore the sea behind his eyes. Even as a boy, if you looked hard enough, you could see it. He was *very* brave."

"But not brave enough in the end," said Douglas.

Ivan cleared his throat uncomfortably.

Fionn backed away from them, a hermit crab scuttling into its shell.

"Fionn," Elizabeth called after him, and despite his better judgment he paused one final time. Her expression was darker now, as though a shadow had fallen somewhere beyond her eyes. "It will *never* be you."

Her words hung over Fionn like a specter as he hurried past the church. He walked so fast his breath punched out of him. His father's name hung like a flashing sign in the back of his head.

Cormac wore the sea behind his eyes.

Cormac was very brave.

And what am I?

What was Bartley going to wish for in that Sea Cave? And why did Fionn have a horrible feeling that it was going to harm his grandfather in some way?

To the lighthouse. He ran and the wind blew with him. Fionn tried to convince himself that the island was on his side, that he belonged here just as much as anyone. That this place hadn't reared up and killed his father twelve years ago. That it hadn't brewed the storm that drowned him.

The land climbed and Fionn climbed too, running and panting past the lake and the deserted fields and the century-old dilapidated stone houses while black birds shrieked in the air above him.

Crows, he told himself. *They're only crows.*

He tried to pretend he didn't recognize those piercing calls as they followed him across the island.

When he reached the cliffs by the lighthouse, he got down on his hands and knees and dipped his head over the edge.

There was no sign of his sister.

There was nothing but his own heavy breaths echoing around him.

Even the birds had disappeared somewhere over the cliffs.

A breeze frittered along the grass and Fionn couldn't help but think the island was laughing at him. Even when he was hitchhiking on someone else's adventure, he couldn't seem to keep up.

He trudged home past shops and boats and endless fields until he found himself at the lifeboat station down by the pier. He slid down on his haunches and pressed his back against the building where his father, and his father and his father and his father before him, had spent every day of their lives between adventures at sea. Between lifeboats. Between bravery.

He stayed like that for a long time, the wind leaving him to his thoughts. Islanders passed by every now and then but he didn't greet them, not even as they paused to take a second look at him—this boy who looked just like his dead father, this boy who would never be half as good as him.

Chapter Eleven

THE WHISPERING TREE

When Fionn finally got back to his grandfather's cottage, Tara was sitting at the kitchen table with Bartley and Shelby, watching a video on her phone. She had changed into her lemon sweater, and her hair was frizzing around newly freckled cheeks. "Where have you been?" she demanded. "I don't care that you were gone, I just hope you weren't filling up on those *disgusting* maple kettle chips. It's your turn to make dinner tonight."

Bartley, who was reading the candle labels in the living room, smirked at Fionn over his shoulder. "Still no friends then, Boyle?"

Fionn couldn't believe his eyes. He had raced across

the island to save Tara from the schemes of this follically gifted Voldemort, and here she sat, lecturing Fionn on basic nutrition as if she hadn't once tasted her coconut shampoo because it smelled so delicious. And also, *as if* this place would sell maple kettle chips. "I thought you were going to the Sea Cave," said Fionn.

"*Ssssh!*" said Tara. "Grandad will hear you!"

"The tide wouldn't go out," said Shelby, through a mouthful of Starburst. "It was too high to see anything and there were all these birds getting in the way, so we gave up and got treats from the shop so we could eat our feelings instead."

"So *that's* why you weren't at the lighthouse," muttered Fionn.

He regretted the words the second they slipped out. He wished he could stuff them back in and chew them into nothingness.

Bartley spun around. "Following us, were you?"

Tara set her phone down. "*Oh my God.* Were you *spying* on us?"

"Yes," said Fionn, surprising himself. "Obviously."

Bartley's grin nearly split his face in two. "That's so embarrassing."

"So's your hair," said Fionn, lightning fast.

"What's got into you?" Tara looked so like their

mother when her eyebrows were pulled close together like that. Her eyes were the same dark brown, but she wore them differently—with anger and impatience.

"What's your wish going to be, Bartley?" Fionn demanded. "I know it's something to do with my family."

Bartley leered at him. "Met my gran, have you, Boyle?"

"Yeah. She's terrible. What's your wish?"

"No, she's not," said Shelby defensively. "She just has a very different ... *vision* for Arranmore. And she makes really delicious gluten-free cookies, which equate to a very passable normal cookie."

"Why do you care about Bartley's wish all of a sudden?" said Tara. "You have no interest in the Irish Olympic Swim Team."

"That's not his wish," said Fionn, his eyes still trained on Bartley. "It's something to do with our family."

Tara turned on Bartley. "What's he talking about?"

"Actually, it's something to do with *my* family," said Bartley, ignoring her. He snatched a thin gold candle from a shelf by the fireplace.

Fionn marched after him. "Hey! That's not yours! Put it back!"

"No," said Bartley, holding it out of reach. "These are *all* mine! Or at least they will be soon. And you'd better believe I'm going to destroy every single one."

"Grandad!" yelled Fionn, but Bartley was already at the front door.

Tara was on her feet too. "Fionn! Don't—"

"*Grandad!* Bartley's stealing from us!"

"Bartley! Come back!" said Shelby, but nobody was listening to anyone now.

Fionn chased Bartley all the way out on to the headland. "Give that back!"

Bartley whirled around, his eyes flashing with determination. "This one has my gran's name on the label!" He jabbed his finger into the candle. "Explain *that!*"

"No!"

"It's *hers!*"

"You're not allowed to burn that!" said Fionn, stalking closer.

Bartley grabbed a lighter from his pocket and flicked it above the wick.

"Stop!" Fionn lunged at him, his fingers circling Bartley's wrist as the flame whizzed to life.

The island inhaled.

The wind swept them up in its current. They were whooshed across the headland so fast Fionn had to gasp air into his lungs to breathe.

"Let go of me!" yelled Bartley.

"No!" shouted Fionn, gripping him like a handcuff. "Blow it out! We don't know what's in it!"

"No way, idiot!" Bartley was jumping like a gazelle, nearly tripping over himself with excitement, as he tried to outrun Fionn. "My gran is in here somewhere!"

"There might be other things in here too!" panted Fionn. He tried to match him stride for stride, but his fear had tossed a lasso around his neck and Morrigan's icy fingertips were tugging on the end. "This is dangerous!"

"Then let go of me and go home, coward!" Bartley was still leaping through the long grass, whooping and laughing, as the island peeled over them.

He couldn't leave Bartley Beasley unaccompanied in one of his grandfather's candles. What if he never came back? Or worse, what if he came back even *smugger* than before?

What exactly did this candle know about Elizabeth Beasley?

An old storm was rising. Thick gray clouds loomed over them, spitting static into the air.

Bartley stopped running. "Let go of me," he said, bending at the waist. "I think I'm going to vomit."

"Good." Fionn used his free hand to yank the candle out of his grip.

"Hey!" Bartley grabbed Fionn's sleeve before he could pull away. "Give that back!"

Fionn brandished the candle above them. "If you think I trust you with *anything* belonging to my grandad, then *you're* an idiot."

Bartley was too weak to argue. He circled Fionn's wrist, his fingers still trembling from his wind-sickness. "Fine."

At least now Fionn had control of the memory. He could blow it out at the first sniff of danger . . .

And if the worst came to the worst, Morrigan could devour Bartley's soul first.

They started walking again, an errant breeze guiding them through rolling plains of grass as the air grew thick with mist.

Soon they found themselves in a meadow of wildflowers. The stalks reached all the way up to their noses, curving around the field in rows that spiraled toward the center.

Bartley bent the head of a purple flower toward him and sniffed. "It's lavender."

"Now is not the time to make soap," said Fionn.

"*Obviously.* It means the Whispering Tree is nearby." He took another whiff for good measure. "That must be where we're going."

The stalks were swaying back and forth, beckoning them into the maze.

"What makes you so sure?"

Bartley released the sprig of lavender and it sprang back into line, like a soldier. "Because the location of the Whispering Tree is ever-changing. You know you're nearby when you find the maze of lavender," said Bartley, in an unusually high-pitched voice. At least his information made him more bearable to be around, if only very, *very* slightly. "Then you just have to follow it!"

"Oh. Cool."

"You really don't know anything, do you?"

"I know you're socially incompetent," said Fionn.

Bartley pulled him into the maze, his chin raised to the heaving sky. "I don't waste my energy on losers."

"Then how do you feed yourself?" said Fionn, striding after him.

They followed the wildflowers, sweeping inward with every spiral until the maze tightened around them. They had to turn sideways then, the flowers brushing their cheeks as the thunder growled like a lion.

At the center of the maze, they stood on either side of a small dark hole in the earth.

"What now?" asked Fionn, glancing at the candle in his fist before peering into the infinite blackness.

Bartley looked around uncertainly. "I think we have to jump into the hole."

"You can still die in these memories, you know."

"The path to the tree is different every time. This must be the one my gran had to take. Otherwise, why would a candle with her name on it lead us here?"

There was only one place to go now. For the first time since they had been pulled into this layer, Fionn was reassured that they were holding on to each other. "All right."

"Don't let go, Boyle."

"Are you afraid I'll hurl you into oblivion?"

He watched with satisfaction as Bartley bit back his insult. "Only slightly."

"Well, don't worry. I'm not a Beasley."

"To your eternal regret. On three?"

Fionn nodded. "*One. Two. Three.*"

They jumped together, their screams rising up in perfect harmony as they plummeted into the earth. It lasted all of six seconds, both boys free-falling through the ancient layers of Arranmore until they emerged from the hole the right way up, their stomachs flipping as they shot out of the earth like rockets.

They landed in a heap of tangled limbs, back in the same field of lavender. This time, there was no maze. The stalks were shorter, brushing against their knees and arranged as wildflowers should be—completely haphazardly. The storm clouds were back, only now they were glittering around the edges.

They got to their feet.

On the other side of the meadow, an ancient oak tree climbed out of the earth. It was prouder and taller than any tree Fionn had ever seen before. Most of its branches wound into the sky, like the gnarled arms of a victorious warrior, while some reached down to the earth like they were searching for something in the soil. The trunk was impossibly thick, and twisting in so many directions it looked as though a hundred faces had been carved into the bark.

"*Cool*," Fionn and Bartley chorused.

Some things you had to agree on. Nemeses or not.

On the ground, in front of the tree, two teenagers stood side by side.

One of the teenagers was Elizabeth Beasley.

The other was Malachy Boyle.

He might have been decades younger with a full head of brown hair but Fionn recognized the slant of his grandfather's shoulders, the way he leaned a little more on his left leg, the profile of his nose as he turned to say something to Elizabeth.

They pressed their palms against the trunk.

The sky ignited.

Fionn and Bartley jumped, their shoulders slamming together as a bolt of lightning whipped down from the clouds and struck the tree right in its center.

Malachy and Elizabeth leaped back as a long, dark fissure cracked the trunk in two.

The tree was set alight, the fire ripping through the bark and exploding along the branches until every part of it was glowing a bright, brilliant gold.

"This is way cooler in the flesh!" said Bartley, and for a precious, fleeting moment, both of them forgot their enmity and watched the burning tree in matching states of wonder.

The branches swayed back and forth, shaking their leaves loose. Pockets of flame dripped onto the grass until Malachy and Elizabeth were enclosed inside a circle of golden light.

Fionn couldn't tear his eyes away. "Are they okay?"

"Of course they're okay, you moron. They're still alive in the present, aren't they?"

"I'm *this* close to kicking you out," warned Fionn.

The oak tree was whispering. It was a loud, hissing noise that rustled in the wind and vibrated in the earth. They crept closer, craning to hear above the whip and crackle of flame. "*Sssspeak or be sssspoken to . . .*"

"This is the part where your grandfather steals the gift,"

said Bartley sourly. The excitement had faded, the adventure of discovery replaced with the very real resentment of their families' history. "My gran said it all happened in a flash."

Up ahead, Elizabeth Beasley cleared her throat, her reedy voice arcing across the meadow as she said, "The island storm has returned. Maggie Patton's time is coming to an end. I want to know if I am going to be the next Storm Keeper of Arranmore."

For a long moment, the tree was silent. Elizabeth grew impatient, drumming her fingers across the bark, her sighs growing longer and noisier.

Then Malachy Boyle fell to his knees and started trembling. His eyes were shut, his face tipped back to the burning tree, while the shadow of its flames crawled across his skin. His body twitched and lurched, and Elizabeth started screaming.

"What's happening to him?" said Fionn in horror.

"What's happening to him," mimicked Bartley. "He's stealing the gift from right under her nose!"

"Malachy! Open your eyes!" yelled Elizabeth. "It's me! Say it's supposed to be me! You don't even want it!"

Fionn and Bartley inched closer, through blackened leaves and wildflowers that tipped their heads to the earth in reverie.

"There hadn't been a Beasley Storm Keeper on the

island for nine generations," said Bartley. "Malachy knew it was time for a Beasley heir but he didn't care. He took the gift from my family all those years ago and now it's time for me to bring it back!"

It started to rain. Big, fat drops hurtled to the earth, like bullets.

Fionn barely noticed. He couldn't tear his eyes from his grandfather, who was still writing on the ground like a snake. It looked like his spine was breaking. He made a mental note never to ask this tree anything.

"Why do you want it so badly anyway?" asked Fionn. Elizabeth Beasley was stomping up and down, screaming at the tree, like it had just murdered her dog. Fionn could feel a whisper of that same desperation in Bartley as he watched her. "I mean, do you *really* care that much about the candles?"

Bartley turned on Fionn. His face blocked out the tree, the flames crowning his head until it looked like his hair was on fire. "You really don't know anything, do you, Boyle?" he sneered. "The Storm Keeper doesn't just make weather candles. The Storm Keeper *controls the elements.*"

"What?"

"The island pours its magic inside you. You have *all* the gifts at your fingertips. You have the island's *power* at your fingertips!"

Fionn stared at Bartley for a long time, the crackle of fire filling up the silence while rain trickled down their faces. This version of Malachy Boyle made no sense to him. He couldn't picture his grandfather away from his workbench, his dusty shelves and pots of wax. He couldn't even begin to imagine him standing in the ocean as Dagda had done, calling the elements to him, pushing the sea, corralling the wind... How would he even *do* it?

How does he make the candles? said a little voice inside his head. *How does he put the weather in wax? Isn't that just as impossible?*

"Why do you think everyone in Arranmore respects Malachy so much?" said Bartley, spitting raindrops from his mouth. "Do you really think it's because he spends all his time making stuffy old candles full of useless rain showers and stupid sunsets?" He didn't wait for Fionn to answer. "Malachy helps the islanders grow crops. He keeps their animals healthy. He calms the tides for the fishermen." He smirked then. "He can't stop *this* storm from coming though."

Fionn shook his head in disbelief. "That doesn't make sense."

Bartley rolled his eyes so hard the irises disappeared. "What doesn't make sense to you, Boyle? The Sea Cave, for that which is out of reach. *Earth*," he growled. "The

Whispering Tree, for that which is yet to come. *Fire.*" He jabbed his thumb over his shoulder in proof. "The Merrows, for invaders that may come. *Water.*" He had raised his hand between them and was counting off his fingers. "Aonbharr, the Winged Horse, for danger that cannot be outrun. *Wind.*" He took a shuddering breath. "And the Storm Keeper. *To wield the elements in Dagda's name!*"

To *wield.*

Not to record. But to *wield.*

To *lead.*

"I think I would know if my grandfather was that powerful," Fionn said uncertainly.

Bartley arched his eyebrow. "Would you?"

"Why would he hide it?" Fionn shot back, not feeling so sure now.

"Because Malachy Boyle is a small-minded old man who's afraid of the past," said Bartley, as though it was the most obvious thing in the world. Fionn could almost hear his grandmother's voice coming out of his stupid pinched mouth. "Do you realize how much better life would be if we stopped hiding Dagda's magic? If we stepped out from behind the scenes for once?" The more Bartley talked, the brighter his crown of flames burned and the wilder his eyes became. He jabbed his finger in the direction of the Whispering Tree. "Think of all the things I could do. I'd be a king. And not *just* here, but outside Arranmore too. People would *love* me! The whole world would know the name Beasley. We wouldn't have to be on the sidelines anymore, standing by and watching while the Boyles squander *our* gift."

The more Bartley talked, the more he sounded like his grandmother. She had drilled the vision into him so deeply, he couldn't see how ridiculous it made him seem.

"You sound deranged," said Fionn, stepping away from him. And yet, he could imagine it too well. Bartley would make himself all-powerful and people like Alva Cannon and Donal would have to obey him. He would make them miserable, all in the name of forgotten Beasley glory. There were the wider implications too—the secret blown wide open for the whole world to see. Morrigan's followers returning in droves, searching for their forgotten souls.

"The magic isn't meant for showing off," said Fionn. "It's meant for protecting the island! There's an evil sorceress buried here!"

Bartley rolled his eyes. "Morrigan hasn't so much as moved in hundreds of years! The past is dead and buried. The Beasleys are the future and Ivan is helping me make sure of that!"

"*Ivan?*" said Fionn. "You don't even know him!"

"He's a long-lost cousin," said Bartley defensively.

"More like a long-lost liar. He looks *nothing* like any of you. And I've never heard that accent before either!"

"You're just jealous because he's on *my* side," challenged Bartley. "He showed us his family tree."

Fionn pulled at his hair. "That doesn't mean he is who he says he is! What if he's not? What if he's a Soulstalker?"

Bartley snorted. "You're more paranoid than your grandad, Boyle."

"And you're more stupid than I thought," Fionn shot back. "Which is really saying something."

"If Ivan isn't a Beasley then why did he tell me where the Sea Cave is?"

Fionn gaped at Bartley.

"Yeah," he said smugly. "He's been studying this place his entire life. Only took him a couple of days to figure it out. Now all I have to do is get to it."

"If he really is a descendant, why doesn't he just take the wish for himself?"

"Because he wants *me* to be the next Storm Keeper. He knows I can put the Beasley name back on the map!" he said, his eyes gleaming. The rain was bucketing down now but he didn't seem to care. "I've been raised for this responsibility my entire life. I'm going to be the next Storm Keeper of Arranmore and you can't stop me!"

"*Watch me,*" said Fionn.

Bartley tightened his grip, his fingers searing hot against his skin. He glanced at the heaving sky. "This storm is on its way back to us. You really think the island will pick you? A *coward*?"

"I am not a coward!" lied Fionn. "And it might not be either of us! It could be Tara or Shelby or any number of others . . ." He trailed off.

Bartley bared his teeth in a terrifying grin. "Make no mistake about it, Boyle. I'm going to get in that Sea Cave before the storm comes in and make that wish. *Then* you'll see what I can do when your stupid grandfather isn't standing in—"

Fionn pushed Bartley so hard he lost his grip and went tumbling backward. "Good luck with that!"

"Boyle—" The air swallowed him with a faint pop, shimmering around his edges as the island catapulted him back to a different version of itself.

Fionn felt instantly better.

If only I could do that all the time.

He was left alone with the very end of the candle, across the field from an ancient burning tree. Elizabeth Beasley was circling his grandfather, her arms folded across her chest.

Fionn stalked toward her, eager to investigate. He could smell the venom in the air, but he couldn't tell whether it was Elizabeth's or Bartley's ... or maybe his own.

Elizabeth planted her shoe on Malachy's chest and pressed down on him, like he was a button.

"Hey!" shouted Fionn. "Get off!"

Elizabeth stumbled backward, her beady eyes flashing as she looked directly at him.

"*Boyle*," she hissed. "Tell me! Is it me?"

Fionn stared at her for a heartbeat, anger pouring out of him, into five sharp words. "It will *never* be you."

Elizabeth started toward him.

Fionn blew out the candle.

It has been a long time since I saw you, Fionn Boyle. A very long time indeed.

The island inhaled, and Elizabeth Beasley disappeared from him, taking her burning tree and her burning eyes with her.

It will never be you.

Chapter Twelve

THE KING'S MEDAL

It took Fionn almost an hour to get home, the sun melting into a flaming sea as he retraced his way across the island. When he arrived at Tír na nÓg, he tried his best to ignore the row of ravens sitting on the roof. He stalked inside and marched down the little hallway, slamming the back door behind him. "I have a lot of things I want to say to you."

His grandfather was hunched over his workbench, stirring a puddle of wax. "I know."

"Just how *much* do you know?"

"Almost everything," he mused. "Although, I do confess, I don't have the slightest idea where Amelia Earhart went."

Fionn took a deep breath, conjured all his frustration and then released the storm that had been brewing inside him since the moment he stepped off the ferry. "When are you going to actually start telling me things I need to know? Or am I not *important* enough to be let in on my own family's secrets?"

His grandfather peered at him over the rim of his spectacles. "Where on earth is this coming from?"

"Your complete lack of respect for me!" shouted Fionn. "Am I doomed to hear every single thing about this island *and you* from a Beasley!" He'd balled his fists so tight his nails were cutting into his palm. "Did you steal the Storm Keeper gift from Elizabeth Beasley?"

His grandfather braced his hands on the edge of his workbench. "Well, you have certainly inherited your grandmother's temper."

"I'm about to tear my hair out."

He tapped the crown of his head. "Careful. It might not grow back."

"*Grandad!*"

"All right, all right," he said, adopting a modicum of seriousness. "The truth is the matter was not up to me, or Elizabeth. The Storm Keeper is chosen to protect the island and, in turn, the world beyond from Morrigan. The *island* chooses the best person for that task. Someone who will lead the islanders against Morrigan should the time ever come. That person can be anyone from any of the five bloodlines. The island is not in the business of taking turns."

"Well, Bartley disagrees," said Fionn pointedly. "He feels the next Storm Keeper should be a Beasley and he's going to use the Sea Cave wish to make sure of it."

His grandfather frowned, the crevices around his mouth deepening. "The Beasleys have always wanted to use the gifts for their own ends. They do not fear Morrigan as they should."

Fionn bristled at the memory of that fathomless stare.

Elizabeth Beasley's burning eyes flashed in his mind.

It will never be you.

Now a human had seen him in the folds of the past too. "Elizabeth Beasley saw me today in a memory."

"Ah," said his grandfather, a deep V forming in the lines on his forehead. "It seems you are not quite as invisible as the rest of us."

"Why not?" said Fionn with mounting dismay.

His grandfather chewed on his thoughts. "I believe your meeting with Dagda might hold the answer," he said, his frown deepening when he added, "But I admit I haven't the foggiest idea what exactly that might be."

Fionn's shoulders had hunched halfway up his neck. He remembered the jolt that had leaped through his fingers when he touched Dagda, the strange spiky warmth that had made him flesh and bone before Morrigan. Was it still inside him now?

"Elizabeth told me she saw a strange boy who looked just like me, standing near the Whispering Tree, when we visited it together a very long time ago," his grandfather continued, more to himself than to Fionn. "I believed it was Cormac that she saw. Well, now we know."

Fionn didn't like how entangled everything seemed to be with the Beasleys, or how little they cared about the biggest threat to Arranmore. How close they were to stealing the island's most important shield. "Bartley says they already know where the Sea Cave is."

"The Sea Cave is very elusive," said his grandfather. "It's extremely difficult to find a way down even if you know where to look."

Fionn's spine unstiffened. "Good."

His grandfather tugged at his jaw. "I'm sorry, Fionn," he said with a sigh. "I've made you feel unimportant and that couldn't be further from the truth. I felt it might be best to let you get used to the island and its peculiar ways before you learned my role in it. But in trying not to overwhelm you, I've kept you in the dark, and here more than anywhere else, the dark is a very unsettling place to be."

Fionn cleared the lump from his throat. "Yeah, it is," he said gruffly. "At least we're on the same page now."

"Indeed we are," said his grandfather solemnly.

Fionn lowered himself on to the stool opposite him, his elbows sliding across the workbench as he studied him at close range. "Can you really control the weather?" he said suspiciously.

"Rarely. And only for the good of the island. It was helpful when I worked on the lifeboats." Fionn gaped at his grandfather, floored by the simplicity with which he had admitted to such wild, incomprehensible power. "I try to keep most of it though."

"But—*what for*?" spluttered Fionn. "Wouldn't you prefer to *use* it?"

His grandfather sat back on his stool, his fingers tap-tapping along the workbench. "What would you have me do with it, Fionn? Release lightning bolts from the highest rooftops? Travel around demanding money and favors, like Bartley Beasley would?"

Fionn didn't have to think very hard about this. "No, but you could throw a rainstorm at him. Or trap him in an ice palace. Or hurl him into an endless hurricane-like oblivion."

His grandfather snorted. "As ever you are a pillar of maturity."

"How do you make the candles? Where does the magic come from?"

"I think this is a conversation for another time, Fionn." He knitted his hands together, his head cocked when he said, "Now that you know what I am, there is the matter of the next Storm Keeper to discuss."

"I want to talk about the candles."

"No. You want to talk about the Storm Keeper's magic," he countered. "And that depends on who the next Storm Keeper is."

"I thought we were on the same page," said Fionn with renewed frustration.

"We are certainly on the same page, but we are not yet in the same paragraph."

Fionn slumped in his seat, defeated. Sometimes it felt like his grandfather thrived on being this annoying. "Fine. Let's talk about the next Storm Keeper. I definitely don't think it should be Bartley."

"Nor do I," said his grandfather, dusting his hands. "Now that that's settled, let's move on to the next order of business."

"Do you want it to be me?" asked Fionn warily. "It sounds like a lot of pressure . . ."

His grandfather's smile was grim. "Responsibility and power, in equal measure. Do *you* want to be the next Storm Keeper, Fionn?"

Power.

Fionn stilled. Being the guardian of this wild and ancient place would mean learning snowstorms instead of long division, composing rainbows instead of acrostics. Everyone on the island would know his name. He would be part of a tight-knit tribe umbrellaed under his sky, bound to protect others from darkness. The elements would shimmer at his fingertips. Earth, Fire, Wind, Water.

The Storm Keeper's magic. He could use it, however he liked.

He had seen what it could do and in that moment, he wanted it very badly.

And then he remembered Morrigan. Her icy hand-print on his heart.

What if she came back in earnest?

His chest tightened.

"I don't think I'm good enough," he said at last. "I'm a Boyle who can barely look at the sea without feeling sick. The island will figure that out soon enough if it hasn't already." He smiled sadly. "I'm not brave enough to be a Storm Keeper."

Fionn traced the swirls in the workbench. The decision had floated out of his hands and back into impossibility, like seafoam scattered to the wind. It left a dull ache in the center of his chest—this destiny worth fighting for, something far greater than his lonely little life.

His grandfather was frowning at him. "And what makes you so sure of that?"

"Because even my dad wasn't brave enough," said Fionn in a very quiet voice. "And he was *really* brave. Even Elizabeth Beasley thought so."

That was the cold hard truth of it all.

Fionn's father had drowned off the coast of Arranmore during one of the worst storms in the island's history. The details were murky, because Cormac never came back to tell them, but sometime in the afternoon, he went out alone in one of the lifeboats. The storm picked up and his boat ran aground, splintering against the rocks. Then the sea swallowed him up. No one remembered a distress call being made, and no one was ever reported missing in the aftermath. By the time they held Cormac Boyle's funeral, Fionn's mother was already on the ferry to the mainland with Tara, and Fionn still in her belly. She hadn't set foot on Arranmore since.

Fionn's fingernails were cutting half-moons into his

palms. "Bartley says the new Keeper is chosen in a storm. That's how it goes. The island gets restless, it brews its own storm and then the gift passes to the next generation."

"Yes," said his grandfather.

Fionn's heart sank. "Well, then that rescue must have been some kind of a test. And my dad failed it. Otherwise, he would be here now with us. He would be the Storm Keeper."

His grandfather stroked his chin, pulling the lines on his face into a grimace. "That storm was so powerful it glittered around the edges. Yes, we thought a new Storm Keeper was rising. Your father had visited the Whispering Tree two weeks before the storm. I thought it had confirmed what we all suspected—that it would be him. But we were wrong, Fionn. Nobody knows what the tree showed Cormac. He took that secret with him in the end." He cleared his throat, gruffly. "Your father was the bravest person I ever knew. The island would have known that better than anyone. It wouldn't have had to test him."

"Then he died for nothing." Here was the ugliest part of Fionn—the shadows and the thorns—spilling out of him, and even though it was sad and painful, there was a touch of relief in it. He could finally talk about the unfairness of losing his father before he ever knew him without fearing he might upset his mother or send her into a spiral that kept her in her room for days. "Why did he go out on that boat by himself?"

"I don't know," his grandfather conceded, and Fionn felt as though he had won something then, only the feeling wasn't warm, but cold and sticky, like gum on the underside of his shoe.

He couldn't forget the sight of his mother fighting the sea. In that moment, as the realness of his father's death rose around them like steam, Fionn couldn't believe an island so magical could be so *cruel*.

"Does it ever give anything back?" he asked bitterly.

"Well . . . Once, a very, very long time ago, when I was a boy much younger than you, the sea took my father from me too. And that time, the island gave him back."

The words landed like a punch in the gut. Fionn was surprised by how fast the tears burst out of him. They rushed down his cheeks like they were racing each other, dripping underneath the collar of his sweater. It felt as though someone was scooping out his insides. His grandfather had asked for his father back, and the sea had bowed to the request. Twelve years ago his mother had done the same thing, and this place had turned its back on her.

His grandfather continued speaking while Fionn

gathered the pieces of himself and tried to glue them back together. "It was December 1940. The weather was as bad as we've ever seen it. Not just hurricane-force winds but sleet and snow and ice too. It was beyond even the Storm Keeper's control. The storm swept in from the north and ran a Dutch cargo ship bound for Liverpool off its course." He splayed his hands wide to indicate the size of the ship, then spread them over his head as though he was yawning. "It ran aground on rocks several miles off the coast of Arranmore."

His brows knitted together and Fionn got the sense he was traveling back inside his head, trying to gather up the memory.

"The ship was called the SS *Stolwijk*," he said. "And by the time my father and his fellow lifeboatmen received the distress call, ten crew members had drowned and many more were in the stormy waters, hanging on for dear life."

Fionn shivered. He could imagine it too clearly—an enormous ship turned belly-up to an angry sky, frantic sailors spilling out like innards.

"The Arranmore lifeboat was the SS *Stolwijk's* last hope." This time his grandfather pinched his fingers close together, until there was just an inch between them. "The lifeboat was small, with sails not meant for hurricane winds, and an engine ill-equipped for such an undertaking. It was a fool's mission, Fionn. And everyone on the island knew it. If you work the lifeboats on Arranmore, you take an oath," his grandfather said. "You swear to put the lives of those in peril ahead of your own. You go, even if you're afraid. Even if you think you won't make it back."

Fionn looked at his feet. To him, the oath sounded like shackles around his ankles, chaining him to a churning sea. He couldn't imagine binding his life to it, the way his father and his grandfather had before him.

"When the call came through that wintry day in December, each of them had a decision to make, Fionn." His grandfather looked at him, the blue of his eyes alive with the memory of an angry sea. "To stay with their families on the island and wait out the worst storm they had ever seen..."

"Or to go," said Fionn quietly. "Despite their fear."

To go the way his father had the day the storm took him.

His grandfather nodded. "They went. All nine of them."

Fionn cleared the cobwebs from his throat. The tears had stopped but he could still feel the prickles underneath his cheeks, the desperate thudding in his chest.

"At 6:30 a.m. they went over the first wave and right

through the next one on their way out of the port. For the rest of the day and most of the night, the women of the island walked up and down the shore dressed in black."

"How did you get them back? Did you go to the Sea Cave?"

His grandfather's eyes twinkled. "Our Keeper, Maggie Patton, led the way to the Sea Cave. It was kind to us that day."

"The island brought them home," breathed Fionn.

"After a long, grueling rescue, they sailed into port." His grandfather shook his head, as though he still couldn't quite believe it. His eyes were alight with a kind of wonder Fionn could only imagine—the satisfying sense of something finally going right for once. "The lifeboat crew rescued eighteen Dutch sailors and returned them to the mainland. Afterward, Queen Wilhelmina of the Netherlands awarded all nine crew members with Dutch gallantry medals for their bravery. The Royal National Lifeboat Institution awarded the men with gallantry medals too." He leaned forward, and Fionn mirrored him without meaning to. The whites of his eyes shone extra bright in the darkness, his smile as wide as Fionn had ever seen it. "King George VI was the patron of the RNLI, so I like to think they got a *king* as well."

Gallantry. Wasn't that the sort of word that only existed in fairytales?

His grandfather sprang to his feet, his finger in the air as though to shush him, even though Fionn wasn't saying anything. "Wait here!" He returned almost immediately. "Hold out your hand."

His grandfather dropped a bronze medal onto his palm. It was not much bigger than a two-euro coin, but it was much heavier than it looked. Fionn held it up to the rising moonlight, picking up its scent immediately. It was tangy and metallic, with a rim of earthiness around the edges. He could tell it was well traveled, and that it had been in more than a few pockets and cupboards over the years. It was unusually shiny despite its age, and had an engraving of a sea rescue on the front. Underneath were the words: *Let Not the Deep Swallow Me Up.*

Fionn traced the curved edges with the pad of his thumb. "Your father's medal."

"And now it's yours." The stool creaked as his grandfather sat down again. It was dark in the back garden, but the moon was creeping into the sky and casting a glow. The birds had deserted them and Fionn was glad of the privacy. "I was going to give it to your dad but, well . . ." Fionn didn't dare blink in case the tears hiding underneath his eyelids slipped out again. "It's too late to wish him back, lad," his grandfather continued, his words turning to careful footsteps on Fionn's heart. "If maybe that's what you were thinking about the Sea Cave. Even Dagda could not raise the dead."

Fionn clamped his fist around the medal, and squeezed and squeezed until the pain in his hand was greater than the pain in his chest.

"He took the oath, Fionn. He knew how it might end. And all the while, as long as I knew him, he was the bravest of us all."

"He didn't get a shipwreck though. He didn't get a story."

"*You* are his story, Fionn. You and Tara. And your mother. And me. As long as there is someone to remember you, you are never truly gone, and neither is your story. That is the wonderful thing about Arranmore. It never forgets."

Fionn opened his fist and released the heat gathering inside it. "I don't deserve this, Grandad." He set the medal on the workbench, thinking of what Elizabeth Beasley had said to him outside the church. "I don't wear the sea behind my eyes."

A cloud split overhead and the moon shone through it, dusting its light along the top of his grandfather's head. He slid the medal back to him. "Bravery is just a matter of forgetting to be afraid, Fionn. Nothing more. Nothing less." He tapped the medal. "You don't have to wear it. Put it under your pillow if you like."

"Why? So the Sea Fairy can visit me?"

He laughed and the wind swirled around them and rustled the hair on the crown of Fionn's head, as though it was laughing too.

"You never know," his grandfather said with a wink.

Chapter Thirteen

THE SEA FAIRY

Long before midnight, Fionn sank into a dream, where the sea climbed up the cliffs and spat its guts onto the land. Merrows with bloody tails and black teeth clawed at his ankles, crooning as they peeled their scales off and stuck them to his skin. *Let not the deep swallow me up,* they moaned as bronze medals tumbled from their gaping mouths. *Let not the deep swallow me up!*

"Hey!" echoed a distant voice.

The Merrows shimmered, flickering in and out like holograms. A familiar lament broke through, the dream changing as the island woman's song floated toward him on the wind.

Come to me, my fearless Boyle,

And see the magic I can brew.

This time the words were clearer, the melody arcing as he slipped down the cliff face in search of the voice.

Visit me beneath the soil.

Come and wish me back to you.

"Fionn!" Fionn woke with a start to find his grandfather's nose less than an inch from his own. "Wakey-wakey, little stormling!"

Fionn groaned. His limbs were luxuriously heavy, the sheets rising around him like quicksand.

His grandfather bounced up and down on the side of his bed. "Are you ready for an adventure?"

"Not interested," said Fionn, turning over.

His grandfather ripped the cover off him. Fionn yelped. The room was *freezing*, his pajamas much too light to stave off the sudden chill of unwanted wakefulness. "Give me my blanket back!"

His grandfather leaped to his feet and pulled Fionn out of bed. He led him from the room, chattering at full volume, despite the fact that Tara was still sound asleep behind them. "Hello, I'm Malachy Boyle and I'll be your Sea Fairy this evening!" He was still wearing his pajamas, and boat shoes that made his footsteps echo down the unlit hallway where the candles peered after them in curious silence. "Please keep your arms and legs inside the vessel at all times."

"What vessel?" Fionn asked the back of his grandfather's head.

His grandfather whistled his tuneless song, only pausing to make sure Fionn put his sneakers on in the kitchen.

"Lace them up good, lad." He plucked a gray cap from the stand by the front door and blew a layer of dust from it. Particles spiraled in the air, catching the light from the candle on the mantelpiece.

Still half-asleep and thus unusually compliant, Fionn bent down to tie his laces. "Why?" he asked. "What's going on?"

His grandfather pulled a candle from his pajama pocket and waggled it back and forth. "I've been looking for this storm all night," he said triumphantly. "It had rolled into one of my shoes!"

Fionn sprang to his feet and tried to knock the candle from his grandfather's grasp. "No!"

His grandfather hopped backward. "Careful, or Maggie Patton will come back and haunt us! She had to sleep for thirty-six hours after recording this one!"

Fionn knew exactly why.

The candle was tall and thick and perfectly round. It was a blue that was as gray as it was green, almost see-through in parts and murky toward the bottom, where the sediment might gather in an ocean. Fionn could smell it perfectly; even unlit, it was sticking to the insides of his nostrils. It was rain-soaked wood and battered sails, the ragged calls of frantic men dipped in seaweed and swirled inside a tide of salt and brine. It was sheets of freezing rain and the burned shriek of lightning striking sea. It was peril and adventure and terror and hope all rolled together, and it was unapologetically pungent.

His grandfather pulled Fionn over the threshold to the cottage and out into the garden. With triumph gleaming in his eyes, he placed the candle in his teeth, twined his fingers in Fionn's and brought the flame to the SS *Stolwijk*. It fizzed to life, and the door slammed shut behind them.

A breeze rippled out from the cottage in an enormous circle. Everything before Fionn—the bushes and the trees and the grass and the flowers—bent their heads to the earth and bowed to the Storm Keeper of Arranmore.

The gate to *Tír na nÓg* creaked open.

"Let's go!" he called, exhilaration tripping through his voice and propelling them down the headland as he plucked the candle from his teeth. He brandished it high above him, the flame waving back and forth at the moon as if to say, *Hello. Remember me?*

"Grandad!" shrieked Fionn as the wind shoved him impatiently. "You're going too fast!"

"Knees up, lad!" his grandfather shouted, his own knees springing to his chest with every stride. "That's it, very good! Lift them higher! Just like this! Good! Excellent! Let's show the island just how brave you can be!"

They raced across the headland, the stars bursting overhead while the moon swam across the sky and shattered the darkness. "Hurry up!" yelled his grandfather, and the wind whooshed at Fionn's back as if to help him along.

"I'm going to be sick!" cried Fionn, tugging at him to slow down.

The island was flying past at an alarming rate, the houses and trees disappearing into the earth. "The bigger the storm, the faster it burns," his grandfather yelled. "Time waits for no one! Not even the Boyles!" He whooped as another of the island's layers peeled over them, the memory slowly taking shape. "Nearly there, lad! We have to get to the pier before morning!"

Fionn was getting a terrible stitch in his side. "Can. We. Turn. The. Candle. Off?" he wheezed. "Please!"

"There's no fear in the doing of it, lad!" His grandfather's words weren't at all strained. His breathing was perfectly even as he charged ahead, the candle brandished high above him like an Olympic torch. "There's only fear in the beforehand, Fionn, and this is the beforehand!"

"If you think this is going to change anything then you're wrong!" yelled Fionn. "I told you I'm not a brave person!"

"Nonsense! How can you know who you truly are until you figure out where you come from?" His grandfather's blue and white pajama bottoms had gathered above his ankles and his pajama shirt was whipping out behind him like a cape. "Watch out for that tree root!"

Right as he said it, a root erupted from the ground. He hopped, clearing it effortlessly, like a gazelle on a nature program. Fionn tripped over it.

His grandfather yanked him to his feet and dragged him onward. "I said watch out!"

"How did you know that would happen?" Fionn heaved, just as he was tugged sharply to the right, out of the way of an old wooden carriage that appeared from nowhere, trundling up the hill and nearly running Fionn over.

"Just as I suspected!" His grandfather waggled the candle back and forth, his eyes glinting with glee. "They can't see you when you're not holding the candle! Our voyage continues!"

Fionn squeezed his grandfather's fingers tighter, trying to keep up. "How did you figure that out?"

"I used my genius sense of intuition!" His grandfather's laughter soared and the wind joined in—the island and its Keeper working hand in hand. "I haven't adventured like this in such a long time, Fionn. I forgot what it smelled like!"

To Fionn, it smelled suddenly and disconcertingly like manure. The layers kept rustling and within them Fionn saw workhorses with flared hooves clopping by, men with strange hats and oversized newspapers and old women in shawls, carrying baskets up and down the headland.

Too soon, the pier rose before them. Morning had come quickly and it had brought winter with it. Fionn's teeth were rattling in his mouth. He couldn't feel the tips of his fingers or his nose. Overhead, the sky was a dark, swirling gray, and just out to sea, beyond the port, the clouds were rumbling.

The memory had crystallized. It smelled like thunder and rain, and it seemed to Fionn less like an adventure and more like a snarling beast.

He tried to pull his grandfather back. "That's enough!" he yelled, almost tripping over himself as he charged on to the long wooden pier. "We shouldn't be here! It's not safe!"

His grandfather cackled delightedly and all the birds cackled with him. "That's just your fear talking, lad! I told you, there'll be no fear in the doing of it!"

At the end of the pier, a group of women and children were huddled around a wooden lifeboat, hugging the men about to board it. Fionn's heart lurched up his throat. The vessel looked more like a giant canoe than a ship capable of saving anything. The men were dressed in black rain jackets that looked like waterproof capes, rain boots, and waterproof hats with brims so wide they hid their faces, so Fionn couldn't tell whether they were scared or not.

The children on the pier were crying.

"No, no, no, no, no, no," Fionn pleaded with his grandfather. "Anything but the boat. I can't go near the water!"

Time tripped again. The huddle of well-wishers splintered apart and Fionn's grandfather charged right through the middle. No one noticed them sprinting by in their pajamas, not even the little boy with big blue eyes who was nearly knocked over as Fionn's grandfather launched himself off the pier.

Fionn tumbled into the lifeboat after him. Time moved them away from the island, the boat bobbing up and down as the men fanned out to opposite sides of the mast. Fionn scrabbled after his grandfather until they were huddled together in the very back of the boat, one arm wrapped tight around the anchor chain in case the wind blew them overboard.

"You nearly killed that child back there!" Fionn roared over the might of the sea.

His grandfather laughed, blissfully unconcerned by the panicked call of men charging up and down the deck, trying to steer themselves out to sea. "That little boy was me!" His laugh was wheezier this time, chilled by the ice water collecting between his toes. "I must have thought it was the wind!"

A fierce wave crashed against the hull and the boat dipped on to its side. Fionn clutched the anchor chain and screamed as a lifeboatman leaned over him and pulled the wayward sail back into position. The pole nearly nicked his shoulder but he ducked just in time, tucking his head in between his knees.

His grandfather squeezed his hand, pulling him closer until they were balled up together, a mismatch of gangly limbs in wet pajamas, the candle blazing defiantly between them. "I'll hang on to the candle, lad," he said, winking at him. "I think every man on this boat would have a conniption if an eleven-year-old boy suddenly appeared before them."

Fionn was glad not to be holding it. Either he'd end up scuppering the rescue mission or the island would kick him out of the layer, and into the sea, before he got the chance to—

"HOLD YOUR BREATH!"

Fionn held his breath as a wave crashed over them, rushing into his ears and down his neck and through his skin into his bones until he could barely breathe from the sudden shivering. Shouts rang out on deck, the sails frantically adjusted as the water dipped and time tripped and they were pulled farther out to sea, into the eye of the storm.

Fionn rubbed the salt from his eyes as a mouthful of seawater spluttered out of him. The island had disappeared behind them and it had started to rain. A chill scuttled up his spine and settled in his chest. *Great. I can cross pneumonia off my bucket list.*

"It's so *cold*," said Fionn accusingly. "Why couldn't we have sailed into a heat wave?"

"Because this is character building," said his grandfather, much too happily. "You know, if you're very careful about it, sometimes you can burn multiple candles at once and stitch entirely separate layers together."

"Why didn't you bring a *Summer Sun* with you then?" moaned Fionn.

His grandfather inclined his head toward the crew. "Best not to chance it with all these people involved. And anyways, it's all part of the adventure!" he said, nudging his shoulder against Fionn's. "We're almost there, lad."

There was no going back now, not through time or over the sea. There was nothing to do but endure the memory and hope it didn't drown them both.

If they survived this, Fionn was *so* telling his mother.

Time was rushing them into the storm, the waves growing big enough to wash them out every time the boat tried to climb over one. Fionn kept his eyes shut and held his breath when his grandfather told him to. "Open your eyes!" he shouted after a while. "I can see the *Stolwijk*!"

"Ship ahoy!" shouted a lifeboatman.

Fionn raised his head. The bellowing man had dropped the sails, his balance firm, despite the chaotic rocking of the boat. His hat had blown off sometime during the journey and Fionn could see his face now. He was impossibly tall, his head was shiny and bald, and his gaze was the same color as the roiling sea. It was a familiar, unforgettable blue.

"That's my dad!" shouted Fionn's grandfather. This time, there was more than just excitement in his voice, the kind of something that pinches the corners of your heart and makes you feel full up all of a sudden. "Isn't he awfully brave, Fionn?"

Fascinated as he was by the man who looked strangely, alarmingly like a younger version of his own grandfather, Fionn was drawn to the beast looming over his shoulder. A gigantic gray cargo ship more than ten times the size of their lifeboat had rolled onto its side. Rocks jutted out of the sea like shards, skewering the end of the ship and holding it in place as the sea devoured it.

A symphony of swear words rippled over the deck as all at once the men beheld the impossibility of the task ahead.

"Showtime!" whooped Fionn's grandfather, a bouquet of fresh rain droplets landing in his mouth.

"Drop anchor to windward!" yelled Fionn's great-grandfather. Fionn and his grandfather scrabbled toward the corner of the boat, away from stomping boots and the overspill of greedy waves. Time whooshed them forward, the anchor chain unfurling as the lifeboat drew level with the SS *Stolwijk*.

The crew of the *Stolwijk* were huddled at the stern of the ship. The wind was shattering their distress calls but they were flailing their arms. A wave broke over them and for a heartbeat they disappeared entirely. A scream stuck in Fionn's throat. "You said there'd be no fear in the doing of it," he shouted at his grandfather. "But I'm more afraid than I've ever been before!"

His grandfather pulled him closer, the candle clutched tightly in his fist. "Just watch!" he said as another wave crashed over them. Time danced and whirled, painted the sky gray and then white and all the while, Fionn watched. He watched as the men in the lifeboat fired a rope across the sea, with an attached life raft suspended, like a harness. The line broke, and broke again, until finally, the third attempt held. The crew on the *Stolwijk* grabbed on to it, pulling it across the stern and fastening it to the ship.

"Excellent! Outstanding! Did you see that, Fionn? Isn't it brilliant!" His grandfather whooped as though he was watching a film and not sitting in a puddle up to his knees, shaking right down to the marrow in his bones.

Fionn glanced at the candle. The flame was still blazing but the wax was more than half melted and he knew if it went out, they'd tumble right down into the ocean without a boat or a buoy to save them.

"Look!" His grandfather pointed the candle. The Arranmore men had huddled along the side of the lifeboat and were ferrying the first survivor along the rope in the buoy. The waves lapped at his knees as they pulled him across. The men heaved and groaned until the waterlogged sailor finally reached them. They dragged him into the boat by his shoulders and the empty buoy swung back out on the rope. "The first survivor, Fionn! And look how relieved he is! He can barely stand up!"

Fionn suspected it was trauma rather than relief that had brought the poor Dutch sailor to his knees. He didn't say as much; he was too distracted. Adrenaline was zinging in his fingers and heating the tips of his ears and he found that he kept forgetting to be afraid.

Fionn watched, as one after another, the eighteen survivors of the SS *Stolwijk* were pulled across the buoy-line and dragged into the lifeboat, their skin tinged blue around the edges, their teeth chattering as they tried to speak. Logically, Fionn knew the process had taken hours, the falling sky a true indicator of evening, but the storm flew past in fast-forward until they found themselves pushing through the water again, headed for Arranmore.

The little boat was still swamped by heavy seas but the rocking wasn't so terrible now and Fionn couldn't tell whether it was the extra weight of eighteen men steadying the vessel or reality overtaking his fear. He hunched against his grandfather beside the motor—the only inch of space left in a boat filled to the brim with twenty-seven seafarers and two secret stowaways.

They sat in silence, watching the Dutch sailors huddling together just the same, while the island men steered them home. Fionn's grandfather's eyes were glassy but it was impossible to tell whether it was the rain spitting down on them or the sight of his father, not twenty feet away, staring through him.

Fionn glanced at the candle in his grandfather's fist. The wax was dripping down his skin and melding it to his hand. It had all but burned into nothingness.

Finally, the storm passed over them. The island crawled out of the sea and the sun flicked its rays through the clouds and blanched the gray from the sky. Fionn's teeth stopped chattering and his fingers began to thaw.

"See," said his grandfather. "There's no fear in the doing of it, is there?"

"I suppose not," said Fionn uncertainly.

The pier rose before them. Huddles of onlookers were crowding at the end of it. Shouts of joy rang out, and floated the little boat toward home. They were almost there when Fionn's grandfather pulled Fionn to his feet. "Remind me, lad. Did you say you could swim?"

"Not very well. Why?"

He glanced at the candle in his grandfather's hand. It had dissolved into a little puddle of wax on his palm. The flame was dying right before his eyes.

"Because I have some unsettling news . . . ," his grandfather said, just as the candle went out.

Fionn screamed as the island took a shuddering breath. The boat disappeared from under them and they plunged feetfirst into the sea.

Chapter Fourteen

THE FALLING SKY

Fionn inhaled a lungful of seawater. His vision blurred as he kicked for the surface, his arms and legs flailing desperately. He couldn't figure out which way was up, and the harder he struggled, the heavier his limbs grew. The lights were winking out inside his head and he knew, somewhere deep inside his panic, that he was drowning.

The sea had come to claim him.

A hand snaked under his arm and tightened over his chest. He was dragged up from the depths of the ocean like a puppet on a string. He broke the surface and hiccuped violently, streams of water pouring out of him as he gasped at the cool air.

His grandfather kept him afloat, one arm fastened

across his chest like a seat belt, the other propelling them toward the sandbank. "You're all right, lad," he heaved. "Lean your head back to the sky. I've got you."

Fionn let his head flop against his grandfather's shoulder. The moon peered over them, a blanket of stars glistening over the water as they moved through it. It was midnight again and the island was eerily quiet.

They crawled onto the sand with their heads bent to the island. Fionn knew they had only been in the sea for a matter of minutes but it had felt like hours. His head was throbbing and his throat was raw from coughing. "You saved me," he croaked. "I thought I was a goner."

His grandfather sat back on his haunches and blinked up at the moon. Then he turned his head and looked at Fionn. "Cormac?"

Something cold and slimy trickled down Fionn's back.

"Wh-what?"

His grandfather looked at the sand, where their shadows bled out around them. He looked back at Fionn, his brows drawing low over his eyes. They were darker than usual. The blue had turned dull and cloudy and the stars weren't catching inside them like they usually did. "What are we doing here, Cormac? It's cold. I'm cold."

Fionn stared wide-eyed at his grandfather. "It's me,

Grandad. It's Fionn." He pointed at himself, and then regretted the absurdity of it. "Are you feeling okay?"

His grandfather shook his head. "I want to go home," he said in a small voice. "Take me home, Cormac."

Fionn rolled onto his feet and held out his hand. "Okay. Let's go home."

His grandfather took it, squeezing tight like he was afraid he might let go.

Fionn led them back up the headland, their way marked by the light of the moon. "I wonder how long we've been gone," he said, picking strands of seaweed from his hair.

His grandfather trudged along behind him, watching his feet.

"Do you think Tara noticed?" Fionn asked him. "I bet she didn't. I bet she's still asleep."

His grandfather didn't say anything.

"She's always been a heavy sleeper," said Fionn. "When I was little I used to take her pulse while she slept to make sure she was still alive."

They crunched onward.

"She's not so bad," Fionn continued, desperation creeping into his voice. "When she's asleep, I mean. She's actually quite tolerable when she's unconscious. Except sometimes she snores and it sounds more like a horse than a human. I told her that one morning and she didn't speak to me for a week. It was the best week of my life." Fionn ignored the pain in the back of his throat, the rough edge of his words as he croaked them out. "Mom made me apologize to her in the end. It was really unfair in my opinion, but I think it's because Mom snores too and maybe she was afraid that she sounds like a horse as well."

His grandfather's grip was so tight Fionn's fingers were turning purple but he didn't dare shake him off.

"Mom doesn't sound like a horse when she snores though. She sounds like an elephant. Especially when she has a cold. But I can forgive her for that because it's not really her fault, and unlike Tara, she has many redeeming qualities."

After a while, Fionn gave up speaking. He couldn't stand the silence that came afterward, or the sound of his own voice getting higher and higher as he jabbered on about nothing. The wind swayed against their backs, the island clearing pebbles and rocks from their pathway as they trundled up the headland side by side.

Thank you, thought Fionn. It wasn't much but it was enough to make him feel not quite so alone just then. *Thank you for helping us.* And in the answering rustle of the trees, the hoot of an owl sprinkling stardust along their shoulders, the island said, *You're welcome.*

When they were almost at *Tír na nÓg*, Fionn's grandfather said, "I hope your mother isn't still up. She hates it when we go out after dark."

Fionn paused at the gate. "Mom's back in Dublin, Grandad."

His grandfather let go of his hand. "Winnie was terrified of the dark when she was small, you know. I don't think she ever grew out of it. But don't tell her I said that, Cormac, or she'll take the wooden spoon to both of us."

Fionn followed him up the path, his turn for silence now. They went inside and he shut the door, sealing them in the cottage. His grandfather drifted over to the mantelpiece, and stood in front of the blazing candle, inhaling noisily through his nose. Fionn flicked the kettle on and went to the bathroom to grab the two biggest towels he could find.

When he came back, his grandfather was sitting in his chair with his eyes closed. The light from the candle danced along his head and painted flames of shadow across his cheeks. Fionn held a towel in front of him. "You should dry off," he said. "We'll catch a cold if we don't warm up."

His grandfather took the towel from him.

"Do you want me to run a bath for you?" asked Fionn.

He shook his head. "Just don't tell your mother where we were. She hates it when we go out after dark."

"I won't," said Fionn quietly.

Fionn removed his grandfather's damp hat and set it back on the coatrack. He helped him slip his shoes off and replaced them with the thickest socks he could find in his suitcase. "Winnie was terrified of the dark when she was a little one, you know," his grandfather told him, flexing his toes inside the socks. "I'm not sure she ever grew out of it, to tell you the truth. But don't tell her I said that, or she'll come after me with the wooden spoon."

"I won't," said Fionn, traipsing back into the kitchen. He made a mug of tea and passed it to his grandfather as his heart climbed up into his mouth.

His grandfather stared into the tea, as though searching for something inside the milky brown liquid.

"Is there anything else I can get you?"

He took a sip, and then shook his head. The blue was returning to his eyes. "You go on to bed. I'll be going soon myself."

Fionn hovered in the doorway, glancing at the candle on the mantelpiece. "Good night, Grandad."

His grandfather smiled, the mug in his hand shaking just a little. "Good night, Fionn."

Fionn got changed into warm pajamas and climbed into bed. Then he pulled the covers up to his chin and stared at the ceiling for a long time. His grandfather was right when he said there was no fear in the doing of something but he was wrong about the rest. There was fear in the beforehand and there was fear in the afterward. In the darkness, it climbed down Fionn's throat and filled him up until he felt like he couldn't breathe.

Fionn had been so distracted by what the island might choose for him that he hadn't stopped to consider what would happen to the old Storm Keeper when a new one came along. As he drifted into an uneasy slumber, he wasn't thinking about the fathomless ocean; he was thinking about the storm clouds in his grandfather's eyes, and the new, burgeoning fear that the sky might be falling somewhere inside him.

Deep in the blackness, the lullaby found him again.

Come to me, my fearless Boyle,

And see the magic I can brew,

crooned the voice.

Visit me beneath the soil.

Come and wish me back to you.

Fionn stood before the mouth of the cave and watched the shadows crawl out of it like skeletons.

Find me where the ravens flock

And wake me from my endless sleep.

The voice grew louder and shriller, the words changing until Fionn found he was not mesmerized, but terrified.

Unbury me from endless rock
And give to me your soul to keep!

Chapter Fifteen

THE SECRET SHELF

The following morning, Fionn waited for his grandfather to come out of his room.

"What's got into you?" Tara demanded, when she wandered into the kitchen just before noon. "How long have you been sitting in that chair doing nothing?"

Fionn tore his gaze from the *Moonbow* candle underneath his grandmother's photograph. He'd been wondering about the memory inside it. His sister was standing in the archway between the kitchen and the living room with her hands on her hips. She was still wearing her pajamas and her hair was piled on top of her head like a bird's nest.

"Nowhere near as long as you've been sleeping," Fionn told her. "I think you've set a new record."

"Don't annoy me today," warned Tara, as she padded into the kitchen and poured herself a glass of orange juice from the fridge. "I'm not in a good mood."

"What a rare and unfortunate occurrence," said Fionn sarcastically. "How come?"

Tara put two slices of bread in the toaster. "Because I haven't been sleeping very well lately. Plus it's *raining*, which means I can't go outside today."

"Why? Are you afraid you might melt?" It had been drizzling on and off all morning, the humidity shifting sometime after sunrise. Mercifully, the weather had been keeping Bartley Beasley away from the cottage.

Tara threw a tea bag at him. "Don't be such a brat."

It sailed past Fionn and landed in the fireplace.

"Pick that up," she said.

"No."

"*Ugh.* I can't believe I'm going to be stuck here all day," she moaned. "It's *so* unfair."

"Burn a heat-wave candle and go stand in it then," said Fionn. "Preferably as far away from me as possible."

"I can't burn any candles without Grandad's super-vision because *someone* wasted the end of *Fadó Fadó*." She cut her eyes at him. "*Allegedly*."

Fionn scowled at her through the archway. "Next

time I'll take a page out of your book and just not tell you *anything*."

The determined scrape of knife-on-bread wafted into the living room as Tara buttered her toast. A sigh whistled through her nose. "We're not supposed to talk about the magic when we're not on the island. Grandad told me not to. Mom doesn't even talk about it to me, just so you know."

Fionn wondered at how much effort it had taken his sister to skirt this close to an apology when her lips had never formed the word *sorry* in her life. "She never mentioned it to you? Not even after you got back?"

Tara set her knife down. "What would she have said? That the island we come from killed our dad? That the storms are magical and the magic swept him away from us? No, Fionny. You have to see it to believe it." She left her toast and wandered into the living room, where she plucked a snowflake candle from a shelf and twirled it in her fingers. "Grandad didn't even tell me until I burned one of these and ended up in a blizzard. I almost got frost-bite in one of my toes."

Fionn regarded her with mounting suspicion. "Is this an . . . apology?"

Tara slid the candle back onto the shelf. "It's a fact. You had to wait. Just like I had to. That's how it's supposed to go."

"Sounds like an apology to me," said Fionn.

"It's not."

"Does this mean I can come with you to the Sea Cave then?" he asked hopefully. He hadn't figured out what he would wish for now he knew he couldn't have his dad, but he still knew for certain he had to thwart Bartley's wish. Even if Fionn wasn't brave enough to be the next Storm Keeper of Arranmore, Bartley would be a disaster.

"No," said Tara firmly. "Bartley says you can't come and it's his thing, Fionny."

"You're really going to let him make that wish, aren't you?" Fionn shook his head in disbelief. "You do realize the cave only grants one wish per Keeper? You're going to let him use it—no, *waste* it—in order to become the Storm Keeper and probably destroy the island while he's at it."

"Oh, don't be so dramatic. Bartley's not a bad person."

"If you believe that, you're more blinded by his ice-cream-cone hair than I thought," said Fionn, leaving the room before the hostility between them spiked again.

In the hallway, he knocked on his grandfather's door and then pressed his ear against it. "Grandad?"

"What's the password?" came his voice from within.

"I don't know."

His grandfather made a noise like a buzzer going off. "WRONG. Try again."

Fionn pressed his forehead against the door. "Abracadabra?"

"Blasphemy!" cried his grandfather.

"Arranmore?"

"Getting warmer," came his grandfather's muffled response. "But you're still in Antarctica."

Fionn sighed. "Is it Malachy-Boyle-Is-Very-Handsome?"

There was a long pause. "You may enter."

Fionn closed the door behind him. Despite the fact the cottage was little bigger than a shoebox, he had never been inside his grandfather's bedroom before. He was always careful about keeping his door closed. The room, now that Fionn was standing in the middle of it, was exactly as he had imagined—complete, organized chaos. It was small and square but he had still managed to cram a lot into it. The wardrobe was wide open, shirts and ties spilling out of the drawers, like they were trying to escape. There were books crammed into every corner, teetering in haphazard stacks, and underneath the floral curtains at the window, there was a wooden shelf, where a small selection of candles had been lined up like soldiers.

Curiosity crept up Fionn's spine and tapped him on the shoulder.

At the other end of the cramped bedroom, his grandfather was half-buried under a mountain of sheets and pillows, surrounded by crumpled tissues.

"Do not worry, Fionn. This is not my deathbed, despite what it may look like. I merely have a terrible cold." Fionn could see that. The tip of his nose was red, and his voice, now that he could hear it properly, was unusually nasal. "And as you are no doubt aware, it is *always* significantly worse when a man catches a cold."

"So Mom says," said Fionn solemnly. Fionn was sorry to see his grandfather ill but he was relieved to have him back to his normal, chattering self. "Can I get you anything? Tea?"

His grandfather flopped back against his pillows. "Fionn, I thought you'd never ask."

"Do you want honey and lemon in it?" Fionn had no idea whether they had these things in the kitchen cupboards.

"Don't offend me," said his grandfather. "I'll have it the right way. One tea bag left in for exactly two and a half minutes and a thirty-milliliter splash of milk."

Fionn edged closer to the bed, studying the lines in his grandfather's face, the blue tinge that lingered around his lips.

His grandfather sighed. "At least one of us survived last night unscathed."

"If it helps, I am definitely emotionally scarred."

His grandfather frowned. "You know, I can't quite remember how it finished." He rubbed the spot between his eyebrows with his index finger, like he was trying to warm the memory up. "The adventure seems to have eclipsed the ending."

Fionn looked at his feet, unsure whether he should remind his grandfather of the forgetting. "Well, it was certainly . . . eventful," he said instead. "I won't be going for a dip in the sea for a long time, that's for sure."

His grandfather sat up and blew his nose extremely noisily until the awkwardness of the moment broke apart. "*Ugh*," he said, balling up the tissue. "Colds are so much worse when you have this much nose to contend with."

Fionn crossed his eyes so he could see his own nose, and then frowned at the reminder of its size. "Tell me about it."

"Then again, a refined sense of smell is no less impressive than baking the best blueberry muffins this side of the Atlantic Ocean," his grandfather mused. "Or perfectly hitting all the notes in 'Bohemian Rhapsody.'"

"I have no idea what that is."

His grandfather regarded him with unconcealed horror.

"I'll get your tea," said Fionn, glancing at the shelf below the window. "And some toast too."

He left the room with curiosity sitting on his shoulder.

His sister spent the afternoon stirring the biggest cooking pot in the cottage the way a witch would tend to her cauldron. "I'm making special soup," she told Fionn when he came to inspect her concoction. "It's going to cure him. Just watch." The rain continued, tap-tapping on the window as Fionn whiled away the hours with the A to F encyclopedia, imagining himself in Camelot, as a knight at King Arthur's Round Table.

When he knocked on his grandfather's door to tell him tea was ready, there was no answer. He eased it open and peeked around it. His grandfather was fast asleep, his breath snuffling out of him in little snores. Fionn tiptoed over to the bedside table to collect the plate from the toast he had delivered earlier. Then he crept across the room to study the shelf.

The rain plinked against the windowpane, and Fionn felt very certain the island was watching him.

There were six candles arranged in a neat little row.

The first two were dyed in varying shades of blue: *Record Low Tide 1959, Record High Tide 1982*. The third, which was pitch-black and punctured with a hundred glistening stars, was called *Perseid Meteor Shower*. The fourth candle, *Blood Moon*, was round as a coin and deeper than crimson. The fifth candle wound upward in a perfect spiral and was rendered in swirling brushstrokes of luminous green. It was called *Aurora Borealis*.

The sixth candle was called *Cormac*.

The plate shook in Fionn's hand, the crumbs tumbling over the edge on to the floorboards.

The candle looked as though it had been carved from the storm itself, plucked out of an angry sky and molded into a column that bubbled along the sides, as though clouds were bursting from it. They were dark gray in the middle and purple around the edges. Along the top, the wax sloshed back and forth like waves, their swirls bleeding into a deep, fathomless blue. The wax was slashed through with a streak of silver that glittered unnaturally in the dimness.

It's just a memory, Fionn tried to tell himself. Even if it was pouring heat into his cheeks and making his lips tremble.

His grandfather was snoring again. It was louder now, like a motorbike revving into gear.

It's not just a memory, said a different voice. *It's my dad! So take it!*

Fionn's fingers hovered over the candle. The wind

rattled the windowpane and his grandfather rolled over, his snore slipping into a sneeze that shook him out of his slumber.

Fionn sprang to his feet as he surrendered to wakefulness, one lazy eyelid at a time.

"Th-there's soup," Fionn said quickly. "Tara made it. It's her own recipe. She's been brewing it for hours. It's bright orange. I wouldn't recommend it, to be honest, but she seems certain it will cure you." He smiled, but it wobbled at the corners. His cheeks were on fire, the guilt of what he had almost done making his words tumble out of him. "I came in here to wake you and I knocked but you didn't hear me so I thought I'd just come in and take the plate sorry if I scared you anyway I just wanted to tell you about the soup do you want some soup?"

"Oh, how lovely," his grandfather yawned. "I was just dreaming about soup. Your grandmother used to make the most delicious chicken broth."

"Lower your expectations."

His grandfather smacked his lips together. "Put me down for a hearty bowl of Soupe du Tara."

Fionn was making every effort not to glance at the candles. "Right. Okay. I'll bring you some then."

His grandfather propped himself onto his elbows. "I'll get up," he said, swinging his legs out from under the sheets and flexing his toes. "I could do with a walk. But only a kitchen-sized one."

Fionn bolted from the room before he could say something incriminating. The windowpanes stopped rattling and the rain tired itself into a light drizzle that splattered silent droplets against the glass.

The three of them ate together. After one miserable spoonful, where Fionn's life flashed briefly before his eyes, he politely declined the soup and made a sandwich instead. Tara made a point of drinking all her soup *and* his, while their grandfather treated them to an unsolicited seven-minute a cappella version of "Bohemian Rhapsody." Afterward, Tara wandered off to the bedroom to watch YouTubers playing pranks on each other on her phone.

Once she was out of earshot, his grandfather thumped his chest like he was dying, wheezing as he pushed the bowl away from him.

"Not to your liking then?" said Fionn lightly.

"Fionn, I would have refused this during the famine."

"Can you detect the secret ingredient?"

His grandfather peered into the orange liquid. "... Is it despair?"

"Close," said Fionn, taking a bite of his crust. "The correct answer is vinegar."

"Carrots and *vinegar.*" The words came out sharp and thorny, like curses. "I thought she liked us."

"She tolerates us. And I did tell you she was the worst."

After covertly disposing of his soup, Fionn's grandfather took himself back to bed. Fionn curled up in the armchair by the fireplace with the encyclopedia on his lap and nothing but the rain for company. As darkness fell, his thoughts turned to his father, and the candles hidden away in his grandfather's bedroom.

Perhaps there was another way to get that wish.

Chapter Sixteen

THE CANDLE THEFT

That night the rain bucketed down with a vengeance. It lasted for several days, lashing from dawn until dusk and smearing the island into an endless gray blur. The monsoon sealed them all inside the little cottage together, Fionn's grandfather sinking into a renewed frenzy of candle-making while ravens gathered on their roof, one by one by one, until they could hear them shrieking down the chimney.

By the end of the week, Fionn had read three boring sports autobiographies and one about a Russian man named Rasputin while Tara had baked eight separate batches of terrible cookies. She seemed to be suffering from cabin fever the most, due in no small part to what

Fionn suspected was withdrawal from one Bartholomew Bouffant Beasley, a boy who evidently did not love her more than he loved his hair frizz-free.

Mercifully, the following Tuesday brought blue skies and warm weather. Fionn woke later than usual, forgetting, as he had done every day before then, the voice that had crooned to him in the darkness. He lay in bed, stretching and yawning, while sparrows chirped happily outside his window. He had almost decided it was going to be a pleasant day when Bartley Beasley's *haw haw haw* seeped into his bedroom like a noxious gas.

Fionn sighed at his ceiling.

He spent an unusual amount of time getting ready, doubling his shower routine and brushing his teeth three times in the hope that when he finally emerged, Bartley would have magically disappeared. Tara had been almost friendly to him over the last few days and Fionn was unsure whether she would continue being tolerable now that their freedom had been fully restored.

When he finally emerged, Fionn was surprised (in the worst way) to find Bartley reclining in his grandfather's armchair, his gangly legs propped up against the fireplace. He was playing his music so loudly Fionn could hear it through his headphones from across the room.

"Hey!" He waved his hand in front of Bartley's face. "HELLO!"

Bartley snapped his eyes open, his foot nearly knocking into the candle on the mantelpiece.

"Careful!" said Fionn, swatting at his feet. "Don't put that out!"

Bartley lowered his legs and kicked them out in front of him, nicking Fionn's ankle. He turned down the music blaring from his iPhone. "Why?" he leered. "What's it doing to us?"

"Mind your own business," said Fionn. A preferable response to the truth which would have been I *have no idea.*

Bartley stretched his arms over his head and rolled his neck around. "I haven't seen you since you threw me out of my gran's memory. It took me *an hour* to walk home, you know. I didn't have phone service for half of it."

"So you had to be alone with your own thoughts? That *is* terrifying."

"I didn't even have the luxury of silence with all those shrieking crows around."

"Ravens, you mean," said Fionn uncomfortably.

Bartley swatted his hand about. "Whatever."

"Where's Tara?"

Bartley jerked his chin to the right. "She's on the phone to your mom telling her how awful you've been."

"My mom called?"

Fionn didn't wait for Bartley's answer. He swung the front door open and went outside in search of his sister. The sky was cloudless and blue, a warm sun hanging overhead. Tara was out on the headland, tracking up and down with her phone pressed to her ear.

Fionn jogged toward her, waving his hands in the air to get her attention. She kept walking, only glancing at him once before abruptly hanging up the phone and shoving it back into her pocket.

"What are you doing?" he said when he reached her. "Why did you hang up?"

"She had to go," said Tara. "She only gets a certain amount of time every week."

Fionn stared at his sister. "What do you mean, *every week*?"

Tara cocked her head. "What part of that sentence is confusing for you?"

"Has she been calling you?" he asked, breathless with unexpected hurt.

"Of course she has. You didn't think she'd just ship us off to this place and forget about us, did you?"

That was exactly what Fionn had thought. "Why hasn't she called *me*?"

Tara turned from him and made her way back to the cottage, her arms swinging purposefully by her sides. "I don't know, Fionn. She said she's been trying, but you obviously haven't been charging your phone."

Fionn followed her. "Why didn't you tell me then? Why didn't you let me speak to her?"

"Because I forgot!" she said, stomping up the garden path. "Just calm down, all right?"

"You should have told me she's been calling!" Fionn said, his voice rising. "You know how badly I've been wanting to talk to her!"

"No, I don't," said Tara, without bothering to turn around. She marched into the living room and collapsed in the chair across from Bartley. "Hey," she said, in a completely different voice, all love-struck and gooey. "Sorry about that."

"Hey." He grinned. "How's your mom?"

"Getting there. She was a little quiet today."

Fionn stood between them. "Am I suddenly invisible or something?"

"What do you want?" said Tara, exasperated.

"Aren't you at least going to *apologize*?"

Tara rolled her eyes. "For what, Fionn?"

"I don't believe you," Fionn said. "I knew you were mean but I didn't think you were *this* bad."

Tara bristled. "My phone calls with Mom are none of your business."

Fionn had the sudden urge to smash something. How could she not see how hurt he was? How could she leave him out like this *again* and not even care? "Why do you have to be horrible to me?" he said, crestfallen. "Are you really so determined to leave me out of *everything* to do with this family?"

Bartley reclined in their grandfather's chair, his arms splayed out on the armrests. "Tell him, Tara. It will shut him up."

"Tell me what?" said Fionn.

"Just leave it," said Tara wearily.

"Go on," pressed Bartley.

Tara chewed on the corner of her lip, the way their mother did when something was bothering her.

"Say it," said Bartley.

"Say what?" asked Fionn.

Tara pinched the bridge of her nose. "It's Dad's anniversary tomorrow. Have you forgotten that?"

Fionn felt himself go very pale. He'd known it was coming up but he must have lost track of the days—they slipped by on the island and he hadn't been thinking about the date lately because his phone wasn't working properly and he wasn't in school anymore and—"Of course not!"

Tara narrowed her eyes. "Well, Mom is extra sad."

"I don't see why you're punishing me for it," Fionn protested. "It's not my fault!"

"Oh, for God's sake," Bartley snarled. "It *is* your fault, Boyle. Haven't you figured that out yet? Don't you get it?"

"Don't," said Tara.

Bartley ignored her. "It's *your* fault because you look exactly like your dad and every time your mom looks at you, she's reminded of his death and that makes her sad. And then it makes her sick!"

"Bartley," said Tara on an inhale. "Stop."

"That's what you told me, Tara." Bartley got to his feet and towered over Fionn, his beady eyes flashing. "Do you understand that, Boyle? Is that making sense to you now? It *is* your fault. So why on *earth* do you think your mom would want to talk to you?" Fionn reeled backward, the words landing in his chest like knives. "That's the reason she shipped you off here in the first place! Next time you burn a candle why don't you do us all a favor and blow away with a tornado?"

Fionn's vision tunneled until it was just Bartley Beasley standing there, red-faced and grinning. "That's not true."

Bartley smirked. "Ask your sister."

"Tara?" said Fionn quietly. "Tell him it's not true."

Tara wouldn't even look at him.

The truth sucked all the warmth out of the room.

How could he not have known?

He had broken their mother.

He was the reason she had to go away.

He was the reason she could never vanquish the shadow behind her eyes—at least not properly and never for long enough.

Bartley flicked his hands like he was shooing a dog. "Now run along and leave us alone. We're trying to track the stupid tide."

"Fionn," said Tara weakly.

Fionn didn't wait to hear what she had to say; her silence had said everything. He left the room, stomping away so they wouldn't hear the strange noises hiccuping out of him.

In the half-light of the little hallway, Fionn tried to steel himself. It was up to him to fix this mess, not wallow in it. He might not be able to wish for his dad back, but his mother was still alive and she was suffering because of him. He owed it to her to take that away. To make her well again. For good.

His grandfather was out in the back garden at his work-bench, but his bedroom door was open a crack and this time Fionn didn't care if the island was watching him or not. He was going to find the Sea Cave today and he was going to fix their mother and then he was going to make Tara eat all those horrible words Bartley had just hurled at him.

We're trying to track the stupid tide.

Fionn was going to go one better. He was going to sink it.

He slid through the door and ducked under the window sill. He grabbed the *Record Low Tide 1959* candle, half expecting something dramatic to happen, but the wind didn't seem to notice and the birds outside continued to mind their own business. Fionn peeked through the corner of the window. His grandfather was leaning over his workbench, stirring a pot of wax.

The candle disappeared seamlessly into the pocket of Fionn's hoodie. He moved the others closer together so its absence wouldn't be obvious. His heart clenched when he touched his father's candle but he forced himself to leave it there. To take two at the same time would be much more noticeable, and besides, today was not a day for remembering—for testing the perimeter of his heart. Today was a day for action.

In the living room, Tara and Bartley had fallen suspiciously silent. Fionn grabbed the box of matches from the mantelpiece without looking at either of them, then he stalked outside and slammed the door behind him.

Chapter Seventeen

THE SINKING SEA

Fionn curled his fingers around the candle in his pocket as he made his way across the island. Time passed quickly, the afternoon sun turning the Arranmore grass a deep, vivid green. He cut through the middle of the island where the fields were wild and deserted, the faraway bustle of island life replaced by wildflowers and birds.

When he reached the lighthouse, Fionn peered over the cliffs. The tide was as high as he had ever seen it but the water was unusually calm. Somewhere far below the surface, the wish was waiting for him. He pulled the candle from his pocket.

"Fionn Boyle!"

Fionn wheeled around to find Ivan strolling across the

headland toward him. He had appeared from nowhere, as though he had just climbed out of the ocean and scaled the cliff edge to get to him. He was wearing his usual black attire, his hair wild in the sudden updraft of wind.

"Where did you just come from?" called Fionn.

Ivan glanced over his shoulder at the sloping grass. Then he looked at Fionn, his lips spreading into a wolfish smile. He crooked his finger at him. "I'll show you."

Fionn didn't move.

Ivan used his whole hand, like he was scooping up the air and throwing it behind him. "I said come *here*."

He was still smiling, but it brought a strangeness to Fionn. He couldn't figure out if it was his grandfather's warnings or Ivan's affiliation with the Beasleys that made him back up a step. And then another.

Fionn squeezed the *Low Tide* candle in his fist as Ivan strode toward him, his arms swinging purposefully by his sides. Fionn was suddenly aware of how alone he was out here. There wasn't another person in sight, or even in hearing distance.

"Do you want me to show you where it is?" Ivan shouted. "Is that why you've come?"

Fionn backed up. "Why would you help me? I thought you were a Beasley."

Liar.

"I need a Storm Keeper," said Ivan, his hair smearing the air with blood-red streaks. "I don't care who it is."

"*Why?*" said Fionn, his eyes never leaving Ivan's.

Ivan grinned. "Why don't you focus on the *where* and I'll focus on the *why?*"

Fionn pulled the matches from his pocket.

"All you have to do is listen!" Ivan doubled his pace, laughter pouring out of him like a song. There was something oddly maniacal about him out here. It was like he had eaten too much sugar and didn't know what to do with himself. Like he couldn't remember how to blink. Like deep inside his delirious laughter, a part of him was screaming. "Why don't you islanders ever *listen?*"

Fionn's fingers shook as he struck a match.

"Wait!" yelled Ivan.

Fionn brought the flame to the wick in one fell swoop.

The island inhaled.

Ivan dissolved into nothingness as the wind rallied around Fionn.

He was pushed out onto the headland, where he found himself alone again on the very edge of Arranmore. An Arranmore that was not quite his own. He loosed a steady breath. The cliffs stretched out on either side of him, the land tumbling into a sinking sea. It was as if someone had pulled out the plug.

The wind coaxed him across the headland, in the direction Ivan had come from. The grass grew past his ankles and the sun climbed higher into the sky. Light edged along salt-crusted stones near the bottom of the cliffs, turning them to crystals that winked up at him.

Keeping his back to the lighthouse, Fionn tracked along the edge of the cliff, searching for openings in the rock. The tide rolled away from the island and wide sandy beaches emerged in its stead.

The grass grew greener as he picked his way down the headland. The tide was so low he could see estuaries of seaweed crawling along the sand. He stayed close to the cliff edge as it dipped and curved around him until finally, he saw it—a gaping hole in the underside of the cliff.

Fionn crept closer, anticipation wringing his throat.

The Sea Cave was hidden beneath a slanted cliff, where the slab of rock bent inward, like it was holding its breath. The opening was almost half a mile away from the lighthouse.

And yet, despite his surprise, Fionn found there was something oddly familiar about this place, as though he had been here before, only he couldn't quite remember when . . .

The sky darkened as a flock of ravens swept in from the sea, circling the mouth of the cave. Fionn pressed a hand to his heart to steady its frenzied beat.

They're just birds.

He shuffled along the edge, humming under his breath—a faltering melody he couldn't quite remember, the words buried somewhere in the back of his mind.

The wind kept rustling, the final layers of *Low Tide 1959* sweeping over him. Steps carved from the rock were emerging from the cliff face, widening and groaning as though the earth was spitting them out. A railing appeared, the rusted metal bars joined together by a fraying blue rope. Fionn watched in stunned silence as a pathway to the Sea Cave materialized, winding all the way down to the beach.

The wind prodded him downward, toward the disappearing tide.

Fionn took his first step. A raven swooped over his head then dived into the cave, as though it was showing him where to go. He swallowed hard, steeling himself. High above him, a seagull screeched. He took the next tentative step. Another gull popped out of the sky and then another, until an entire flock was squawking at him.

"Don't start, please," muttered Fionn.

The seagulls swooped lower, circling him as they

cawed. Some broke off and plummeted toward the cave, chasing the startled ravens inside it.

Fionn took another shaky step. "J-just l-let me get down."

He upped his pace, stumbling down the steps as the birds surrounded him, beating their wings to push him back.

"I need the wish," Fionn gritted out. "Let me have the wish."

Far below, someone was singing. Fionn tried to concentrate on the quiet lilt and not the chaos around him as he followed the song.

The wind howled and the rock groaned and when Fionn was almost halfway down, a seagull dropped away from the others and came straight for him. He waved the candle at it, the flame pointed like a sword. The bird grabbed it with its talons and dropped it into the sea.

The island inhaled.

Fionn released the railing and pressed his cheek against the rock as debris tumbled past him, chunks bouncing off his shoulders and nicking his arms on the way down. The sea climbed above the mouth of the cave while the steps crumbled away. Some disappeared entirely, including the slab just below the one he was standing on. The railing fell into nothingness, pulling the rope with it, until Fionn was left clinging to the edge of a cliff, stranded in the middle of an ancient, broken stairway.

Fionn picked his way back up, scrabbling for the tufts of grass sprouting from the rock. His gaze was glued to his feet, given that any potential missteps would prove fatal now. After what seemed like forever, he dragged himself over the edge and lay there panting until the wind settled.

He had failed. His best chance of helping his mother had been taken from him by a seagull and now that *Low Tide* was gone forever. He scrunched his eyes shut until his cheeks stopped prickling. He would not give up. Not when it was his fault. Not when there was still a chance to fix it.

He blew out a breath. At least he knew exactly where the Sea Cave was. He could easily find the hidden cliff steps now that he knew where to look for them. If he waited for low tide, *real* low tide, he might be able to get all the way down without candle-intervention.

But there was something else needling him as he traipsed back up the hill: the island might not let him. If he wanted to pull that wish out of the cave, he would need Arranmore on his side and right now that was far from the case.

When he made it back to the lighthouse, Fionn was relieved to find that Ivan had taken off. The reprieve had lasted less than a minute when Bartley Beasley leaped into his path with all the confidence of Peter Pan. "I knew I'd catch you!"

"Go away," said Fionn, stalking past him. "I'm not in the mood for you."

Bartley jogged along beside him. "I *knew* you'd try to go to the cave," he said accusingly. "Did you burn a candle? I've been looking for a low tide one all day!"

Fionn doubled his pace to get away from him. "I'd say great minds think alike but you're a moron."

"Did you find a way down?" shouted Bartley.

"Yep."

"Did you go inside by yourself?" he asked, his long strides keeping him level with Fionn. "You're a fool if you did!"

Fionn marched onward.

"Did you take the wish?" he asked, sounding panicked now.

Anger was surging inside Fionn, the memory of what happened earlier still rattling around in his head. All those things Bartley had said about his mother, the way he had sneered at Fionn like he was worse than nothing.

"Yeah," he shouted over his shoulder. "I found the Sea Cave and I wished for your hair to turn green."

"Not funny," snapped Bartley. "What the hell is wrong with you, Boyle?"

"Specifically, *you*. Both generally and right now, since you're in my face," Fionn said, breaking into a run. The wind was back and this time it was blowing him along, a shiver of it curling around his ears. There were birds in the sky again and Fionn could swear that pesky seagull was circling them.

"Tell me where it is, Boyle!" Bartley was still chasing after him. "You may as well. We both know you're too scared to go yourself."

"I got further than you, didn't I? And I didn't need your *cousin*'s help either. But tell him thanks for the offer!" At Bartley's splutter of surprise, Fionn added, "I thought you were supposed to be on the same side."

"We are," he said quickly. "He's rooting for *me*."

Fionn glanced over his shoulder. "Are you sure he isn't rooting for himself?"

"You're just bitter because I told you the truth about your mom," snarled Bartley. "It's not my fault she can't take care of you anymore."

Fionn skidded to a stop. If he was stronger or taller he would have punched Bartley then and there. "*Don't* talk about my mom," he warned, his finger raised. "*Ever*."

Bartley slapped it out of the way. "I'll talk about whoever and whatever I like, Boyle."

Fionn's breath was ratcheting out of him and the

color red was seeping into the sides of his vision. He had forgotten all the words he wanted to say. There was only rage and frustration and determination and the infuriating smirk on Bartley Beasley's face and suddenly a seagull was swooping over their heads, squawking triumphantly as it released a torrent of bird poo all over Bartley's hair.

"*Eeeeeeuuuugh*," shrieked Bartley as it dripped down his face and onto his hoodie. He pressed his hand to his cheek and then stared at it in horror. He looked at Fionn, his cheeks blooming redder than a tomato. Then he turned on his heel and bolted.

Fionn stood stock-still with his mouth open and watched him go. Then he bent over and laughed so hard he nearly passed out.

Chapter Eighteen

THE MELTED MOONBOW

Fionn was still laughing to himself when he got back to the cottage. He had considered trying to be mature about the whole thing but the sight of Bartley Beasley's face, all gooey and red, was seared into his brain and he was still bursting with the mental image. If only a rogue storm would sweep that moment up. Fionn would keep it in a trophy case above his bed.

When he swung the front door to *Tír na nÓg* open, his laughter evaporated. His grandfather was folded over in his armchair with his head in his hands. There was a puddle of wax bleeding across the armrest, midnight blue mixed with red and yellow and violet.

Fionn glanced at the photograph of his grandmother

and felt the whisper of her presence in the hairs on the back of his neck. The *Moonbow* was gone, the last of it dripping along the armrest of his grandfather's favorite chair.

Fionn took a tentative step, the floorboards creaking under his weight.

His grandfather raised his head.

"S-sorry," said Fionn. "I didn't realize you were going to . . . I just . . . I'm sorry."

He blinked and a tear striped his cheek. "She was as giddy as a child that night. Woke me up well after midnight and dragged me out onto the headland. It was below freezing." He shook his head, his eyes glazing as he traveled somewhere else inside his head. "I had never seen a moonlit rainbow before. Didn't even know moonbows were possible. Winnie said she had wished it for my birthday. The island gave it to her . . . of course it did. She was impossible to say 'no' to . . . It was that smile. That beautiful smile."

Fionn cleared his throat. "Can I make you some tea or something?"

He blinked at Fionn. "What time is it?"

"Oh. Uh. I don't know. Mid-afternoon, I think," said Fionn, glancing through the window where the sun was still high in the sky. "Maybe three or four?"

He frowned. "Is it that late in the day already?"

"I suppose it is."

"Goodness," he muttered. "Have you seen my glasses?"

"They're on your head."

He nodded thoughtfully, but didn't remove them.

"Are you hungry?" asked Fionn a little breathlessly. "Did you and Tara eat lunch?"

His grandfather frowned. "Tara . . . ," he said slowly. "I don't know."

Fionn didn't like the feeling that was creeping over him.

"What time is it?" asked his grandfather.

"I think it's three or four."

"Already? It's later than I thought."

"Are you feeling okay?" asked Fionn.

His grandfather studied the puddle beside his right arm. "I burned the *Moonbow*."

"I know."

"I wasted it," he said mournfully.

"No, you didn't," said Fionn. "You got to see her. How could that ever be a waste?"

He shut his eyes tight. "They're supposed to be for the boy. All for the boy. He's going to need them. And I know that. I do. I'm trying. But sometimes . . . sometimes I forget . . ." He trailed off.

"Grandad?" said Fionn anxiously. "What are you talking about?"

"She was even more beautiful than I remember." He leaned back and stared vacantly at the ceiling, lost in the memory. Fionn glanced at the candle on the mantelpiece. The flame was as high as he had ever seen it.

He went into the kitchen and made up a sandwich for his grandfather. There was nothing else to do.

"Here," he said, when he had cobbled together some brown bread and cheese and ham. "I think you should eat this."

His grandfather took the plate from him, surprised at its sudden appearance. Fionn had cut the sandwich into triangles because his mother said they tasted better that way and he was inclined to agree.

"Thank you . . . Fionn." The word came slow and wavy, like he had only just remembered it. He looked up at his grandson, the sea bleeding back into his eyes. "I'm not having a very good day."

"I know," said Fionn softly.

"I find myself forgetting," he said in a quiet voice.

"That's okay." It really was the furthest thing from okay but Fionn knew the many faces of fear and he could see that his grandfather was already frightened. It was etched in the hard edge of his mouth, the spiky inhales between his words.

His grandfather picked a triangle up and stared at it.

"Eat it," said Fionn. "It will make you feel better."

Fionn sank into the chair across from him and watched him eat while the candle between them tried to climb its way to the ceiling.

"Tell me something that will cheer me up," his grandfather said, his mouth half-full of bread.

"I just saw a seagull poo all over Bartley Beasley's head."

He nearly choked on his sandwich. He thumped his chest as he gulped it down, laughter spluttering out of him like a sneeze. "*What?*" he said delightedly. "I don't believe you."

Even though the incident didn't seem quite as hilarious to him now, Fionn was glad his grandfather was enjoying it. "It was the best thing I've ever seen."

His grandfather beamed at him.

Fionn watched him devour the rest of the sandwich, relieved when the color returned to his cheeks. It was just like Tara to take off without making sure he had something to eat.

When he finished the sandwich, he kissed his fingers. "Delicious. Thank you."

"The secret is in remembering to include the bread."

His grandfather nodded, his expression thoughtful. "What time is it?"

"It's about four o'clock."

"Is it, really? That's awfully late." His knees creaked as he unfolded himself. "I think I might take a little nap. Will you wake me in about an hour?"

"Of course," Fionn called after him. "I'll take care of dinner too, if you want."

"Lovely," came his grandfather's response. "Thank you, Cormac."

* * *

Fionn let his grandfather sleep for two hours before he went to wake him. A part of him was hoping the extra time would help with the jumbled memories; the other part was just too afraid to confront the possibility that it wouldn't.

At six o'clock, he knocked on his grandfather's door. Tara was still out, and he was glad not to have to share the cottage with her as he cooked. "It's time to wake up!" Fionn called through the door. "I made spaghetti bolognese!"

"From scratch?" came the muffled reply.

"Uh, no," said Fionn, prizing the door open.

His grandfather was sitting up in bed, still dressed in his shirt and trousers. He chuckled. "That was a joke, Fionn. I know you're my grandson but I haven't lost *all* objectivity on your talents."

Fionn smiled weakly.

His grandfather's eyes were a bright, unclouded blue. "Did you have something to tell me, Fionn?"

"What do you mean?"

"Oh, I think you know very well what I mean."

Fionn stood very straight. For a heartbeat he considered lying but he couldn't bring himself to do it. "I burned the *Low Tide* candle so I could find the Sea Cave," he admitted. "I'm really sorry."

"No, you're not," said his grandfather.

Fionn looked at his shoes. "How did you know I took it?"

His grandfather pointed at the shelf. "The truth is you left a very obvious trail of breadcrumbs. It was a bit of a Hansel and Gretel situation."

There was indeed a large smattering of crumbs on the floor in front of the shelf.

"Oops."

His grandfather sighed. "As much as casual thievery offends me, I'm more concerned that you burned that candle despite everything I said last week, and *worse*, that you went to the Sea Cave by *yourself*."

Aside from that night in the cottage when Fionn had blown out the candle on the mantelpiece, this was the closest his grandfather had come to being truly angry with him. It was an entirely uncomfortable experience.

"I'm sorry," he said in a quiet voice. "I didn't really think about it too much in the moment. And if it makes it any better, I didn't even reach the cave. When I got halfway down the steps, a seagull stole the candle out of my hand and I nearly fell into the sea."

"Good."

"Good?"

"As I have *told you* until I'm blue in the face, you're not supposed to go to the Sea Cave. And *especially* on your own."

"But the cave has been helpful in the past. You said it yourself."

"It has also claimed a life, Fionn."

Fionn's jaw dropped. "Are you serious?"

His grandfather was indeed wearing his serious expression, the wrinkles around his eyes rising to the surface. "A boy called Albert Cannon died in that cave thirty years ago. He was in your dad's class at school. He managed to get down by himself when the tide was low but didn't tell anyone where he was going. By the time the lifeboat crew finally found him, he was dead. He had got lost in the darkness, had run out of food and water and, in the end, hope, I suspect. He was so far in, no one heard him when he called out." He shook his head mournfully. "Something went wrong with the Sea Cave a long time ago, Fionn. There's a strange darkness there and if you're not careful, you can lose your way inside it. That's why you're never supposed to go there by yourself." He paused, his gaze meaningful when he added, "There's a reason I've kept my low tides hidden. The cave is not to be trifled with. The island is volatile enough as it is—I don't want you to go *looking* for trouble. Do you understand me?"

Fionn blew out a breath, a cocktail of guilt and shame swirling inside him. "Yeah."

"It's a good thing the island likes you," he added. "Otherwise you'd be—"

"Dead," said Fionn.

"Or well on your way, at least."

Fionn felt very dizzy all of a sudden. He had been so close to taking that next cliff step, so close to plummeting into the ocean when it disappeared. And what would have happened if he had reached the cave? Would he have lost his way like Albert Cannon had? Would the lifeboat crew have found him in time?

His grandfather patted the bed beside him in invitation, his face softening when he said, "Why the sudden wish urgency? Does this have something to do with your dad's anniversary tomorrow?"

Fionn slumped down beside him, the hurt from earlier bubbling back up. "Tara and I had an argument. She said it was my fault that Mom is sad all the time. She said it's because I look like Dad. I just wanted to help. I wanted to get to the wish before Bartley, so I could make Mom better."

"Ah." His grandfather leaned back on his palms, his shoulders hunching up around his neck. "Well, that makes sense."

"Does it?" said Fionn, horrified.

"Not the part about your mother, Fionn. The part about you taking the candle and going by yourself," his grandfather amended. "Tara's theory is far from the truth."

"But how do you *know*?"

"Because I just do," he said with full confidence. "Tara might believe that explanation because it's simple and it's neat but matters of the heart and matters of the head are never straightforward, Fionn. Your mother loves you both. She's been bombarding me with photographs and stories of you two for as long as I can remember. Quite frankly, if I wasn't so emotionally invested myself, I would have reported her for harassment a long time ago." He smiled at Fionn, his eyes twinkling in the duskiness. "She adores you. Can't you feel that?"

"Only sometimes," said Fionn truthfully.

"You and Tara are the sun in your mother's sky. The truth is she never really said goodbye to your dad, nor to Arranmore. She took her grief and her fear with her on the ferry boat that day, and all of that darkness became a cloud. Sometimes it moves across the sun and eclipses it for a time. You are not the sadness, lad. You are the *antidote*. The fact that you look like Cormac is a gift, Fionn. It is not something you should ever regret, no matter what your sister might say in the heat of the moment."

Fionn looked into his grandfather's eyes and saw the clear blue of a summer sea, the truth shining just beyond it. He believed him, and that belief shifted the weight on his heart. "I just want her to get well again. For good."

"There are many different kinds of bravery, Fionn. Often the journeys we take inside ourselves are more difficult than the stormiest seas." He ruffled his hair, his voice soft and sure when he said, "Your mother has a warrior's heart and an islander's soul. Some day it will lead Evelyn McCauley home. Some day that sky will clear."

Fionn pressed a shaking hand to his chest to steady it.

"You must try and forgive your sister, Fionn," said his grandfather gently. "She was speaking from a place of sadness. Tara has a good heart despite what you may think."

Fionn nodded glumly. "Can I at least ignore her for a while?"

"Of course. You don't have to be a saint about it."

For the rest of the day and the night that followed, that is exactly what Fionn did.

When Tara tried to speak to him in bed that night, he put his earphones in and turned over, keeping his back to her. In his dreams, he made it all the way to the bottom of the cliff steps and found the Sea Cave glittering with possibility. Inside, his mother was waiting for him with open arms, her smile wider than he had ever seen it.

Come to me, my fearless Boyle,
she crooned.

And see the magic I can brew.

She took a step toward him and the blackness of the cave came with her until she wore it around her shoulders like a cloak.

Visit me beneath the soil.

Come and wish me back to you.

Fionn felt the earth crack beneath his feet. He blinked to find it wasn't his mother standing before him, but someone else entirely. The ravens came and buried him in darkness, and Fionn went willingly, desperate to forget what he had seen.

Chapter Nineteen

THE SYRUPY TASTE OF REMORSE

"I made breakfast," Tara announced the following morning from the doorway of their bedroom. "French toast. Your favorite. I thought we might have it out the back, like a picnic."

Fionn peered at his sister from underneath his quilt. "Why..."

"There was bacon too, but I burned it." Tara shuffled from one foot to the other. "I did get a grapefruit from the shop though. But it might be a melon. I don't really know the difference. Sorry."

Fionn sat up, the quilt pulled around him like a shawl. "That's all right..."

Tara cleared her throat. "Not about breakfast, Fionn. I meant … I'm sorry about yesterday, about what Bartley said."

"Oh."

"I did say those things to Bartley," she admitted, not quite looking at him now. "But I don't think I really meant them. I was angry and upset. Dad's anniversary always makes me feel strange. Sometimes it's easier to blame someone for what's happened with Mom and … I don't know. I didn't mean to hurt your feelings and will you please just eat the French toast and let's put it all behind us?" she asked, before hastily adding, "I promise it's not poisoned."

The momentousness of this moment was not lost on Fionn. This was the first time Tara had ever apologized for anything. He swung his feet over the side of his bed and stretched. "I will eat the French toast," he informed her. "And I will enjoy the syrupy taste of your remorse."

Tara rolled her eyes. "You don't have to be weird about it."

Fionn grinned at her. "But who knows when this might happen again? It could be another fifty years before I get to experience an authentic Tara Boyle apology."

Tara smiled crookedly. "That's because I'm never wrong."

A one-*ha* laugh burst out of Fionn.

"Come on then," she said, sashaying out of the room. "Before it gets cold."

In his pajamas, Fionn followed her outside, where the sun was beginning its ascent into a cerulean sky. Tara had transformed their grandfather's workbench into a makeshift picnic table, covering it with one of their grandmother's crocheted blankets and planting a little vase of dandelions in the middle. Fionn didn't have the heart to tell her they were weeds. "Did you hear what happened to Bartley yesterday?" he asked.

"I heard," said Tara, pouring three glasses of orange juice. "He's very upset about it."

Fionn picked up a slice of melon and popped it into his mouth. "I can't believe he actually told you."

"He didn't." Tara uncovered a steaming stack of French toast and plonked two slices onto her plate. "Shelby and I were at his uncle's house when he got back. The bird poo was . . . hard to miss."

Fionn didn't bother to hide the glee from his face as he forked a slice of bread and dropped it onto his own plate. It smelled delicious, warm and buttery, and just like home. Since he wasn't entirely ready to let his sister off the hook (she did still have terrible taste in boyfriends) he resolved not to be too generous with his praise. "Well done, Tara. These look edible."

"I'll take that as a compliment." She sat down across from him, before screeching "GRANDAD, BREAKFAAAAAST!" at the top of her lungs.

Fionn winced. "He's in the next room, not Siberia."

"Yeah, but he's old," she said, squeezing an alarming amount of maple syrup onto her French toast and using a slice of melon to wipe up the overspill.

Fionn unscrewed the cap from the bottle of maple syrup and began to pour, twirling it around and around as rivulets of sticky sugar drizzled on to his own toast.

"Bartley says you found a way down to the Sea Cave." Tara shoveled a bite into her mouth, her words sticky and muffled when she said, "How did you manage that?"

Fionn took a swig of orange juice. "I used my natural sense of adventure."

"How, really?"

"I found a *Low Tide* candle in Grandad's room and burned it," he admitted. "The whole sea drained away and I found a pathway to the beach. I didn't get inside the cave though. The island kind of freaked out when I was halfway down the cliff."

Tara stared at him. "Does Grandad know?"

"Unfortunately."

"He must have been livid."

Fionn nodded as he chewed. "Turns out I could have died in a lot of different ways."

"I can't believe you tried to go by yourself."

Fionn grinned at his sister through syrupy teeth. "Not such a coward now, am I?"

"Just an idiot." Tara shook her head in disbelief. "I'm relieved nothing bad happened to you. It could have been a *lot* worse."

"So I hear."

"Can I know where it is then?"

"Nah," said Fionn. "I don't think I trust you."

Tara considered this while she chewed. She dipped her chin then, as though this was a fair conclusion. "What if we go together next time, just you and me? We can use those steps."

"Why would you want to do that?" said Fionn suspiciously. "I thought you wanted to go with Bartley."

Tara laid her fork down and leaned toward him, dropping her voice like she was afraid the birds might hear her. "Look, I don't care about Bartley's wish, Fionn. I know he's obsessed with being the next Storm Keeper and his gran won't give him a minute of peace about it, but it seems to me that the island should make that decision, not the Beasleys. And, anyway, as long as it's not me, then I don't really care who it is."

"You wouldn't want it?" said Fionn with surprise.

"I'm too young and too talented to be tied to this rock forever. How would I ever kick off my Hollywood acting career?" She swallowed her smile, the seriousness returning to her voice, when she said, "I was thinking we could use the wish for Mom. I want her to come out here and be with us."

"Why didn't you tell me this before?" asked Fionn. "I thought you'd lost all your brain cells."

Tara glowered at him. "Because you were being annoying."

Fionn rolled his eyes.

"And it made more sense to go without you anyway," Tara added. "That way, Bartley wouldn't be worrying about us ganging up and tricking him."

"Making it easier for *you* to trick him," said Fionn with admiration. "Your poor, stupid boyfriend."

"It makes sense that we go together now that we know exactly how to get to it. We both want the same thing. There won't be any ugly arguments when we reach it."

"I don't think Grandad would be happy with either of us trying to get that wish." Now that he was properly considering it again, Fionn's uneasiness was rearing its head. "He says the cave might swallow us."

"Not if we're together," said Tara dismissively. "It's

only a matter of time before the tides behave again. Bartley's as close as we are. Maybe even closer, with that weirdo Ivan helping him. If the wish is going to be used up either way, why can't we have it?"

Fionn chewed on his bottom lip, considering.

"I mean, we've spent so long looking for it already, are you really going to give up now that it's within reach?" Tara went on, expertly playing his resolve like a violin. "The cave is part of the island, Fionny. Dagda *left* it for us. How dangerous could it really be?"

"I don't know," he said uncertainly.

"Grandad won't know until it's over." She looked at her plate, her voice wobbly when she said, "We owe it to Mom, Fionny. We're all she has."

Fionn's heart thumped painfully in his chest. Tara was smiling sadly, just the way their mother did, and in that moment, she looked so like her that Fionn melted. If there was a chance to help their mother, then they owed it to her to try.

He dropped his voice so he couldn't be heard from the next room when he said, "Let's go tomorrow morning then. That'll give us enough time to look for another *Low Tide* while Grandad's asleep."

"What if Bartley gets to it before then?" Tara whispered.

"The tides are all over the place." Fionn took another bite of his French toast, the sugary syrup exploding in his mouth and dancing along his taste buds.

And he doesn't know about the secret steps either, he thought with satisfaction.

"Okay." Tara ate another forkful, her eyes blazing with determination.

When there were only three pieces of toast left in the stack, their grandfather appeared in the doorway. "Well, well, well. Do I detect the sweet smell of reconciliation?"

"That's the syrup," said Fionn.

"We saved these for you." Tara clinked the edge of the plate with her knife. "They're a bit cold now."

His eyes lit up. "Ah, French toast. My *favorite*." He seated himself at the head of the workbench, and made quick work of the French toast, drowning the slices in maple syrup and then adding a shake of powdered sugar, just for good measure. Fionn watched him eat, drawn to the wrinkles along his forehead and the deep creases underneath his eyes. He seemed so much older than he had been only days before.

Fionn thought again of the wish ... of their mother back in Dublin wrestling with the shadow inside her ... of all the things that had been slipping through his grandfather's fingers recently, spectacles and hours and people . . .

One wish and two heartaches.

"You know it's been years since I've had a picnic," his grandfather was saying. "What a lovely idea, Tara. And what a fitting way to honor your father's anniversary today. Winnie and I used to take Cormac for picnics on the beach all the time. We'd have to take turns tackling him when he ran off to find the Merrows."

There was a sudden flash of violet in Fionn's periphery. His attention was pulled skyward, where a rainbow was shimmering into being. "Hey, look."

His grandfather turned his face to the sun. It sprinkled its rays along the crevices in his face until he seemed not quite as old as before. "Ah, a gift."

The seagulls circled them in muted silence, the rainbow glinting off their wings and painting color wheels along the ground.

"And there's another one!" said Tara excitedly.

There, just a breadth above the first one, a second rainbow was painting itself into the sky.

"One for each of you," said their grandfather.

"They're right over the cottage!" Tara was wearing her own special shade of wonder; it softened her smile and glistened behind her eyes. Fionn realized he hadn't seen her like this in a very long time. He wondered if perhaps she had a shadow too, somewhere inside her. If perhaps they both did. "It seems like it's only meant for us."

"It does, doesn't it?" said their grandfather, a twinkle in his eye.

Tara and Fionn watched the rainbows until they scattered their shades across the sky and dissolved into the ether.

Their grandfather ate his toast, chomping happily to himself, as though there was both a rightness and a distinct expectedness to this moment.

"Does this happen every year?" asked Fionn.

"Of course it does."

Fionn understood then why his grandfather had dedicated his entire life to protecting the secrets of this strange place, why he didn't resent Arranmore for the loss of his son. The island remembered. It cared. And Fionn thought that perhaps it was sorry too, for what had been taken from them.

"So," said their grandfather, once he had licked every last drop of syrup from his fingers. "What's on the agenda for the rest of the day then?"

Tara pushed her stool away from the workbench.

"Shelby wants to make a cake for her aunt's birthday. I said I'd give her a hand."

"Well, that's all very altruistic, Tara, but you must remember to smuggle me at least three slices."

"I will," she said, skipping back inside.

Fionn's grandfather pointed his empty fork at his forehead, gold-spun threads of syrup dripping off the end. "And what about you, Fionn? Do you have some time to spare for your dashing grandfather this afternoon?"

"What did you have in mind?"

"I thought I might show you how the candles are made. Would you be up for that?"

Fionn swallowed the sudden dryness in his throat. "I am *definitely* up for that."

His grandfather winked at him, the promise of enchantment lingering in his smile.

Chapter Twenty

THE STORM KEEPER'S SECRET

" I 'll just be a minute," Fionn's grandfather called from inside the shed, his words punctuated by a cacophony of clanging and banging and thumping. "*Where* has all this trash come from? I can barely see past my own nose in here . . ."

After rummaging around for what seemed to Fionn like an eternity, he finally unearthed the box he was searching for. It had been hidden under a broken beach umbrella and wedged between a collection of old music records. He carried it back to the workbench, setting it down with a satisfying thud. On one side of the box, in black felt-tip pen, it read: *Candle-making for beginners*.

On the other side, names were scrawled in different handwriting, most of them blurry and faded by time. Fionn recognized his grandfather's name nestled between *Maggie Patton* and *Ferdia McCauley*. There were other Boyles too, and Cannons and McCauleys and Pattons, but it took Fionn almost a full minute to find a Beasley entry—a woman called Bridget—which was scrawled along the other side.

Fionn peered over the lip of the box. It was mostly full of candle molds—stars and spheres and squares and hearts—and old whittling knives. There were half-used bags of wax chippings and wax pebbles piled along the bottom, bits of branches and strips of seaweed strewn haphazardly on top. Nothing to suggest how his grandfather got all the right ingredients jumbled together, how he distilled the smell of a storm or the scent of lightning at sea.

His grandfather pushed his glasses up onto the bridge of his nose. "You once asked me why I chose to record the weather."

"Yeah," said Fionn.

His grandfather placed the metal pot on the grid over the burner. "Our weather is raw elemental magic, Fionn. It runs in the Storm Keeper's veins just as sure as our skies. It is the source of the Storm Keeper's power. To store it is to store magic."

Fionn blinked in surprise. "So you're *saving* it?"

"Aye." His grandfather dangled the bag of wax pebbles. "We keep the magic behind a flame, so that we can use it against Morrigan's darkness if she returns."

Fionn took the bag of wax, his hands trembling a little. This moment was bigger than it first appeared—the simple rattle of wax on metal, a flame hissing in the wind—it might one day be his legacy. "Does that mean there's a way to use it?" he asked as he poured the wax. "To get it *out*?"

His grandfather held a wick between them—a long, thin rope ending in a round silver disk. He flicked the disk with his finger, then pressed it against the bottom of a mold, rolling the wick back and forth between his fingers until it stuck straight up. "We haven't even put it in yet and you're asking me how to get it out."

Fionn set the bag back into the cardboard box without taking his eyes from the chippings in the pot ... watching, waiting ...

"You—" His grandfather went rigid in his seat. He sniffed the air, licked his bottom lip. "Oh," he said, frowning into the melting wax, instead of up at the sun, like it was inconsequential to the matter when he said, "The storm is coming in a little earlier than I expected."

Fionn went very still. "How do you know?"

"I can feel the shifting inside me," he said, shifting on

his stool just the same. The wax in the little pan was bleeding into a creamy white puddle and his grandfather's eyes were glistening. He looked at Fionn. "The new Keeper is rising."

"Now?" Fionn pulled his sleeves down as a cloud appeared from thin air and moved in front of the sun. Shadows danced across the workbench. There was a flock of birds circling them, appearing as if from nowhere. Not just seagulls and ravens but swallows and finches and thrushes, all jumbled together. The longer he stared, the more appeared, watching over them with rapt curiosity. Waiting. "Are you sure?"

His grandfather nodded grimly. "Believe me, lad. You know when the magic is dribbling out of you, just as sure as you know when it's thrumming inside you, beating your heart like a drum."

"Do you feel okay?"

"I feel very full and very empty." His grandfather's spectacles inched down his nose as he dipped his chin to examine him. "Do you feel okay?"

"I don't feel anything," said Fionn, discounting the dread that was hopscotching over the notches in his spine. "What if it isn't me? What if it's someone else?"

His grandfather set the pot down on the bench and turned the burner off. "Fionn, the day you stepped off the ferry, the island woke up. It has been more restless these last few weeks than I have ever known it to be."

Fionn stared at him.

"The candles react to you in an entirely different way," he went on. "Unburnable wax burns for you. The wind chaperones you wherever you go. It's as though Arranmore recognizes you, not just in this layer, but in all of them ..." He grew very quiet then, his chin resting on his chest like he was talking more to himself than to Fionn. "I believe it has been expecting you for quite some time."

There was such enormity to his grandfather's statement, more than enough wonder and impossibility to drown in, and yet he seemed not intrigued or surprised ... but resigned. And it stoked the uneasiness that had long been kindling inside Fionn.

Fionn stared at the melted wax. "What will happen to you when the storm comes?"

To this, his grandfather said nothing.

In the sudden absence of birdsong and breeze, Fionn could hear his own ragged breathing.

"You should hold on to the gift. Tell the island you're not ready to give it up yet." He pushed his stool back from the bench and got to his feet. "I can wait. Bartley can wait. We can *all* wait."

"Fionn," his grandfather said.

"No, honestly, I'm fine."

"Fionn."

"I'm cold. I'm going to just go inside and—"

"Sit down."

Fionn sat down.

His grandfather stirred the wax. "I can't do it anymore, Fionn. My memory is fading."

"No," said Fionn softly, but he couldn't say anything else. The lie was too big to push past his tongue.

"I have spent my whole life remembering, Fionn. It stands to reason that at some point, I would reach capacity. That I would start to forget."

The sky was growing dark; thick clouds of gray and black had rolled in from nowhere and had stubbornly hung themselves in front of the sun. It felt exactly like what was happening inside Fionn. He stared at the wax in the little pot and felt the insignificance of a thousand sunsets and snowstorms rise up between them. His grandfather had spent so many years capturing the island's magic, toiling with red-wired eyes and tired fingers, that he had forgotten to record himself. Now he was slipping away, like sand through splayed fingers. Who cared about magic if this was where it ended?

"Then stop putting the weather in the wax, and find some way to put *yourself* in it instead."

"I already have, Fionn."

The clouds sank lower, and another layer emerged behind them, yawning across the sky in great pockets of gray. Darkness crept across the workbench, cloaked hands and faces and arms and fingers and understanding crawled over Fionn. It had been there all along—the edges of it, but he could never make sense of it. "The candle on the mantelpiece. The memory . . . it's *you*."

His grandfather's answering smile was small and true. "The Storm Keeper's secret."

Fionn looked a little closer at his grandfather, this man who lived with the island inside him. This man who had somehow found a way to record his own conditions so that he might anchor himself to the world. For a little while at least. "What happens when it runs out? Can you make another one?"

"I am already changed, Fionn. When the candle goes out, I will forget, for good."

Fionn slammed his teeth into his bottom lip to stop it from shaking. "But that's not *fair*."

And that was the truth of it: heavy and full and dark as the rain clouds hanging over their heads. It wasn't fair at all.

His grandfather continued to stir the wax, counter-clockwise, then clockwise, back and forth, back and forth.

"There are worse things to fear, Fionn. A life without love. A path without meaning. A heart without courage."

"Are you afraid?"

"No, Fionn. I am not afraid."

Somewhere in the distance, a lone crow weaved its caw between the sinking clouds. "The sky is falling," said Fionn.

"The sun will break through again," his grandfather replied, and there was much more in those two sentences than there had been in everything else that came before them.

Fionn wanted to say something more; he wanted to say that he loved his grandfather fiercely, that he was the only person in the world who made him feel better about living in his own skin, that he was the brightest star in Fionn's sky, that he couldn't bear to see him forget a single thing or to find that in all the forgetting, he would come to forget him too. The words crowded together on his tongue until he felt too full to speak at all.

"Don't feel sorry for me, lad," his grandfather said softly. "I have filled my head with adventure and laughter and love, and all the stories of those who have gone before me . . ." He leaned toward Fionn so all he could see was the roiling sea in his eyes, not the storm clouds sweeping in above them. "In truth, I've been quite greedy about the whole thing."

Fionn couldn't summon a smile.

His grandfather sighed. "If you *insist* on pity, then really you must pity yourself. Your head is still very empty."

Fionn frowned, indignation jostling the urge to cry for a precious, fleeting second.

His grandfather chuckled. "Start filling it up, lad. That is your greatest responsibility. To live a life of breathless wonder, so that when it begins to fade from you, you will feel the shadow of its happiness still inside you and the blissful sense that you laughed the loudest, loved the deepest, and lived fearlessly, even as the specifics of it all melt away."

A slant of light broke through the gathering dark, tiptoeing across the workbench and sliding into the pot of wax.

"Is that *really* how you feel?"

His grandfather withdrew a small leather pouch from the cardboard box and pulled a silver pin from inside it. "That is exactly how I feel, Fionn. Which is why I can afford to be so smug about the whole affair." He pricked his finger and held it over the pot. The movement knocked all the words right out of Fionn's head.

There was only wonder now.

Wonder, and an angry sky.

"Sometimes they come slowly," said his grandfather as

they both stared at his pricked finger. "The more incon-sequential ones, the rain and the clouds and the snow you can coax out ... but the big ones, oh, the magic-dripping storms and the fiercest blizzards, Fionn, they swell inside you until it feels like a wave and you feel like you might fly if you tried hard enough."

He tapped his finger on the edge of the jar.

"What exactly is supposed to happen?" Just as Fionn said it, a single droplet squeezed itself out of the tip of his grandfather's index finger and tumbled into the pot of molten wax. It landed with an unmistakeable *plink!*

Fionn's eyes grew. "That wasn't blood."

The truth was simply this: it was the sea. His grand-father had pricked his finger and the sea had come out of it. The droplet was clear; the scent of salt and brine and seaweed climbed into Fionn's nostrils as it rippled into the wax.

It was a drop of ocean. A drop of magic.

"The first one is the island," said his grandfather, licking the second drop from his finger. This one was blood. "And the second drop is you."

Fionn tried not to think about how much of his grandfather's blood had gone into that candle on the mantelpiece. He watched the wax change, from white to sunshine yellow, streaks of golden brown threading its way through it like estuaries, until it looked like cracked marble. The wax shimmered and then changed again, as if it couldn't quite make up its mind. Now it was whorls of red and orange and yellow. Wisps of green and blue bled into indigo and indigo twirled into violet.

The scent changed; instead of the sea, there were other things: warm toast sizzling in a buttery pan, sticky strands of sugary syrup, and slices of fresh grapefruit. No. Not grapefruit—the scent wavered, melon creeping over it. There were aromas of fresh rain and blue skies. Fionn could picture it perfectly: a mild summer sun slanting through two perfectly curved rainbows. And deep down, underneath all of it, the whisper of shared smiles and love at its fiercest.

Fionn found himself grinning like a cat. His grandfather had bottled their picnic.

"You know, I often wonder whether there is more magic in humanity than a skyful of rainbows." He held the wick straight and poured the wax into the side of the jar, the colors swirling and crystallizing against the glass.

"That's it?" said, Fionn. "That's all it takes?"

His grandfather dusted his hands. "That's it, Fionn. All it takes is a drop from *the island that lives and breathes inside you.*" He snorted. "Most people would be impressed by that, you know. I think you play too many video games."

Fionn looked at his fingertips, waggling them back and forth. "I might have the sea inside me?"

"Now doesn't it seem silly to be so afraid of it?"

Just as he said it, the heavens opened and the first drop of rain catapulted to earth. It landed on the tip of Fionn's nose. The next one slid over his ear and down his neck. The third one brought the storm with it.

His grandfather stowed the box in the shed and pulled a blue tarpaulin over his workbench, while Fionn grabbed the candle and shoved the stools under the rain cover. The clouds were skimming the sea and bringing salt water with them, until it tasted as though the ocean was falling from the sky.

It took three attempts to get the back door open against the sudden raging wind. When they managed it, the direction changed and it nearly swung off its hinges, flattening Fionn against the wall of the cottage.

"It will get worse before it gets better!" his grandfather yelled, as Fionn shimmied out from beneath it and darted inside, both of them heaving the door closed behind them.

It slammed shut with a bang, and they rolled backward, panting. The windows rattled as a fresh onslaught of rain bucketed down on the cottage. They had barely made it into the kitchen when the front door flew open, clanging against the coatrack and knocking hats and scarves all over the ground. Fionn looked up to find Shelby Beasley standing on the threshold, her long hair stuck to the sides of her face, as though she had just climbed out of a horror film.

"You have to come with me right now!" she shouted, as a fork of lightning struck the headland over her shoulder. "It's Tara. The island's taken her!"

Chapter Twenty-One

THE SEA CAVE

Fionn's heartbeat roared in his ears. "What happened?"
"She went to the Sea Cave!"

"No," his grandfather said almost at the same time.
"She wouldn't have."

Shelby was nodding furiously. "The tides changed.
Bartley came home when we were baking and said he'd
found some kind of secret cliff steps but he couldn't go
down to the cave alone! Tara went with him!"

"She promised she would wait for me!" said Fionn
frantically. "We were supposed to go together!"

Shelby was sobbing so hard it looked like someone was
shaking her by the shoulders. "Th-th-the t-tide w-wasn't
l-low e-enough s-so they had to swim inside the—"

"Is Bartley with her now?" Fionn's grandfather interrupted.

Shelby shook her head, silent tears streaming over her cheeks as she tried to gather herself. "Bartley said the cave started to swallow them and he wasn't able to pull Tara out. There were all these birds blocking the way and then the storm began . . ."

Fionn's grandfather bit off a curse. He darted from the living room, muttering to himself as he disappeared into his bedroom.

Shelby stumbled into the cottage, her teeth chattering furiously in the silence.

His grandfather emerged less than a minute later with an old schoolbag in his hand.

"We have to be quick about it." He pulled a lighter from his pocket and dropped it inside before leaping onto the armchair in the living room and sweeping some candles from the top shelf into the bag.

He thrust the backpack into Fionn's chest. "Do you know what you have to do, lad?"

Fionn snatched the bag from him. "Can't you come with me?"

His grandfather glanced at the candle still blazing on the mantelpiece, then at the storm outside. His face crumpled.

"It's all right," said, Fionn quickly. His grandfather couldn't leave his anchor—not anymore. If he did he would lose himself long before they reached the cave.

Fionn slung the bag of candles on to his back. "I'll go," he said, steeling himself. "I'll go."

His grandfather gripped him by the shoulders. "The cave will have buried her somewhere inside. The tide is too high now. You'll have to enter by a different layer to find your way in. Start with *Ebb Tide*. It's the thinnest one. It will pull the ocean out." Fionn tried to focus on the words and not the fear gnawing at his bones. He glanced past him, out the window. The sky was darker than he had ever seen it, the clouds glittering around the edges. "No matter what happens, do not let yourself be alone inside that cave, Fionn. When you find Tara, you must stick together, do you understand me?"

Fionn gripped the straps of his backpack. "I understand."

They tumbled into the storm, Shelby's hand finding Fionn's as the gate swung open for them. His grandfather stood in the doorway, his fingers gripping the frame as he leaned out.

"Be careful, Fionn!" he shouted over the roll of thunder. "The island will answer to you if you ask the right questions!"

Fionn dragged Shelby out onto the headland before he had time to change his mind. Lightning struck the sea ahead, a crack of fire curling into smoke that beckoned them onward.

"I can't believe Bartley left her in there by herself!" shouted Fionn.

"He said it all happened so fast!"

"I bet he had enough time to make his dumb wish though!"

"It's all my grandmother and my uncle go on about," Shelby panted. "Bartley wants it so badly, he talks about it in his sleep. He can't think about anything else!" They cut through the middle of the island, their feet squelching in the long grass, slipping and sliding from field to field as the rain swamped them. "I know it doesn't make it okay."

Fionn could barely see through the freezing sheets of rain. His heart was thumping wildly now and he couldn't tell how much of it was fear for his sister and how much of it was longing for the opportunity that had been whipped from his grasp at the last second.

They ducked under a sopping wooden fence and waded through mud up to their ankles. "Look!" yelled Shelby. "We're nearly there!"

A string of seaweed tumbled from the sky and lashed

Fionn across the face. He kept his head down, clambering over another fence as blood dripped down his cheek.

When they reached the lighthouse, they found Bartley huddled into a ball behind it.

"Hey!" Fionn kicked him in the shin. "Where's my sister!"

Bartley snapped his head up, his face blotchy with tears. "The cave took her! I couldn't save her! There wasn't enough time!"

Fionn kicked him again, harder this time. "You had time to save yourself though! Some Storm Keeper you'll make!"

"Where's Malachy?" said Bartley, turning his panic on Shelby. "I told you to get Malachy! He's the Storm Keeper!"

"He's not coming! We're on our own!"

"*We?*" said Bartley, staggering to his feet. "What can *we* do?"

"We can *help!*" shouted Shelby, louder and fiercer than Fionn had ever heard her. "We can go back down there and *do* something!"

"I almost *died!*" said Bartley, his eyes wild. "I'm not going near that thing again! I've called Gran! She and Douglas are on the way! They'll know what to do since Malachy clearly doesn't care enough!"

"Coward," spat Fionn. If it was any other occasion, he'd lay into Bartley for speaking badly about his grandfather but the sky was glittering violently and the storm was turning purple around the edges. They were running out of time.

He swung the schoolbag over his front and dug around inside. His fingers were shaking badly and his mind was racing a mile a minute.

The storm was twisting around the island like a tornado. It looked like it might rip the lighthouse up at any moment and fling it out to sea. The tide was bobbing up and down, high one minute and low the next, as though it couldn't make its mind up. The waves were hurling themselves against the cliffs below, thrashing and hissing as they broke around jagged rocks.

Shelby screamed and flattened herself against the lighthouse as something small and hard hurtled past her shoulder. "Is that a *crab*?"

Bartley picked a clump of neon coral from her hair and held it up to his face. "Where did *this* come from?"

Fionn found the *Ebb Tide* candle and clamped it in his fist.

"Which one's that?" said Bartley, his attention flitting to Fionn.

"Go and find shelter," said Fionn, one eye on the tornado as he searched for the lighter.

"What are you going to do?" Shelby asked, jumping to the side as a pink jellyfish arced over her head.

Fionn unearthed the lighter and flicked it open. "I'm going to sink the sea."

Bartley yelped as a school of mackerel soared past them.

Fionn was already stalking away from them. He followed the headland down to the coast, sliding over mud and grass as the sea rained down on him.

"Let me come too!" shouted Shelby, slipping down after him. "I can help!"

"Are you both insane?!" called Bartley from his perch by the lighthouse. "There are people coming to help us!"

Fionn knew better. There was no one in the world who could save his sister now. No one but him. "Don't try to follow me into the cave!" Fionn called over his shoulder. Shelby was far behind him already, stumbling through the soupy mud. "Wait until the tide settles again. We might need someone to pull us out!"

When he reached the edge of the cliff, he curved his shoulders over the candle to keep it dry and then brought the flame to *Ebb Tide*.

It lit up immediately.

The island inhaled.

The sky quieted. The rain sputtered into a light drizzle and the thunder faded as Fionn sank into a different layer of Arranmore. The water was dragged away from the cliffs, the waves trickling back out to sea until the beach emerged below him.

Fionn lowered himself onto the crumbling staircase.

He kept his eyes firmly on his feet. The steps were still broken, while some were no longer there at all. He crept down, down, down, following the sinking tide, as ravens swooped from the sky and beckoned him onward. Unease grumbled in his stomach. It was a warning, painted in shrieking black feathers, but he couldn't turn back now. Not while Tara was in trouble. He took a deep breath and kept moving.

The mouth of the Sea Cave emerged from the retreating sea. Fionn kept clambering, his fingers scrabbling against the rock face as he lunged over gaps in the stairway. The rain had stopped, and a thick mist hung like a veil over the sea. The stairway grew steeper, growing more complete near the bottom where the steps were unweathered by time and would-be explorers.

When Fionn reached the end of the stairway, the island fell eerily silent. He could feel its eyes on him as he stood at the entrance to the Sea Cave. It was much bigger now that he was standing in front of it, and so tall it dwarfed him.

A trickle of seawater crossed the sandbank and slithered inside, like a snake. Fionn followed it into the cave.

The island watched him go.

"Tara?" The word echoed back at him, punctuated by his own ragged breaths.

The cave was unnaturally dark, the blackness unfeathered by the flame in his fist. He couldn't see his own feet as he shuffled forward, knocking against rocks and slipping over seaweed. He held the light up to the wall and saw nothing but droplets sliding down the carved rock.

"Tara!" he shouted.

"Tara!" the cave called back.

Fionn's grandfather was right. There was something else here—something beyond the island's ancient magic. It made the air heavier, the darkness denser, and as he walked onward, into the abyss, it caressed his ears and whispered to him.

Come to me, my fearless Boyle.

The longer Fionn walked, the less he believed there was an end to this ancient, rustling place. He could barely see his own nose in here and he was afraid of the voice calling to him in the darkness. He swung his bag around and fumbled inside until he found *Sunrise*, barely discernible by its dim amber glow. He had never done this before—burned two candles at once and stitched two completely separate layers together, but he knew it wasn't impossible. He just had to be very careful.

"Please," he whispered, appealing to whatever magic was tucked away inside the cave, whatever tendril of it was inside the candle. "Please let this work."

Fionn held his breath as he set *Sunrise* alight. The island took another heaving breath. The flame fought its way into the darkness, the wind changing around him as he held a candle in each hand, like battle swords.

Somewhere in the distance came the lilt of birdsong. The voice in Fionn's ears quieted as the rising sun poured its rays into the cave and the rock face lit up in yawning pockets of sunlight. He exhaled with relief, the air shimmering around him as the layers melded together, the tide low, and the sun rising.

Now he could see everything.

Crystal stalactites hung from the ceiling like chandeliers. They glinted at Fionn as he passed between them, navigating the spires that wound up from the ground. The scent of salt and brine hung heavy in the air, dampness clinging to his skin as he pushed onward, into the belly of the cave. There were shells everywhere—pearl and silver and blue and gold, and as he walked, more sprouted up from the ground like coins, ripe for the taking.

He didn't dare.

He could feel the island's presence more keenly now. Sunrise had illuminated everything—both the seen and the unseen. Magic rose from the ground like steam and hummed in the air like wind chimes.

The cave was definitely enchanted.

And in the unknowable, unignorable magic, he could hear his sister sobbing.

It was an echo. Tara was not quite here in this strange layer, the one that Fionn had cobbled together with *Sunrise* and *Ebb Tide*. But she was nearby. He tried to follow the sound, but it wavered in and out, like a radio station struggling for signal. The cave grew steeper, tunneling downward into the heart of island.

The candles were burning too quickly and the sunlight behind Fionn was disappearing, ray by ray. The farther into the cave he got, the faster the wax melted. By the time Tara's echo had faded entirely, the candles had pooled all over his fists.

The flames went out, one after another. First *Ebb Tide*, and then *Sunrise*. Fionn came to a stop, his heart hammering in his chest.

He couldn't hear his sister anymore.

He couldn't see the entrance, or even the path that had led him here.

He was lost.

Outside, the tide would be coming in. Inside, the darkness was growing denser. Time was running out.

A droplet fell from the ceiling of the cave and landed in a puddle at his feet, its *plink!* echoing around him. The water rippled, turning a deep, shimmering blue. Fionn stared at the blueness, until the blueness stared back, and then it winked, and Fionn understood with sudden clarity.

The island will answer to you, if you ask the right questions.

Fionn took a deep breath and with all the courage he could muster, he said to the magic and the cave, and the rustling island above: "My name is Fionn Boyle, son of Evelyn McCauley and Cormac Boyle, grandson of Winnie and Malachy Boyle, and I wish for my sister back."

A stalactite came crashing down beside his left ear. It shattered into a thousand crystals that sank into the ground and disappeared. Fionn raised his chin. "I wish for my sister to be returned to me," he said, more loudly this time. "I come on behalf of the Storm Keeper of Arranmore and I want my sister back!"

The island groaned.

It seemed for a heartbeat that Fionn was not in a cave

but in the belly of some great and terrible whale. He crushed his wax-stained fingers into fists as the ground bubbled beneath his feet. Shells tumbled over shells, sapphire and ruby twinkling in the darkness. Bejeweled stalactites formed around him, crawling down around his ears. They fused with stalagmites that crept up from the ground until Fionn was surrounded by a hundred glittering columns—the makings of a marbled palace underneath the island.

The cave settled and then there was nothing but silence.

"Tara?" The wind swirled around him and carried it deep into the cave.

Five heartbeats.

Ten heartbeats.

And then—"Fionn?"

Fionn's heart leaped in his chest. "Tara? Where are you?"

"I . . . I d-don't know," came his sister's voice.

At one end of the strange chamber, the walls tapered into a narrow passageway. Fionn had to flatten himself and squeeze through, holding his breath and raising his chin so as not to scrape his face. He inched along, his arms splayed on either side of him, until he came to the very end, where a small hole had been carved into the rock. He pressed his face to the opening and peered inside the crack. "Tara?"

Tucked inside a hollow barely bigger than himself, Fionn's sister was huddled into a little ball. She blinked up at him, the whites of her eyes shining in the darkness.

Then she burst into tears.

Chapter Twenty-Two

THE LAST LIFEBOAT

F ionn's relief was short-lived. "Come out of there," he
said, shuffling backward.

Tara pressed her face through the gap and stared at
Fionn with eyes made round with fear. "We'll drown," she
whispered. "The cave will drown us for this."

"Not if we hurry," Fionn insisted, reaching inside and
tugging at her hand. "The tide is coming back in!"

Tara squeezed through the tiny gap, yelping as she
nicked her shoulder on the rock. Her sweater was pocked
with holes and there were tracks of mud on her cheeks.
"I'm sorry, Fionny. I know I shouldn't have come without you but Bartley was going to take it, with or without

me." Her fingers tightened around his, as though she was afraid he might let go. "I wanted to out-wish him."

"You shouldn't have risked it," said Fionn tightly.

The walls reclined from each other, the gap opening out into the cavern of jeweled columns and glittering rock. They hurried into the belly of the cave, crunching over seashells as salt water trickled into their sneakers and pooled between their toes.

Shadows slunk down the walls and crawled over them.

The island was shifting.

Tara lurched against him as the sea began to rush in. "The tide is rising!"

Fionn pulled her after him, the arms of his hoodie slashed open by columns of rock as they stumbled in the darkness. He could feel blood trickling along his skin, the fresh cuts on his arms stinging from the salt water. The cave felt bigger now, and much deeper than before. The darkness was toying with them.

And then—a flicker of hope.

"There! Look!" shouted Tara, gesturing up ahead.

Fionn spied a pocket of gray sky glowing in the distance. "Hurry!"

The water climbed to their shins and then their knees as they ran, and when it was at their hips and the entrance was still out of reach, Fionn fumbled in his bag for another candle. His skin was mottled with wax, slipping and sliding over the last tools at his disposal. A candle rolled out into the darkness and landed with a *plop!* in the water.

"What are you doing?" said Tara frantically. "Go faster! We have to go faster!"

The water was at their belly buttons now. Fionn found a candle, but it slipped from his grasp as he scrabbled to light it.

The water was almost up to his chest.

"There's no time!" shouted Tara, as Fionn tried to reach for another candle. "We have to keep moving!"

Fionn eyed the slash of gray sky before them.

He pushed his sister in front of him, his hand curled in her hoodie as they half swam, half waded toward the mouth of the cave. "You go first."

"But—"

Fionn pushed her with all his might. The bobbing tide pushed them back. Somewhere in the back of his mind, the cave was beginning to whisper again.

Come to me, my fearless Boyle . . .

"Try to swim," Fionn heaved, failing to break through the waves pooling at the mouth of the cave.

"I can't," Tara gritted, knocking back into him.

And see the magic I can brew . . .

Outside, the sky was shimmering, streaks of gray and purple slashing through the clouds as Arranmore broke through again.

The tide was rising higher and higher.

Visit me beneath the soil . . .

And then Shelby Beasley appeared. Her hair was sopping wet, her body submerged in the water as she bobbed up and down at the mouth of the cave.

"Tara! Fionn! There you are!" She anchored herself to the rock as she leaned inside.

She flung her arm out. "Quick! Take my hand!"

Fionn shoved his sister, using every last ounce of his strength to propel her through the surging current. Tara reached out, her fingers scrabbling in the half-light, before finally closing around Shelby's. Fionn stumbled forward, releasing the back of her hoodie as Shelby pulled her from the other side.

Come and wish me back to you . . .

Tara turned back to Fionn as the waves lapped over her shoulders.

Fionn grappled at thin air as froth exploded between them.

The current pulled him back.

"It's sealing you in!" cried Tara.

"Swim!" shouted Shelby from over her shoulder. "Try and swim to us!"

It was too late for that now. Fionn was a poor swimmer even at the best of times. The current was too strong, the tide too high, and still it climbed. If they stayed any longer it would swallow them all.

"I have candles! Save yourselves!" screamed Fionn, as a wave washed over him and poured salt water down his throat. He jumped and spat it out, frantically hoisting the backpack over his head. Two more candles tumbled out and floated into the blackness. The current dragged him back, toward the voice that called to him from that strange shadow layer inside the rock.

Find me where the ravens flock . . .

The ravens were shrieking outside the cave. They swarmed in front of the entrance, blotting out Tara and Shelby. Fionn could only hope they had listened to him and saved themselves.

And wake me from my endless sleep . . .

Another wave swept over him. In the murky water, he scrabbled for another candle, his dread spiking when he realized it was the last one. He clamped it in his fist before it could wriggle free.

Fionn pulled the lighter from his pocket as the schoolbag floated away from him. He held his breath as another wave pushed him back, a spire of rock ripping the kneecap from his jeans.

The voice was getting impatient. It rose up like a terrifying aria as the shadows climbed out of the cave like skeletons.

Unbury me from endless rock . . .

The sea was pushing him back and the darkness was pulling him in. He wasn't alone now. No. He had never been alone in here.

And give to me your soul to keep!

There was something else with him and it was not the island's magic. Not anymore.

Coward!

Fionn imagined talons scraping along his neck, icy breath shivering in his ear. Fear closed a fist around his heart and dragged it into his stomach. He couldn't breathe properly. He couldn't think straight. There was only terror and an ache deep in the center of his soul. The shadows were swarming around him, their edges twisting into hunched, skeletal forms.

You belong to me! cried the voice. *You have always belonged to me!*

Fionn squinted at the final candle. It was too dark to know if the last memory would bring the water to the cave ceiling and herald his certain death, or worse, an eternity without a soul, but the odds were stacked against him already and despair was crawling over him like a shroud.

Fionn touched the lighter to the wick and the flame came alive in his hand. The tide rose above the mouth of the cave. He held the candle in the last foot of space above the waterline as he attempted to swim toward the entrance. The wind was tugging at his collar, trying to help him along.

Fionn's lungs were burning. He started to sink. The cave threaded seaweed into his hair and hid cockleshells in his shoes as it drowned him. Eels stroked his face, and all the while, the voice crooned to him in the blackness. It was gentle now, the careful whisper of a smiling serpent.

I *know* you, Fionn Boyle.

I *remember you.*

Do you remember me?

The words rattled through his bones until they were in every inch of his skin, every drop of his blood. The fist around his heart tightened.

The voice grew louder.

I *remember you,* it cooed. *Your soft heart. Your quivering soul.*

I *have a place for you in the darkness.*

No. Fionn squeezed his nails into the wax. He would not surrender to the darkness. No matter how leaden his legs, how heavy his head ... no matter how tempting it was to give up, to inhale one lungful of water and float away into the eternal blackness . . .

I have a place for you beside me.

The ravens swept inside the cave, canopying over him in a plume of shrieking feathers. They pecked at the candle, stabbing his fingers until they bled.

Fionn tightened his grip. No.

He would not give in, even though he was exhausted.

He would not give in, even though he was afraid.

He would not give in, not yet.

Fionn pushed off the ground and kicked his legs, the candle in his fist bobbing dangerously along the waterline. He surged upward, his head cresting the water and slamming into frenzied wings and vicious beaks. The wind pulled at his hair. *This way*, it seemed to be saying. *Follow the memory.*

Up ahead, a streak of white sky arced across the mouth of the cave. Somehow the waves were being held back, just enough that Fionn could stand on his tiptoes. He gulped at the air, jabbing the blazing candle at the ravens as he squinted at the shard of light.

There was a lifeboat angled across the entrance to the cave. It was small and flat and bright orange, with ropes looped along the side and a motor whirring at the end of it.

Standing in the middle of the lifeboat was Fionn's father.

Fionn understood with sudden, deafening clarity.

The candle in his fist was *Cormac*.

And Cormac had come to rescue him.

Fionn waded toward every wish he had ever made turned to flesh and bone before him. Through beaks and feathers and darkness, his fingers fastened tightly around the wax. When Fionn had almost made it to the mouth of the cave, with two liters of salt water now gurgling in his stomach and a flock of angry ravens at his back, Cormac Boyle leaned over the side of the boat and flung out his hand. "Let me pull you in, lad!"

Fionn blinked the water from his eyes—he couldn't tell whether it was the ocean or his own tears that were stinging him now, only that the candle was burning too quickly and his father was speaking to him in a voice that was both foreign and familiar.

Fionn took his father's hand and something exploded in the center of his chest.

Every chamber of his heart was thrumming with recognition.

"Watch that candle!" Cormac shouted, one eye on the sputtering flame as he heaved him up. "Keep it lit! That's it, lad. I've almost got you. Up you come!"

He pulled him up over the lip of the lifeboat. Fionn tumbled in and rolled onto his back, panting at the glittering sky. His father peered over him, wearing the same burning curiosity. He had the same nose as Fionn, the same dark hair that curled a little at the ends, the same long legs and narrow shoulders.

The same sea-blue eyes.

It was like looking up into a distorted mirror—a spectre of Fionn's future and his past standing over him.

"Are you all right, lad?"

"I—" The boat lurched and Fionn nearly slid out of it. He grabbed on to a rope, brandishing the dying candle like a sword as his father pulled him back in. The storm flung them out to sea, the boat dipping to one side as the rain beat down on them.

Cormac hunkered over the edge and steered it alongside the island as the tide pulled the vessel down, down, down. There was a gaping hole in the lifeboat. A rock must have slashed it lengthways when it was hovering in the mouth of the cave.

They were sinking. And fast.

As the sea rose to meet them, everything fell into place with sudden, sickening clarity.

Today was July 14th, 2006.

Today was July 14th, 2018.

His father was about to die, all over again.

Fionn staggered to his feet, the flame no bigger than a

peppercorn as he wobbled across the little boat. "My name is Fionn Boyle!"

Time stuttered for one long heartbeat.

His father looked up at him, a glint sparking in his eyes. "I know your name, lad."

The sea hiccuped, and Fionn stumbled.

Cormac flung his free arm out to steady him and Fionn clutched his sleeve so hard he ripped a hole in it. The candle was a puddle of wax now—he had ten, twenty seconds at the most.

"You'll be brave now, won't you, Fionn? I need you to be brave for what's to come."

The tide turned and a mammoth wave smashed up against the side. Fionn almost tipped over. His father pulled him back, his hand clasped around his middle so that he was anchored to him.

Fionn looked up at him.

"Please don't let go," he said, his throat bobbing painfully. "Please don't leave me."

"You'll be all right, lad," said his father, his blue eyes glistening. "You're the strongest of us all. You'll see."

The water lapped at their knees. "Are you ready, son?"

Fionn shook his head. "No, no, no, no, no, no, I'm not ready, I'm not ready."

His father threw him out of the sinking boat.

Fionn tumbled through the air and landed on the cliff steps with a painful thud just as the candle went out.

The island shuddered.

The storm howled its goodbye.

Chapter Twenty-Three

THE WARRING WISHES

Fionn scrabbled up the steps on his hands and knees, the sea nipping at his ankles. The world reset itself, the clouds moving through the layers above him, until he was home again with the same storm hanging over him. When he was almost at the top of the steps, where the stairway bled back into the cliff, he sneaked a glance over his shoulder. The waves were starting to settle and the rain had run itself dry.

The lifeboat had been swallowed up in the salty layers of the sea.

His father was gone too.

It was as though he had never been there at all.

Are you ready, son?

Fionn replayed those words over and over as he climbed.

Faces peered over him, Douglas Beasley's mustache twitching vigorously as his voice boomed across the island. "He's alive! He's right here on the steps!"

At the top of the cliff, Ivan pushed through the gathering crowd and extended his hand to Fionn. "Well, this is a miracle."

Fionn took his hand, and a jolt sparked in his fingertips. Ivan's eyes grew wide as moons and behind them Fionn saw the jarring emptiness for the first time. There were no irises, just the all-consuming blackness of a soulless existence. His grip slackened and Fionn wobbled on the edge of the cliff. He grabbed Ivan's sweater, the neckline stretching to reveal a tattooed swirl underneath.

"I *knew it*," he gasped.

Ivan stumbled backward, pulling Fionn with him, up over the cliff and onto the sodden grass. They stared at each other for one horrified moment, before Ivan peeled his lips back and said, "Did you hear her? Did she speak to you?"

Fionn staggered to his feet. "Sh-she's buried," he said, his chest heaving. "She's gone."

"Then why has she summoned me?" Ivan sprang up after him, his eyes bright with glee. "*She will wake when the boy returns.*"

"Wh-what?" said Fionn, backing away from him.

"*She will rise when the Storm Keeper bleeds for her,*" he said giddily. "*She will come to power with descendant souls. And the darkness will rule again.*" He glanced once at the clearing sky and then sank back into the gathering crowd, a grin painted across his face. "We'll meet again, Fionn Boyle."

Fionn had barely managed to catch his breath when Elizabeth Beasley pushed her way through the search-and-rescue party and seized him by the shoulders. She pulled him close until they were almost nose-to-nose, her coal-like eyes flashing. "Is it you?" she said, shaking him. "I can't see. I can't tell."

Bartley appeared beside her. "Gran," he said, trying to tug her away. "Let's just give him a minute."

"Oh, be quiet, Bartley! You almost lost it for us today! I'm trying to see if you managed to do it right!" She narrowed her eyes, spittle foaming at the sides of her mouth. "No, you don't look very different at all," she said in a low voice. "It must have worked then, Bartley. I think it must have worked."

"Gran, just leave it."

Tara shoved Elizabeth Beasley out of the way. "*Unhand* my brother, Betty. He's been shaken enough for one day."

"Fionny!" She flung her arms around him and hugged him tighter than he had ever been hugged in his life. "I thought you were *dead*!"

Shelby was hovering over Tara's shoulder. She swung the towel from her shoulders and draped it around him like a cape. "I knew you'd make it back!"

"I was so scared," cried Tara. "I thought you were gone!"

"I'll tell you about it when we get home," said Fionn, his voice shaking just as badly. "We need to get back to Grandad."

The storm had taken a chunk out of the cliffside and dropped the sea out of the sky—what had it done to *Tír na nÓg*, the little cottage on the headland? What had become of the Storm Keeper?

The same dread was dawning in Tara's eyes. "Let's go," she said.

"Let's run!"

And they did.

Chapter Twenty-Four

THE UNEXPECTED EMERALD

Talk of storms and sea caves traveled after Fionn and Tara on the wind, the day made brighter by the Boyles' triumph over the sea, a story that would go down in the annals of Arranmore like so many that had gone before them.

The sun chased the clouds from the sky and poured warmth back into the island as they ran far away from Ivan and the Beasleys and the dark imprint of Morrigan rippling somewhere deep in the earth.

When they reached the gate of their grandfather's cottage, Fionn and Tara froze. The front door had been blown off its hinges and one of the windows was broken. The storm had uprooted the briars and flung them all over the garden path.

Inside was just as bad. There were candles everywhere, coats and hats and chairs strewn across the floor like confetti, and the cupboards in the kitchen had been turned upside down. Most of the shelves in the living room had toppled over and one of the armchairs had been thrown against the wall.

In the middle of it all sat their grandfather. He was on the floor by the fireplace, staring vacantly out of the window. Above him, the candle on the mantelpiece had gone out.

"Grandad?" said Tara nervously.

"I'll talk to him," whispered Fionn.

Tara picked her phone up from the kitchen floor, one end of her charger still dangling from it as she wiped the screen with a tea towel. "At least *this* survived," she muttered.

Fionn hunkered down in front of his grandfather. "Grandad?" Fionn waited for the storm in his eyes to pass, for the recognition that didn't come. He took his hand and squeezed it. "Where are the matches, Grandad? I need the matches."

His grandfather looked at his hand as though he was only just noticing it. "I don't know."

Candles carpeted the ground, rolling this way and that in the breeze that had followed them inside.

"Here," said Tara, tiptoeing over the mess. She held

out her hand, a small box of matches sitting inside it. "I found these in one of the cupboards."

The glass trough on the mantelpiece was still half-full with wax but there were two inches of water along the top. Fionn heaved it across the room and tipped it out of the front door, then dried the surface with his towel. He set the trough back above the fireplace and lit the wick inside it. It flickered softly, at first, as if it couldn't quite remember how to burn. *Come on*, thought Fionn. *Burn better. Burn faster.*

The flame climbed and began to thrash, and finally the scent trickled back in, filling his nostrils with the sea. Fionn righted the armchair and moved it as close to the fireplace as possible. "Sit here a minute, Grandad. You'll feel better soon."

His grandfather sank into the chair, his eyes closed as the scent pushed itself back into the living room.

Tara brought him a cup of tea. "One tea bag left in for exactly two and a half minutes and a thirty-milliliter splash of milk, just the way you like it."

He took it without saying anything.

Tara and Fionn set to work re-stacking the candles on the shelves. They tidied the coats and hats back onto the rack and put the kitchen back to the way it was supposed to be. They boarded up the cracked window with a piece of wood they found in the shed and managed to put the front door back on its hinges after four attempts. It creaked awfully, and left an inch gap along the bottom, but at least it closed. They could worry about the rest of it tomorrow.

When they finished fixing up the cottage, Fionn helped his grandfather into bed, removing his boots and giving him a clean, woolly sweater to wear. Back in the kitchen, Tara's phone was ringing.

Fionn fanned the quilt over his grandfather and tucked it up to his chin.

"Thank you," said his grandfather.

Fionn hovered uncertainly. He felt like he had swallowed the island and it was trying to climb back out of him. There was so much he wanted to tell his grandfather—the story of his first adventure, how his father had come to rescue him, how he had looked at Fionn with eyes full of recognition, how they had fought the sea together until the very last moment, and how in the end, Cormac Boyle had been the bravest of them all.

And then there was the After—Fionn's fingertips jolting at Ivan's touch, the emptiness in his eyes, the sound of Morrigan's voice, too awake. Too near.

She will wake when the boy returns.

He swallowed hard, remembering the words his grandfather had spoken to him only days before.

Fionn, the day you stepped off the ferry, the island woke up.

And so did Morrigan.

There was only one person in the world who could understand any of this, and he was a million miles away now.

Fionn peered down at his grandfather and in a small voice he said, "Do you know who I am, Grandad?"

His grandfather looked at him for a long time. The clouds shifted inside his eyes, streaks of blue trying to push through the storm. The lines in his face grew deeper, the ghost of the storm stealing the last fleck of color from his cheeks. "You know, it's a funny thing, lad. I don't know who you are."

Fionn's face crumpled.

"But I do know that I love you," his grandfather said as he closed his eyes. He smiled then, and it seemed as though the sun was rising somewhere inside him. "How very peculiar."

Fionn waited until he felt like he could breathe again. "I love you too, Grandad."

Back in the kitchen, Tara was sitting at the table with a plate of hastily made ham sandwiches, scrolling through her phone. "Is he okay now?"

Fionn slumped into the chair beside her. "I hope so."

She slid a mug of tea to him, the milky liquid sloshing over the side. "Bartley and I never got to make our wishes, Fionny."

"What?"

"I pushed him out of the cave before he could open his mouth. It took every bit of my strength ... then the cave dragged me into the darkness and I couldn't fight it. Wherever I went, I wasn't near that magic. At least not the good kind." She tapped her phone, her voice barely more than a whisper when she said, "But what if my wish came true anyway? Mom just rang me. She's heard what happened."

Fionn froze with the mug in his hand.

"She's coming out on the first ferry tomorrow morning." Tara's dark eyes were shining in the dimness. "She's coming back to Arranmore, Fionn."

* * *

In the bathroom, Fionn turned the shower on and peeled his clothes off. He had to tug extra hard to get his jeans off, and when he finally managed to fling them across the room, something flew from the pockets and landed in the sink with a *plink!*

He peered over the bowl and found an emerald winking back at him. It was exactly the size of his palm— big and heavy and almost perfectly round.

In bed that night, he put the stone on the bedside table, marveling at the tinge of green that hung like mist around it.

"What's that?" yawned Tara, her lids already at half-mast.

"I'm not sure," said Fionn, blinking at it in the darkness.

Sleep was tugging at him, the day's events floating away until only one thought remained: He didn't feel any different now than he did that morning when he woke up. If Tara's unmade wish had worked, then perhaps Bartley's had too somehow.

Or perhaps Fionn had never deserved the gift in the first place.

If he had been any less exhausted, he might have dwelled on this a second longer, acknowledged the frustration that was niggling at him, but sleep was calling out to him, and so he went willingly, the emerald winking him goodnight.

Chapter Twenty-Five

THE ST⊕RM KEEPER'S ARSENAL

Fionn woke up at midnight, feeling like he might take flight. His skin was tingling all over and his teeth were vibrating in his mouth. He was full up with something that made him want to shout at the top of his lungs and laugh until all of his breath ran out.

The emerald was still sitting on the bedside table, its green glow filtering into the darkness. He picked it up and clamped it in his fist until the heat walked up his arm. Was it doing this to him? He glanced at Tara, who was snoring happily, then surveyed the stone again with suspicion before shoving it into his pocket.

He couldn't stand to be lying down anymore. He

was buzzing from the tip of the hairs on his head to the undersides of his feet and he was afraid his hiccuping energy might fling him against the ceiling and splat him like a fly.

He hopped out of bed and made his way to the living room, where he paced up and down and waited for his bones to stop singing. Relief didn't come, but his grandfather arrived shortly after him, padding into the room in the same clothes he had been wearing earlier.

His eyes were clearer now, but there were still clouds around the edges, creeping into the blue. "Can't sleep, Fionn?"

A grin broke across Fionn's face and a strange, giddy laughter tumbled out of him—joy and sadness and relief and exhilaration all rolled together. "I can't even lie down!"

His grandfather crooked his finger at him. "Come with me."

Fionn bounced along behind him, down the dark hallway and out into the back garden, where a full moon peered over them.

His grandfather busied himself at the workbench, unearthing the candle-making box and unfurling the burner flame. He eased himself onto his stool and extended his hand to Fionn. "Congratulations," he said quietly.

Fionn stared at the old weathered hand, calloused by years of being at sea and adventuring in places buried long ago in the past. He took it eagerly, his own fingers thin and delicate in comparison. "I'm the Storm Keeper?"

"You are the Storm Keeper." His grandfather squeezed his hand. "And I am unbearably proud of you."

I *am the Storm Keeper.*

Fionn sank onto the stool opposite him. "Poor Bartley," he said delightedly.

His grandfather set the pot down and poured the wax pebbles into it. "Poor Betty."

Fionn plucked a seashell mold from the box and stuck the silver disk to the bottom, rolling the wick between his fingers. There were other things to discuss now, things that were far more important than Elizabeth Beasley's burning eyes when she woke tomorrow to find her grandson had lied about his wish.

"I saw my dad today," said Fionn. The words sounded strange out loud, as though he was still half-asleep in the most impossible of dreams. "He saved my life in the Sea Cave. He went through his storm and into mine and he knew who I was, Grandad. He told me so!"

His grandfather set the burner to light and peered at Fionn over the lip of the pan. "I've always wondered what the Whispering Tree told Cormac. He was so quiet when he came back ..." He trailed off, his lips twisting. "I suppose, at last, we know."

Fionn tried to swallow the hard lump in his throat. His father had known the price of his son's survival and he had paid it willingly. Fionn couldn't imagine anything more selfless, anything *braver*. How could he ever have doubted his father's courage?

His grandfather looked past him, into the night sky. "You know, I tried to burn that storm candle at least a hundred times since Cormac was swept up in it." He shook his head, his eyes misting. "And not once did the wick light for me. It was not meant to."

You'll be brave now, won't you, Fionn? I need you to be brave for what's to come.

They stared into the melting wax, both of them wondering exactly what the Whispering Tree had shown Fionn's dad and why the island had decided Fionn must be saved over him.

She will wake when the boy returns.

The reflection of a thousand dancing stars winked up at them, united in their silence.

When Fionn looked at his grandfather again, his face was pale as the moonlight, the blue of his eyes still blurring around the edges. He took a new pin from the leather pouch and burned it over the flame. He passed it to Fionn. "Are you ready?"

Are you ready, son?

Somewhere far away, an owl hooted. The moon sank lower in the sky and Fionn tasted the sea on the wind.

Fionn took the pin from his grandfather.

He pricked his finger and everything he had been feeling bubbled to the surface at once, until it felt like he might explode into a million pieces. He held his finger over the pan and watched as a single drop of seawater tumbled out of him and landed with a satisfying *splat!*

An owl soared over them, its wing sprinkling starlight across the bench. A breeze rustled Fionn's hair as his grandfather clapped his hands together and smiled.

For one euphoric moment, Fionn felt a hundred times taller and a thousand times older. He swore if he looked hard enough at the wind he would see all the Boyles who had gone before him, smiling just the same.

"Very *good*, lad!" his grandfather whooped.

Very good, lad! the island whispered, and Fionn imagined his father's voice threaded somewhere deep inside its tapestry.

Fionn slumped in his chair. His bones had stopped vibrating and the heat had drained from his cheeks. He was suddenly *exhausted*. He exhaled as the sea crept into the wax and turned it every shade of blue he could imagine. It glowed purple around the edges, a dark tornado scattering rivulets of color along the surface, until it was the exact shade and design of the last candle Fionn had held in his fingertips.

"There's a touch of relief in it," his grandfather muttered. "In pricking your finger and bleeding the magic from you ... but it will return again tomorrow. And the next day ..." He cast his gaze along his fingers, waggling them back and forth. "I think I will miss it, you know. When you get very used to a thing, it's not so easy to say goodbye to it."

A line of silver threaded its way through the wax. Fionn wasn't giddy anymore, but he wasn't unhappy either. He felt ... oddly settled. There was a sense of rightness to this moment, to the glow of the moon on their backs, the breeze rustling his hair.

You'll be brave now, won't you, Fionn? I need you to be brave for what's to come.

Fionn lifted the pan and carefully poured the rivers of wax into the seashell mold. "What will I call it?"

"I believe that is a decision for the Storm Keeper." His grandfather tapped the side of the mold, and all the colors jumped over each other, threading themselves into the wax until it looked like a shell made of a hundred choppy waves all tumbling after each other.

Fionn held the candle in his fist, the wax warm against his palm, and suddenly the answer was obvious to him. "*Fionn.*"

It was a twin to *Cormac.*

The scent of adventure rolled over them as the wick changed color, from white to a column of emerald green.

"And from the drop of water comes a drop of magic," his grandfather murmured. "I don't know if this has ever happened before, Fionn. Islanders bursting through the layers and threading them all together like that—future and past and present interacting under the same sky, two heirs meeting somewhere in the middle, one hoisting the other up. The island has broken so many of its rules. Do you know what that means?"

He didn't wait for Fionn to respond.

"It means it has been looking out for you since before you were even born." He cocked his head, his gaze suddenly searing. "It means there is a task for you here. Something that is much bigger than you. Bigger than all of us."

And the darkness will rule again.

The snake in the pit of Fionn's stomach writhed its way to the surface. He pulled the emerald from his pocket and set it on the workbench. "This followed me home earlier. I think it belonged to Dagda."

His grandfather stared at the emerald with wide, unblinking eyes.

"Morrigan was in that cave with me." Fionn was surprised by how simply the words slipped out, how little fear there was in speaking the absolute truth, in knowing it could not be undone now—whatever was to come, whatever had already happened.

I *know you, Fionn Boyle.*

I *remember you.*

Do you remember me?

"Did you hear her?" asked his grandfather.

"I *felt* her. She's awake, Grandad."

And I *was the one who woke her,* he wanted to scream.

His grandfather went very still. "So, we are sure, at last, of where she's buried. We've always suspected it but could never be certain."

Fionn blew out a breath. There was a dull throbbing in the base of his spine, terror tripping over his vertebrae and pooling at the bottom. How close had he and Tara been to death, or worse, to death everlasting? How close had Fionn come to floating right into her clutches, to surrendering to fear and pain and sadness until every shard of light inside him winked out, every thread of his soul unspooled and devoured in the shadows?

"Ivan is a Soulstalker."

His grandfather swallowed a swear word.

Fionn waited a beat, then he mustered the last dregs of his courage to give voice to the thing he feared most. "He's here to resurrect her. And I don't know how to stop him."

His grandfather rose abruptly, beckoning for Fionn to follow as he marched back into the cottage. Fionn plucked the emerald from the workbench and trailed after him. Already, he felt better with it in his fist.

In the living room, they stood apart from each other in the duskiness, a thousand and more candles peering over him.

"When I was fifteen years old, I looked into the future and saw great darkness on these shores," said his grandfather. "I saw you too, Fionn. Exactly as you are." His face crumpled. "And like the Storm Keepers who visited the Whispering Tree before me, I learned that my destiny was part of a greater one, that my power was not my own. I have bled my magic out of me, drop by drop, storm by storm, since the day it was poured into me. But the time for recording has come to an end." His face darkened, and somewhere behind his eyes a shadow fell. "I'm afraid your task will be different from mine, Fionn."

There was an awful, loud silence.

A drumbeat pounded in Fionn's heart.

"You will not bottle any more of Dagda's magic." He took Fionn's hand and turned it over, the blue of his veins stark against the skin on his wrist. "You will keep it all inside you, where it can gather and build. You will learn how to endure it, how to stoke it, and then you will learn to master it. So you can defend this island from Morrigan should she free herself from that rock."

She will rise when the Storm Keeper bleeds for her.

Fionn had bled inside that cave, in nicks and gashes and scrapes. Had it been enough? Or would Ivan come back for him, now that he had finished grooming Bartley like a pig for slaughter?

Fionn took his hand back, his fingers circling his wrist as he stared at all the shelves. "What about the candles?"

His grandfather plucked a crayon-sized candle from the shelf and rolled it along his palm. "You don't need this magic, Fionn. You already have it in your veins."

"Then who is it for?"

"Even Morrigan has her followers. You will have to see about yours when the time comes, but I have made you an arsenal. There will be a role for everyone, for Tara and Shelby and Bartley and Betty and anyone else who will stand up for Arranmore." He dangled the candle, like a fish by its tail. "Of all the things I cannot promise and all the moments I cannot change, I can say this at least: you will not have to face this darkness alone and the island will not have to face it unprotected."

Fionn swallowed the dryness in his throat. The world was tilting, and it was too late to turn back now—he had to go with it. To a place he was being dragged to by the blood in his lineage and the sea in his veins. Without even realizing it, he had stepped onto the most dangerous lifeboat of all, and now he was sailing into the greatest storm of his life.

"Did I ever have a choice?"

I remember you, Fionn Boyle. Do you remember me?

His grandfather only said, "I'm sorry, Fionn. I wish it wasn't you."

Fionn peered at the shelves, at all that precious, gleaming wax. His grandfather's blood. His grandfather's life.

Red-wired eyes and wax-stained fingers.

Memories slipping away, face by face, name by name.

All for this: the Storm Keeper's arsenal.

There are many different kinds of bravery, Fionn.

"How do we get the magic out?" said Fionn.

His grandfather raised the candle between them, its brassy coat glinting in the half-light. In one quick movement, he dug his fingers into the underside of the wax and ripped the small silver disk out of it. "You remove the anchor." The wick unfurled from the bottom. "You reverse the flow of magic."

He lit the wick from the opposite end, and held it upside down as it burned. The flame disappeared, burrowing up inside the wax, against gravity and reason. His grandfather lurched, as though something in his chest was trying to punch its way out. "Instead of the magic drawing you into the memory," he heaved, "you draw it out, into yourself."

The flame consumed the wax from the inside out, Fionn's grandfather's eyes growing wild with power as he clamped it tightly in his fist. He turned his attention to the candle blazing above the fireplace, his breath whistling through his nose. With his free hand, he caressed the flame until it swelled in size and danced its way toward the ceiling. He crooked his finger and it changed direction, pouring over the mantelpiece in a burning waterfall. It leaped into the empty grate and rushed up the chimney in a neat blaze.

"Smoke," said Fionn quietly. "From an empty fire-place."

"The Storm Keeper's magic," said his grandfather, raising the disintegrating crayon candle. "Brewed and bottled."

Fionn traced the veins in his palm as a new weight shifted on his shoulders. They were darker now, bluer. Already, he could sense a flicker of that same power gathering inside him. The tide was coming in. "What do I do now?"

His grandfather crushed the remains of the candle in his fist, his eyes glittering in the duskiness. "Let your magic build up. Let's see what it can really do."

Chapter Twenty-Six

A VERY SPECIAL
HOMECOMING

Fionn Boyle stood at the end of Arranmore pier and watched the morning ferry wade into port. He was doing his best to ignore his sister, who had been chattering nonstop since they left their grandfather's cottage.

"When Mom comes off the ferry, I'm going to hug her first because I'm the oldest and I think she'll be happiest to see me, just because she's known me for longer."

"Fine."

"And don't start telling her the story until we get back to Grandad's, because he'll want to hear it too and then you'll have to tell it all over again and Mom will probably get bored of it."

Fionn rolled his eyes. "Okay."

"And let me tell most of it because I have a really good narrative flair and sometimes you include unnecessary details and it makes the story kind of boring and then people lose interest."

"I thought saving your life meant you would be nicer to me."

Tara glared at him. "This *is* me being nice!"

A flock of seagulls swooped over their heads and flew out to sea. They circled the ferry as it trundled its way into port.

The horn sounded.

Fionn winced. "I don't think I'll ever get used to that sound."

"It sounds a bit like a dying cow, doesn't it?" said Tara.

They studied the passengers as they stepped off the ferry, dragging suitcases behind them as they drifted this way and that, into outspread arms and waiting cars along the pier.

Fionn didn't exhale properly until his mother appeared on the lip of the ferry. She hovered uncertainly, caught between the boat and the island, with her arms pulled tight around her. She seemed much smaller than Fionn remembered, dwarfed by the boat looming at her back, the island sprawled before her. She was wearing her favorite green cardigan. Her hair had been swept up in a ponytail, wisps curling around her face as the wind tried to coax her from the ferry.

"She looks scared," said Tara.

"She is scared," said Fionn.

"Maybe we should hug her at the same time."

"I think that's a good idea."

They made their way through the arriving crowds. When they reached the bottom of the port, their mother's eyes lit up. "My beautiful children!"

Fionn coiled his fingers in the back of Tara's T-shirt to keep her from bounding on to the ferry. "Just wait," he murmured.

Their mother flung her arms wide, her smile flickering at the edges. She hesitated for the briefest moment—Fionn might not have noticed it at all if he hadn't been looking out for it.

Then she stepped off the ferry and the island sighed with relief.

"I've missed you both so much!" she told them as they slammed into her.

Fionn pressed his face into her cardigan and held her tight enough to stop her trembling. "We missed you too, Mom!"

"Wait till you hear what happened to us!" said Tara

from the other side. "We've had the biggest adventure already!"

Fionn couldn't tell whether his mother was laughing or crying. They stood like that for a long time, between the sea and the shore, their shoulders shaking as they hugged each other. Fionn's fingertips were crackling, the magic thrumming giddily inside him. He curled them in on themselves and pushed the swirl of power down, down, down. The wind whipped up and enveloped them, and Fionn heard that voice again in his ears—this time, it was as familiar to him as his own. "Come here," it was saying. "Come home."

This time, it wasn't talking to him.

There were still clouds in the sky, and a strange darkness gathering somewhere on the horizon.

But they were all here now.

They were home.

EPILOGUE

In a tiny cottage on the headland of a storm-ravaged island, Fionn Boyle was smiling in his sleep. He was dreaming of a flying horse, his fingers curled inside his snow-white mane as they dipped and tumbled through purple clouds that glittered around the edges.

Tomorrow, he would be twelve years old.

The island watched over its new charge, contented with its decision. Though he was the youngest Storm Keeper in Arranmore history, he would have the hardest job of all of them. It would take every drop of sea in his veins and every ounce of courage in his heart, but he would give it willingly. He was his father's son. The island knew this well. It had broken many rules to get him here—almost all of them, in fact—but the time for fairness was over. There would be no surprises when the darkness returned.

For now though, the island let the boy sleep, dulling the wind and silencing the seagulls so that he might find peace in the safety of his dreams. For a little while at least.

A note from the author

A visit to Arranmore Island is the beginning of Fionn Boyle's story, just as it was the beginning of mine. Nestled a few miles off the northwest coast of Ireland, where a once-bustling population has been whittled down to just 500 people, this beautiful, half-forgotten place is where my maternal grandparents were born, grew up, and eventually fell in love. When my grandfather Captain Charles Boyle left Arranmore as a young man, he took a piece of it with him. My grandfather could predict the weather from the peculiar clock-like instruments that hung on his kitchen wall, read storms as easily as books, and catch a fish faster than I could tie my shoelace. He kept a captain's log long after he retired, beginning each day with a description of the weather, and adding details of family life, the comings and goings of his grandchildren as we traipsed through his house wearing his captain's hat over our eyes, tapping the barometer to make the storm come out, grasping shamelessly for the ship's wheel mounted in his hallway. Even when we were on land, it felt like we were at sea— sailors on an enchanted ship, our very own captain steering a course for Arranmore.

While on a recent visit to the island, the beginnings of a story unfurled inside me. I wanted to write about adventure. I wanted to write about magic. But most of all, I wanted to write about a very special grandfather. For several days, I explored the secret cliff steps and the haunted cottages, the lone lighthouse and the music-filled pubs, and the towering, terrifying cliffs. In the evenings, I traveled around the island, sharing cup of tea after cup of tea, learning the stories of my ancestors.

Walking in the footsteps of his own ancestors, Fionn experiences firsthand the incomprehensible power of nature. But *The Storm Keeper's Island* is as much about the storms we must sometimes weather inside ourselves as it is about the ones that blow in from the Atlantic. Not too long ago, my grandfather developed Alzheimer's disease. I have spent the past couple of years trying to navigate the difficult long goodbye, learning to reconcile the person I love with the version of him that is slowly fading away. Fionn faces the same challenge: the struggle to view his grandfather as a man who is losing part of himself but is not diminished by it. A man who is still the sum of all his experiences, despite his inability to recall them. If Malachy Boyle cannot remember his own adventures, then Fionn must remember them for him. He learns, as I am learning, that for all the transiency of memories, love is not so easily erased by the winds of time.

The Storm Keeper's Island is a story of bravery and adventure, of ancient magic and nature at its most powerful. It is about a love that will always anchor us, no matter the changing tides of memory. I hope you enjoyed reading, and I can't wait to share Fionn's next adventure with you.

Catherine

TURN THE PAGE FOR A SNEAK PEEK AT
THE LOST TIDE WARRIORS...

THE TICKING CLOCK

Fionn Boyle lay sprawled on an old, threadbare couch and tried to scream himself awake. Somewhere in the back of his mind, he knew he was dreaming, but he couldn't open his eyes. He could only listen to the crooning voice that had made a home inside his head. It was hissing like a snake, burrowing deeper into his brain.

Tick-tock, the voice whispered. *Can you hear me, little Boyle?*

Fionn could see Morrigan in his mind's eye—her leering grin, too wide in her angular face.

Tick-tock, crumbling rock.

Three days, watch the clock.

She cackled, and a shadow came skittering toward him, its fingers reaching through the blackness of his mind. *Tick-tock, tick-tock, tick-tock . . .* The words grew frenzied, the pitch climbing until it was no longer a laugh but a scream. TICK-TOCK, TICK-TOCK, TICK-TOCK.

Get away from me! Fionn tried to yell, but the words bubbled in his throat.

His body was spinning like a tornado, his arms thrashing blindly as he tried to pull himself back to consciousness. The couch groaned underneath him, the rusted springs heaving from the effort. *Help me! She's going to claw my eyes out! Please—*

There was a loud *splat!*

Fionn jerked awake as something cold and slimy slid down his nose.

He sniffed. Was that . . . ?

"Ham," came a familiar voice. "It's crumbed."

Fionn peeled the slice from his face.

His grandfather peered over him, his blue eyes twinkling in the dawn light. "I'm afraid you were cycloning again." In one hand he held an open packet of sliced ham, and in the other a bright orange block of cheese. "I thought the ham might be more humane."

Fionn pushed the matted hair from his eyes. A familiar fist of heat was blazing in his chest, the knuckles of it rolling against his rib cage as if saying hello. The Storm Keeper's magic awake, just as he was.

Fionn sighed. "Couldn't you have called my name, like a normal person?"

"When have you ever known me to be normal?" said his grandfather, nibbling a corner off the block of cheese. "But besides that, I called your name eight times. I poked you three times and I shook you by the shoulders exactly once. The next logical step—"

"—was ham," said Fionn, dragging himself into a sitting position and laying the offending slice on the armrest.

"I'm afraid so, lad." His grandfather was watching him too closely, his brows raised above the tip of his horn-rimmed spectacles. "Was it the same again?"

"Tick-tock," said Fionn, with a grim nod. "The countdown continues."

Morrigan had been living in his head for many months, but two weeks ago his dreams had taken on a new sense of urgency. The voice, once disembodied and distant, now came with a countdown, grasping hands and clawing fingers, bloodless lips held too close to his ear. She was growing stronger, giddier.

"The countdown," said his grandfather now, "is somewhat concerning."

A breeze slipped underneath the window and

wreathed the couch. Fionn pulled the blanket close around him. Last month, winter had crept over the island, sewing itself inside the wind and howling through the cracks in the walls. There were ice crystals webbing the windowpanes, and sometimes in the night, when Fionn woke gasping, he could see his breath hovering like clouds in the darkness.

"Why don't you go and lie down in my room, lad?" suggested his grandfather. "The energy in there is very benevolent and handsome. And there's a nice storage heater that'll blow the socks off you."

"I'm awake now anyway," said Fionn, stretching his arms above his head and rolling his neck around until it clicked. Back in the summertime, he had surrendered his twin bed to his mother, insisting instead on taking up residence on Donal the shopkeeper's donated couch, which looked like it had been exhumed from a haunted house and smelled not unlike abiding despair. It creaked awfully in the night and made the little sitting room seem even smaller than it was, but Fionn knew it wouldn't matter where he slept—Morrigan would still find him.

He rolled onto his feet. "What time is it?"

"Time?" His grandfather was striding back into the kitchen. "You know very well I don't adhere to such arbitrary concepts."

Time.

Fionn drifted toward the candle flickering on the mantelpiece, the only lit flame in a room full of candles. The wax was growing shallower—less a candle now, and more a milky blue puddle. Of course, it wasn't *just* a candle to begin with. It was his grandfather's essence, all of his memories gathered up in one magical concoction, borne of blood and sea, burning all day and all night, racing toward its end.

Time. His grandfather had borrowed an awful lot of it.

The reminder made Fionn queasy. Lately, it felt like everything was out of his control. As the nights ticked by and Morrigan crept closer to his days, he couldn't help imagining himself as the controller of a runaway train. He felt the darkness seeping in around the edges of him, the sorceress's countdown ticking in time with his pulse. Something was going to happen. Soon.

She will wake when the boy returns, Ivan had told him once, all too gleefully. *She will rise when the Storm Keeper bleeds for her.*

Fionn had not bled for Morrigan since the day she had awoken, but he had not succeeded in putting her back to sleep either. His journey to the Sea Cave during the summer still haunted him. He had come so close to losing his sister, and then to drowning all alone in that endless darkness, with Morrigan laughing in his ear. The memory had grown hard and spiky, and often, when his thoughts wandered, he would find it digging into his ribs.

"Sandwich?" called his grandfather from inside the kitchen. "I'll share the ham but the last of the mustard is all mine, I'm afraid. It's whole-grain. And French. Très expensive."

"No, thanks." Fionn stared at the little flame on the mantelpiece. The magic inside him flared in recognition. He stuck his hand out above the glass trough, willing the flame to dance for him.

Come on . . . Come on . . .

Fionn was the Storm Keeper, the one the island had chosen to wield the elements in Dagda's name, for as long as his mind and body could bear it. The one to command earth, wind, fire, and water, at little more than a simple thought.

It was supposed to be easy. It was *supposed* to be seamless.

He ground his jaw, wriggling his fingers the way his grandfather had taught him. *Come on.*

The flame ignored him.

His face started to prickle.

Grow, he willed it. *Dance.*

His magic hiccuped in his chest, nearly toppling him over.

Fionn dropped his hand with a sigh.

The sitting room filtered back into focus, and he found his grandfather hovering beside him. "It will come, lad."

"It's been five *months.*"

"Maybe it will take one more."

"I don't have one more!"

"For all we know, Morrigan is bluffing," said his grandfather unconvincingly. "Spooking you, for her own amusement. Trying to get in your head."

"She's already in my head, Grandad. I need to figure out my magic. *Now.*"

His grandfather frowned at his sandwich. "It wasn't like this for me ... It didn't require much concentration, really ..." He moved his gaze to the candles filling the shelves around them—the Storm Keeper's magic—years of it, brewed and bottled. The same magic that now ran in Fionn's veins. "You could always try burning one ..." He trailed off at Fionn's expression.

"The last time I used candle magic, I vomited and passed out," Fionn reminded him. "I'm already full of magic. I just have no idea how to get it out of—"

Fionn's attention snagged on the bookcase over his

grandfather's shoulder—the one he had pored over last night, restlessly counting the columns of wax, name by name, wick by wick, until he fell into a fitful slumber. Every night he studied them meticulously, like a general cataloging his arsenal, while his own weapon chugged and sputtered in his veins.

There was something not quite right about it now.

Halfway down the case, where the usual array of blizzards and snowstorms jostled for space between sunsets and sunrises, there was an almost imperceptible gap. Between *Saoirse*, which meant "freedom," and *Suaimhneas*, which meant "peace," *Spring Showers 2008* was missing.

Fionn crossed the room in three strides, jamming his feet into his sneakers without stopping to untie the laces first.

His grandfather peered after him, chomping on his sandwich. "Where are you off to in such a rush?"

Fionn shrugged his coat on and pulled his woolly hat over his ears. "There's been a theft!"

"Good grief. Of what sort?"

Fionn narrowed his eyes at his grandfather. "I think you know exactly what sort of theft I'm talking about. And thief too, come to think of it."

His grandfather smushed the rest of his sandwich into his mouth all at once until his cheeks swelled up like a blowfish and crumbs tumbled over his lips, then he pointed at his own face as if to say, *I can't talk right now, my mouth is suddenly very full.*

Fionn swung the front door open, and winter gusted right through it, curling the dark strands peeking out from underneath his hat. "We're supposed to *save* them!" he said angrily, before slamming the door behind him and taking off down the garden path.

The gate swung open for him, and the shrubs, skeletal without their summer foliage, *click-clack*ed a goodbye. Outside, a canopy of clouds smothered the rising sun. Fionn could see the usual flock of ravens patrolling the headland, chasing the seagulls back out to sea. The icy wind whistled alongside him, drowning out their faraway shrieks. It cleared stones from the roadway and tipped the flowers in reverie as he wound down the headland toward the strand.

He saw the whirlpool first. There, in plain sight of anyone who bothered to look, was the Storm Keeper's magic, skipping and dancing along the shoreline. Water twisted round and round, seafoam flying from its edges like cream from a mixing bowl. The longer Fionn watched it, the taller it became.

He swung his legs over the wall and stalked across the sand. "Hey!" he shouted. "Stop that!"

Across the beach, his sister turned to face him. She kept one hand outstretched toward the whirlpool, the other clenched around a turquoise candle that was burning upside down, devouring itself from the inside out. "Hey, loser," she said, through a wide grin. "What are you doing down here?"

Fionn marched toward her. "I told you a thousand times, you're not supposed to waste the candles!"

"I'm *practicing*," she said, turning back to the ocean. Her ponytail whipped through the air behind her, the ends of her winter coat flapping in the wind. "Grandad said I could have it, so just take a chill pill."

"It's not up to Grandad; it's up to me!" Fionn yelled. "Blow it out!"

Tara's laughter soared into the air. "You're so *dramatic!*"

"Coming from the girl who held a candlelit vigil the night Bartley Beasley went back to the mainland!"

She threw him a withering glance. "I told you I'm not ready to talk about that yet!"

Fionn yanked her by the arm.

The whirlpool faltered.

"Get off me!" Tara barked, shaking him off. "I'm concentrating!"

"The sun's almost up! Anyone could see you out here!" He glanced over his shoulder to where an old woman in a gray shawl was pottering along the strand. "See," he hissed.

"Don't be so paranoid," said Tara, not bothering to look. "You're *always* down here. You're just afraid the islanders will see how much better than you I am at this. How the waves actually *listen* to me. And then they'll start to wonder about *your* magic. Why they've never *seen* it. *Oooh.* The Storm Keeper's sister—maybe they'll say the island should have chosen me." Her lip curled in amusement, knowing she had touched a nerve. "Maybe they're right."

"No," said Fionn quickly. "You're just an idiot who's going through our stash of weapons faster than a bag of Skittles, because you're incapable of thinking of anyone but yourself!" He took a shaky breath. "If you didn't have less than ten brain cells, you'd *realize* that."

Tara stuck her chin out. "I have *loads* of brain cells. I always beat Grandad at Scrabble."

"Then prove it," said Fionn, glancing over his shoulder again. The old woman was gone. "Put it out."

"Fine." Tara crushed the remains of the candle in her fist and swung her free hand around until it was no longer facing the ocean but his face instead. In one icy deluge, the whirlpool leaped from the ocean and crashed over his head, soaking through his hat and pouring itself down his neck and into his clothes until streams of icy water gushed out of his pant legs, bleeding into puddles along the sand.

"Happy now?" she said, smirking at him.

Fionn glared at his sister, his words chattering violently through his teeth. "I wish, just once, we could bury *you* under a rock for all of eternity."

"Try it," she said, sashaying away. "I'd be back before the week was done."

THE ROTTEN WAVE

An hour later, Fionn lingered outside Donal's corner shop, glowering into his hot chocolate. The sun had fought its way through the thicket of clouds, bringing an icy chill with it. It settled in the gaps between his toes and clung to the tip of his nose. All around him, fellow students milled by in scarves and hats and heavy winter coats, their bags *thu-thump*ing against their backs as they chatted animatedly along the strand. It was the last day of school before Christmas and there was a giddiness in the air.

Fionn hardly noticed it; he was too busy staring at the marshmallow in his cup.

Do something. Anything.

He ground his teeth together, refusing to blink.

Give me a bubble. Just one little bubble.

His vision was starting to go funny.

Come on. Come on. Come on.

A horn sounded in the distance, making him jump. Fionn discarded his cup and rolled his neck around, blinking the tears from his eyes. Up ahead, the morning ferry was gliding into port.

He blinked again, this time in confusion. Not one ferry, but *two*—the second one following in the wake of the first.

Fionn frowned. In all the months he had lived on Arranmore, he had never seen one ferry so full, let alone two. He stepped out onto the strand and nearly crashed into the Aguero sisters. They divided around him, tossing identical veils of black hair in affront, as they made their way toward Fionn's sister, who was lingering outside the school gates. Tara caught his eye, then tapped her wrist, as if to say, *Hurry up, loser. You're going to be late.*

Fionn ignored her, turning instead in the opposite direction and tracking toward the pier. The boats were heaving with passengers. Most of them had spilled out onto the decks, where they stood shoulder to shoulder, like tightly packed sardines. When the second ferry horn blasted, they turned as one, suddenly standing to attention. There was something eerily familiar about it all—this strange sea of faces, moving silently across the water, each one marked by wide, unblinking eyes.

Soulstalkers.

Fionn stared in silent horror as the first boat docked. A wave rolled out from under it, swelling and frothing as it galloped toward the beach.

It brought a shoal of rotting fish with it. There were so many that Fionn could hear them splatting against the sand from where he stood up on the strand. He could even see their fleshy insides, their gloopy eyes and tarnished scales piling up and up and up, with every towering wave that came after.

Down on the beach, someone screamed. Douglas Beasley tore out of the post office with a parcel under his arm and Donal appeared in the doorway to his shop, his hair floating about his head like a cloud. Up by the school, teenagers discarded their conversations and craned their necks in curiosity.

The rotten waves kept coming, dead fish filling the air with a putrid, clinging stink.

Fionn clapped his sleeve over his mouth to keep from gagging, but he could do nothing about the accompanying panic. It rose up in his chest, pounding its fists against his heart until he felt like he couldn't breathe.

She had finally done it. Somehow, Morrigan had called

her followers home, and they had brought the shadow of death with them.

The thunder of nearby footsteps interrupted his rising hysteria. It came with his name, thrown up into the air like a football. "Hey! FIONN!"

Fionn snapped his head up to find his best (and only) island friend furiously sprinting toward him.

This was not usually the way of Sam Patton. Of the two of them, Sam was the unflappable one. He had seen so much more of the world than Fionn and was used to a less conventional life. It was what had drawn Fionn to him in the first place. That and the fact that Sam, despite growing up in London, was from one of the original five families of Arranmore. He had all but announced as much when he first alighted on Fionn in September, emerging from a gaggle of zombie-tired teenagers and stalking across the schoolyard with the confidence of a celebrity. "Storm Keeper!" He had scanned Fionn up and down, as though making sure of it. "You're a bit scrawnier than I expected but you do have a certain *look* about you. You remind me of my great-grandmother."

"Sam Patton," he had announced then, sticking out a leather-gloved hand. "Great-grandson of the one and only Maggie. She was a Storm Keeper too. I've been waiting to meet you all summer."

Sam was several inches shorter than Fionn, but his

sense of ease made him seem ten feet tall. He had big brown eyes, brown skin, and curly hair. It bounced along his forehead now, as he pelted along the strand, a flute case tucked under his left arm, the other flailing around him like a windmill. He skidded to a stop. "Look at the size of those waves!" he panted, before slapping his free hand over his mouth. "Ugh, that smell. It's getting *worse*."

The waves were still piling on top of each other, crashing and foaming as they painted the shoreline silver. "Where do you think they're coming from?" asked Sam, through his fingers.

"*Them*," said Fionn, gesturing at the pier. "It looks like Morrigan's minions have finally found her."

Sam turned on the heel of his boot. "Do you mean those passengers are—"

"Soulstalkers," said Fionn. "Can't you tell?"

Sam narrowed his eyes in suspicion. The first ferry was releasing its passengers onto the island. They scuttled across the pier like crabs, men and women dressed in scarves and coats and hats and suits, all moving in the same direction, one after another after another. "They don't blink," he said, with a shudder. "They just sort of *stare*."

"I *told* you something was coming." Fionn's insides were twisting and twisting. "I've been saying it for weeks now."

Tick-tock, tick-tock, tick-tock.

Morrigan hadn't been bluffing; she'd been gloating.

Sam shuffled uncomfortably. "Is this really an I-told-you-so moment?"

"I suppose not." Fionn swung his schoolbag around and pulled out his notebook. "Come on. We don't have much time. Let's get out of here before the beach fills up." He tucked it under his arm and gestured for Sam to follow as he stalked off up the strand and right past the school gates.

They left the bell ringing into the sky behind them.

"Ms. Cannon's bringing pies in today," said Sam, looking forlornly over his shoulder as he hurried to keep up with Fionn's determined strides. "They're my favorite."

Fionn passed the notebook to him. "If you help me save the island from oblivion, I'll make you a batch myself," he promised.

"I'm holding you to that," said Sam, slowing down to open the notebook. "And I want gingerbread men too. *With* buttons."

"Fine. Just read, please."

On the first page, Fionn had numbered and annotated the five Gifts of Arranmore in his messy scrawl. Sam read them aloud as they walked.

"One—**The Storm Keeper of Arranmore: to wield the elements in Dagda's name.** You said, '*Aka me. See also: useless.*'"

Fionn nodded grimly.

"Two—**The Sea Cave (earth): for that which is out of reach.** 'Used that one on Tara already. Very ungrateful.'"

"Understatement," muttered Fionn.

Sam continued. "Three—**The Whispering Tree (fire): for that which is yet to come.** Says 'Probably should sort out the present before I go snooping around the future.' Yep. Let's stay focused here.

"Four—**Aonbharr the Winged Horse (wind): for danger that cannot be outrun.** 'Might get in a bit of trouble if I fly away from the island by msyelf and leave it to die?' Wow, Fionn. You think?

"Five—**The Merrows (water): for invaders that may come.**

"Ah yes, the terrifying mer-people of Arranmore," said Sam, before reading out Fionn's note. "'This looks like the only option that can help us.'"

"I'm afraid it is," said Fionn.

Sam hmm'd. "But the merrows are way scarier than mermaids. What if they eat us?"

"What if they help us?"

After a moment of contemplation, both boys trudging up the headland in silence, Sam slammed the notebook shut. "Right, then," he said, adjusting the lapels of his blue peacoat. "The merrows it is."

JULIA DUNIN

Catherine Doyle grew up beside
the Atlantic Ocean in the west of Ireland. Her love of reading
began with great Irish myths and legends, which fostered in
her an ambition to one day write her own stories. The Storm
Keeper's Island series was inspired by her real-life ancestral
home of Arranmore Island (where her grandparents grew up)
and the adventures of her many seafaring ancestors.

www.catherinedoylebooks.com

@doyle_cat